Praise for
The Wife Stalker

"Thrillers with a big twist near the end make for good reading, and that's what Liv Constantine's *The Wife Stalker* provides. It saves lots of its ammunition for the denouement, making it a page-turner—not surprising considering its authors, the sister duo Lynne and Valerie Constantine as Liv Constantine, have written nothing but bestsellers." —*Washington City Paper*

"By their very nature, thrillers and novels of suspense typically have any number of twists. However, *The Wife Stalker* is teeming with them. . . . Once you've reached the aha moment, you'll want to go back to the beginning to see the perspective in a whole new light. Liv Constantine really is that clever."
—*Book Reporter*

"Skillfully constructed and fast-paced—a mischievously tense and engaging novel filled with plenty of twists and turns that keep readers spellbound and guessing until the very final page."
—*New York Journal of Books*

"Exciting. . . . Strong storytelling draws in the reader—hook, line, and sinker. . . . Constantine keeps the suspense high. A clever twist pulls *The Wife Stalker* in a unique direction that readers will savor." —*Sun-Sentinel*, South Florida

"If you're looking for an entertaining binge-read, this book is for you. . . . Readers will not see the twist coming, and the nuances of the writing will ultimately come together in not one, but two 'what just happened?!?' moments." —*Portland Book Review*

"In true Liv Constantine fashion, this story wraps with a twist that you just won't see coming, no matter how hard you try. This one is definitely a must-read!" —*Suspense* magazine

"The Constantine sisters are as astute observers of class as any literary writer I can think of; they understand how people signal their social status both consciously and subliminally. And class is really at the heart of *The Wife Stalker*, which I don't want to spoil, so I will just say it's about a woman who has a habit of marrying rich men who then have fatal accidents."

—*CrimeReads*, "10 Novels You Should Read This Month"

"A psychological thriller that keeps readers squirming until the last harrowing page. . . . Readers will enjoy the twists, turns, and surprises as the story unfolds." —*Library Journal*

"The story's swift pace and twist in the final act should keep domestic thriller fans engaged." —*Shelf Awareness*

"A twisty, engrossing house of mirrors. . . . Smart, propulsive, and tricky-in-all-the-best-ways psychological suspense."

—Lisa Unger, *New York Times* bestselling author of *The Stranger Inside*

"Tense and deliciously twisty, *The Wife Stalker* is a hall of mirrors in which Liv Constantine delivers sinister surprises with characteristic sleight of hand."

—Gilly Macmillan, *New York Times* bestselling author of *The Nanny*

"Wickedly entertaining. With *The Wife Stalker*, Liv Constantine proves once again to be a master of domestic malice."

—Riley Sager, *New York Times* bestselling author of *Lock Every Door*

"*The Wife Stalker* is a daring, dastardly story with complex characters and a sinister plot. A read-through-the-night thriller that mesmerizes to the final page. An absolute must for your [reading] list!"

—Samantha Downing, *USA Today* and *Sunday Times* bestselling author of *My Lovely Wife*

"Suspenseful and mesmerizing, Constantine's third novel is a breakneck thriller that keeps you riveted from the first page to that explosive, jaw-dropping twist."

—Jennifer Hillier, award-winning author of *Jar of Hearts* and *Little Secrets*

"Oh, you sneaky sisters. Liv Constantine got me in the best possible way with *The Wife Stalker*, a wicked, whip-smart bag of tricks."

—Kimberly Belle, internationally bestselling author of *Dear Wife*

Praise for
The Last Time I Saw You

"Murder, threats, and forgotten friendships come together in this thriller, from the author of the hit book *The Last Mrs. Parrish*." —*Newsweek*, "Best Books of 2019 So Far"

"From murder and madness to secrets and fraught family relationships, the nonstop glitz gives this tale a soapy sheen that makes for perfect escapist summer reading."

—*New York Journal of Books*

"Elegantly constructed. . . . [A] terrific tale of brooding noir that echoes Patricia Highsmith and her classic Ripley series, as complex as it is ambitious." —*Providence Journal*

"Another clever whodunit jam-packed with enough twists, turns, and secrets to keep avid thriller readers second-guessing until the bitter end." —*Library Journal* (starred review)

"An absorbing tale. . . . Fans of *Gone Girl* and its successors will appreciate an ending that puts a pricey shoe on one foot and then changes it again . . . and again." —*Booklist*

Praise for *The Last Mrs. Parrish*

"Filled with envy, deception, and power, it's a great reading escape. And there is a thrilling twist at the end!"

—Reese Witherspoon

"[A] wicked debut thriller. . . . You'll relish every diabolical turn."

—*People*

"Utterly irresistible. . . . Pivots on an enormous and satisfying twist . . . the pages keep flying, flying, flying by."

—*USA Today*

"*The Last Mrs. Parrish* by Liv Constantine will keep you up. In a 'can't put it down' way. It's *The Talented Mr. Ripley* with XX chromosomes." —*The Skimm*

"Wonderfully plausible, hypnotically compelling, and deliciously chilling and creepy—some of the best psychological suspense you'll read this year." —Lee Child

"[A] haunting psychological thriller. . . . Engrossing."

—*Real Simple*

"Fabulous. . . . I read this book in a flash, devouring every twisty delicious detail." —*Milwaukee Journal Sentinel*

"To the pantheon of *Gone Girl*–type bad girls you can now add Amber Patterson, the heroine of this devilishly ingenious debut thriller. . . . Readers would have to go back to the likes of Ira Levin's *A Kiss Before Dying* or Patricia Highsmith's *The Talented Mr. Ripley* to find as entertaining a depiction of a sociopathic monster." —*Publishers Weekly* (starred review)

THE
WIFE
STALKER

ALSO BY LIV CONSTANTINE

The Last Mrs. Parrish

The Last Time I Saw You

THE WIFE STALKER

A NOVEL

Liv Constantine

HARPER

NEW YORK • LONDON • TORONTO • SYDNEY

Lynne's dedication: for Nick and Theo

Valerie's dedication: for my sons

HARPER

A hardcover edition of this book was published in 2020 by HarperCollins Publishers.

HarperCollins books may be purchased for educational, business, or sales promotional use. For information, please email the Special Markets Department at SPsales@harpercollins.com.

FIRST HARPER PAPERBACKS EDITION PUBLISHED 2021.

Designed by Elina Cohen

Library of Congress Cataloging-in-Publication Data has been applied for.

ISBN 978-0-06-296729-9 (pbk.)

21 22 23 24 25 LSC 10 9 8 7 6 5 4 3 2 1

| 1 |

PIPER

Piper Reynard pulled into the parking lot of the Phoenix Recovery Center and parked in her reserved spot. When she'd been forced to leave San Diego ten months ago, she wasn't sure where to go, only that she wanted to be as far away from the West Coast as possible. It had to be somewhere near the water, though, so that she could still sail on the weekends. And it needed to be a place where she could start over without standing out. After extensive research, she'd settled on Westport, Connecticut, a jewel of a town on the coast of Long Island Sound. The former home of Paul Newman and other celebrities, it had a sophisticated vibe and was just over an hour away from New York City by train. But best of all, it was the kind of place that attracted people from all over, rather than the kind of small town where everyone's family had lived for generations, making them nosy about newcomers. She'd found the perfect house—a sprawling white clapboard on the water—and joined a yacht club, where she kept the sailboat she'd bought as soon as she came east.

The one problem she had to overcome was how to reinvent herself. She couldn't continue with her counseling practice, as her license was in her real name, so the next best thing was a business in a similar field. She'd been incredibly lucky to find an existing one for sale and bought the Phoenix Recovery Center a few weeks after moving to Westport. All she'd had to do was have a lawyer set up an LLC for her under the name Harmony Healing Arts. It had already been a thriving business, offering meditation retreats, mindfulness, recovery programs, and nutrition and yoga classes.

She grabbed her briefcase from the passenger's seat, slid out of her Alfa Romeo Spider, and walked toward the entrance of the building, feeling a sense of pride as she looked up at the sleek, two-story building of glass and cedar. She unlocked the front door and went directly to her office. It was still early, six thirty a.m., but Piper liked to be there well before the center opened at eight. It gave her time to get centered before she thrust herself into her busy day. She took a quick look at her calendar to check the time of her appointment with Leo Drakos. He'd called her out of the blue last week and asked to discuss a client he was defending in a murder case. He spoke to her about Fred Grainger, who had been in one of the center's support groups for the last four months and was about to go to trial for the murder of his actress girlfriend. She'd googled Drakos and seen he was a well-known defense lawyer, prominent or perhaps even famous in his field. Based on her knowledge of Fred, she didn't think he was guilty, and she was glad Drakos had taken his case.

She opened her laptop to check the social media accounts for Phoenix. Instagram first. Another three hundred followers. Excellent. It must have been the podcast episode she'd uploaded yesterday on filling your well before trying to fill someone else's. Twitter next. Thirty-five retweets of her blog post on selfishness being the new selflessness. And on Facebook, the center had hit ten thousand likes. A very good morning indeed.

She dimmed her office lights and pressed Play on her iPad. As the soothing sounds of Debussy filled the room, she closed her eyes and leaned back in the chair. Maybe things were really going to be different here. They had to be. She couldn't keep starting over and finding new places to hide.

| 2 |

JOANNA

Leo's finally coming out of his depression. After three long months of his barely communicating with me, lost inside his head, he suddenly seemed to perk up. He was starting on a new murder case next week, and I could see that having it to immerse himself in was a good thing, but I knew from experience that it would also be exhausting. I convinced him that a few days away at the house in Maine before the trial started would be a nice break for all of us. The bracing sea air and magnificent views were always restorative, so I'd already called ahead to Lloyd, the caretaker, to ready the house for us.

As soon as we drove up and opened the front door, fresh flowers greeted us on the entry table, and the rooms seemed to welcome us back. Stelli ran through the house ahead of us like a tornado, and when I heard a whoop of delight, I knew he'd found the surprise I'd arranged to have waiting in his bedroom. A minute later, he came barreling down the stairs holding two remote-control bumper cars and ran to his sister, Evie.

"Look what was in my room! Come on, let's go play."

Evie, a grown-up eight to his six, gave him a measured look, then spoke. "Let me put my things away first."

She was such a sweet child that she didn't ask if there was anything waiting in her room, which of course there was. I'd ordered her a pink wireless karaoke microphone and asked Lloyd to place it on her bed.

As Leo unloaded the car, I went through the house, turning lights on, unpacking our bags, and getting us settled in. Opening the door to the deck, I took a deep breath of Maine air. It was a perfect spring day, 62 degrees, according to the thermometer on the outside wall, but the sun made it feel warmer. The sea was calm and the sky a brilliant, cloudless blue. I sat in one of the white lounge chairs and breathed in the salt air, closing my eyes as the warmth of the sun spread across my body.

"Are you asleep?"

Leo's voice startled me from a light slumber, and I sat up, turning to look at him standing at the open sliding glass door. "No, just resting," I said. "Where are the children?"

"In their rooms, playing."

"Why don't you sit down and join me?"

He shook his head, his expression serious. "No. I think I'll go inside and rest for a bit."

I tried not to show my exasperation. "Leo. The sun and sea air will do you some good. Come sit."

He sighed reluctantly. This is how he'd been the last few months—keeping to himself, sleeping most of the time, or staring off into space. Finally, he stepped onto the deck and took the lounge chair next to mine, but he looked straight ahead at the water, not saying a word. I put my hand on his arm.

"Leo, let's try to make this trip a good one for Stelli and Evie. They love it here. It would be good to make some happy memories for them."

He continued to stare at the water. "I'll try, Joanna. I know I've not been the easiest person to be around these last months." He turned to look at me and attempted a weak smile. "You've been wonderful, you really have, and I'm grateful. I don't know what I would have done without you."

Even though we'd been together for many years, it was still a thrill to hear those words, to know he appreciated me. There was no one I cared about more than him and the children, and I was relieved to see that he was starting to come back to me.

"I will always be here for you, Leo. No matter what," I said.

Tears filled his eyes, and he blinked, then turned to hide them from me. Seeing him like this made me hope he was emotionally prepared for this case, which would be another high-profile one. I'd been telling him it might be good for him to get counseling, but he wasn't interested, even when I reminded him how much it had helped me. My therapist, Celeste, advised me not to push him, so I'd backed off. But after something he'd said in passing, a possible solution occurred to me. I just had to figure out a way to frame it so that it sounded like a good idea to him, too.

| 3 |

PIPER

After teaching her nine o'clock yoga class, Piper went back to her office to work on her new blog post. The alarm on her phone sounded, reminding her of her next appointment, and she barely had time to throw a shirt over her sports bra and yoga pants before there was a tap on her office door.

"Hello, come in," she said, rising from her chair.

As Leo Drakos walked in, she was immediately struck by his dark good looks and brooding eyes, and when he put his hand out to shake hers, she took in his well-groomed nails and firm grip. Then her eyes traveled to his perfectly tailored gray suit and starched white shirt, silver cuff links, and paisley Zegna necktie—the same brand Matthew had always worn. In the pictures she'd seen of Leo Drakos online, she had thought he was nice-looking enough, but his charisma came across in person in a whole different way.

"Thank you for making time for me so quickly, Ms. Reynard." His voice was deep and pleasant, and she felt herself not wanting to let go of his hand.

"Of course. I'm glad to help in any way I can. But please, call me Piper. Won't you have a seat?" She indicated a deep-cushioned armchair, and Leo waited for Piper to sit before settling himself into it.

"As I told you on the phone, my client, Fred Grainger, has authorized me to speak with you about the time he's spent here, in addition to his work in AA."

Piper nodded. "Yes, when he told me, I had him sign a release."

"He worked through some addiction issues here with you, is that right?"

"Yes," she said. "He was very committed to the process. Worked very hard."

"Was he receiving any counseling here in addition to the recovery work?"

Piper shook her head. "We don't offer one-on-one therapy sessions here, but work on a group approach." She could have filled him in more but didn't want to sound like too much of an expert. Her new identity here in Westport didn't include a master's in clinical psychology from Pepperdine and her work at a private practice in San Diego.

"He's been coming here for six months, right?"

"Regularly—twice a week, in addition to his AA meetings. I have the records here." She indicated the file folder in her lap. "He needed a place that was safe, where people listened without judgment or condemnation." She paused and smiled at Leo. "You know, it's what everyone needs, really—a place where they can spill their insides and let it all out. It's like a cleansing of the soul. All of us have wounds we bury deep inside, and they affect us without our even realizing it."

He stared at her for a moment. "Do you . . ." He put a hand up and shook his head. "Back to Fred. Did he do well here?"

She sat up straighter, giving him a professional nod. "Fred made great progress and stayed clean and sober. I believe he truly wants to turn his life around."

"I agree," Leo said with a nod. "We're going to need character witnesses. Would you be willing to testify?"

Piper shifted in her chair, thinking of all the possible ramifications of taking the stand in a high-profile murder case. "Well . . . it might be better if some of my staff did, specifically Morgan Timmons. He worked more closely with Fred. I oversaw his progress, but Morgan had more direct interaction."

"Okay, then. Could I speak with Mr. Timmons today?"

"Of course. He'll be in this afternoon. I'll have him call you as soon as he gets here. In the meantime, if you'd like, I can take you on a tour of the facility so you can see what services Fred participated in." She stood, annoyed with herself for her gym clothes and messy ponytail. If she'd known how attractive Leo Drakos was, she'd have taken more care with her appearance today.

He glanced at his watch. "I'm pressed for time. I'll take a rain check."

Though unsettled by how disappointed she was to see him leave, she nodded. "I understand, I'll walk you out."

When they reached the door, he stopped and handed her a business card. "If you think of anything else that would help, you have both my cell and office number here. And again, thanks for passing it along to Mr. Timmons."

After Piper returned to her office, she leaned back in her chair and took several deep breaths. She was sorry that she couldn't testify—it would certainly have given her an excuse to get to know him better. She was a little surprised by how strongly attracted to him she was, but she couldn't deny it felt good. There was something strong and powerful about the way he carried himself and how he spoke. She'd read that he could mesmerize a jury, and she could see why. She pictured him now, as he'd sat across from her, handsome and debonair. Piper had taken in everything about him—especially the gold ring on his left hand. That was the one detail that troubled her.

| 4 |

JOANNA

Sometimes life has a way of taking care of things for you. It was serendipitous that Leo's case had led him to the Phoenix Recovery Center right here in Westport. With this trial imminent, Leo needed to be able to focus and not dwell on things he couldn't change. He'd always been the one to light up a room, his infectious laugh and passionate way of speaking drawing everyone in, but the spark in his eyes had dulled, and he barely looked at any of us when he got home at the end of the day. Even Stelli's antics failed to perk him up lately.

Keeping one eye on the kids, who were bouncing on their trampoline, I checked the time on my phone. Almost six. Leo would be home from the office any minute now.

"Time to get off. Daddy will be home soon."

Stelli kept jumping, ignoring me, but Evie scooted off and came toward me.

"Can we have ice cream for dessert tonight?" she asked.

I smiled at her. "Sure."

Stelli yelled and continued bouncing. "Can I do one more flip? Please."

I pushed away my frustration at Stelli's pushing the boundaries, reminding myself that boys needed to work off their energy. "Okay, one more. Should we rate you?"

He bounced up and down, his face scrunched up in concentration. He bounced higher, put his hands up in the air, and executed a perfect somersault. When he landed, I applauded, and Evie joined in.

"Fantastic! An eleven," I pronounced.

He jumped off and ran to me. "It only goes up to ten, silly."

"Well, it was so super-duper that a ten wasn't enough."

I let them watch a show while I finished making dinner. There was a roast in the oven, and I opened the door to check it. Leo was a meat-and-potatoes man, and though I'd tried to get him to eat a little more adventurously, in the end it was easier to cater to his tastes.

I'd just uncorked a bottle of Stags' Leap cabernet when I heard the door chime.

"Daddy's home!" Stelli jumped up from the sofa and went to greet him. I always loved to see their special bond. No one could make Stelli's face light up the way his father could. Of course, lately, it'd been a little more difficult, but I knew Leo was doing his best.

"Hi, buddy," he said to Stelli before looking to me and Evie. "Good evening, ladies," he called, sounding a little like his old self. Evie ran up and hugged him. I was encouraged by the enthusiasm in his voice, but when he smiled at me, it didn't quite reach his eyes. "Smells good in here."

I poured a glass of wine and handed it to him. "Your favorite."

"Thanks." He took a sip. "Ah, nice."

I put out a small platter of olives and cheese. "To tide you over until dinner." I knew he would have skipped lunch—he always did when he was close to the start of a trial—but I also knew that he needed time to unwind when he got home. The kids went back to their show, and Leo took a long swallow.

I decided to plunge in. "I noticed that there's a meditation workshop at that recovery center this Saturday. Maybe it would help with the Grainger case if you spent a little time there to better understand what they do and how it helped him."

He looked at me, his brow wrinkling. "What do you mean?"

"It's nothing weird. Just a day to try to focus on what's good in your life. You know, taking a look at the positive."

He took another long swallow of wine and set the glass down. "You know I don't go in for that kind of New Age thing. And weren't we planning to take the kids to the beach?"

I shrugged. It was more important to me that he get better, and I could handle them on my own. "It's only one day. I'll take them to the beach, and we can all go back on Sunday."

"I don't know. Sounds like a waste of time. I already spoke with Fred's counselor and got everything I needed from him. No need for me to waste more time going back there."

"Maybe it would be a waste. But maybe not. The website says their techniques can help you to clear your mind and improve your focus and concentration. You've got a big case coming up. Every little thing helps."

He was quiet, seeming to consider this. "You really think this kind of stuff works?"

"I think it can work. I know you've been feeling better, but can you honestly say you're at a hundred percent? The worst that can happen is you waste your day, but it could be the thing that gets you all the way over the hump."

He nodded. "I guess it can't hurt."

I was relieved that he was finally going to take a step toward health. Little did I know that it would be his first step out of my life and right into hers.

| 5 |

PIPER

Piper was surprised and pleased to see Leo's name on the roster for the meditation workshop—she hadn't pegged him as someone who'd take the time for such things. She allowed herself a moment to wonder if he'd signed up because he felt the same attraction to her as she did to him, but then dismissed the thought. He'd been nothing but professional when he'd come to the center. Regardless, though she hadn't even been planning to attend the workshop, she quickly cleared her schedule.

She made sure to dress more attractively this time, in navy knit pants that showed off her trim figure and a champagne-colored silk shirt revealing just the right amount of cleavage. She spritzed on some Wild Bluebell perfume and checked her makeup before leaving her office and heading to Studio One, where the workshop was being held.

She entered the studio to find fifteen chairs set up in a semicircle, but no Leo, and she felt a pinch of disappointment. She hoped he hadn't decided to skip it. Taking one of the empty chairs, she put a program down on the seat next to her, saving it in the hopes he would show up. She sat and took in the room, which she had redecorated with a mural of clouds on the ceilings and soothing sky-blue walls. The next few minutes crawled by as her eyes darted to the door every time it opened and a few more attendees straggled in. And then, finally, he entered, casually dressed in khakis and a white button-down shirt. He was even more attractive than she remembered.

She smiled at him and motioned for him to sit next to her, and he returned her smile and strode over, settling into the chair. For a moment his leg brushed hers, and she felt the heat of desire go through her, but she reluctantly turned her attention to the facilitator when he began to speak.

"Welcome, everyone. I'm Zodiac, your guide for today." He put his hands together in a prayerful pose.

Leo looked at Piper, cocking a sardonic eyebrow. She shot him a look that said *Behave*.

As Zodiac explained a breathing technique, then prompted everyone to close their eyes and clear their minds, all Piper could think about was the man sitting next to her and how much she wanted to spend more time with him.

"Okay, everyone," Zodiac said. "Mindfulness is more than just a—"

The ringing of a cell phone interrupted him, and he scanned the attendees to see who the culprit was.

Leo made a face, pulled the phone from his pocket, and silenced it. "Sorry."

Zodiac nodded and cleared his throat. "As I said before . . . silence or, better yet, turn off your cell phones. They are a major obstacle to living in the now." He stood and walked over to a woman across from Piper.

"You are not your thoughts," he yelled. The woman jumped.

"Yes, that's startling. But true. Your essence has nothing to do with what you're thinking." He tapped a finger to his temple. "Clear away the clutter. One way to do that is meditation. We'll focus on the basics of that soon. But for now . . . sit and be in this moment. Look around you. How does it feel to just be?"

Leo shifted in his seat, and Piper, feeling his restlessness, had to resist looking at him. She did her best to concentrate on Zodiac and force her thoughts away from Leo.

An hour later, as they filed out of the studio for a ten-minute break, she turned to him. "So, what do you think?" she asked.

As they moved to a corner of the hallway, he gave her a measured look. "No offense, but it sounds like a bunch of mumbo jumbo to me."

She put a hand on his arm. "It's hard for everyone at first. It takes practice. But meditation can be very soothing."

He held up a finger and pulled his phone from his pocket. "Do I get points for putting it on vibrate?" he joked before answering. Piper walked away to say hello to a few of the other attendees and give Leo some privacy. By the time the break was almost over, he was still on his phone.

He looked up as the sound of wind chimes came through the speakers on the wall, and ended the call. Piper walked back to him.

"Sorry. Work," he said sheepishly.

"No worries. The next session is only thirty minutes," Piper told him. "You game?"

"Why not?" He was quiet as they followed the group back into the studio. Piper found she couldn't concentrate on the mantras the group was repeating, and the half hour passed slowly again. When the session was over, Leo rose from his chair.

"Sorry, Piper. All this is doing is making me think of everything I need to get done."

She bit her lip. "You're leaving?"

"Yeah. I'm sorry, this just isn't for me."

"I understand. Would you like to join me for some lunch here before you go? After all, you've already paid for it."

He tilted his head. "Tell you what, tofu and green drinks are not really my thing. Why don't you let me buy you lunch at the Spotted Horse? You do eat regular food, right?"

She laughed. "That I do. I'd love to. Let me just tell Zodiac that I'm leaving."

He raised his eyebrows. "That's a made-up name, right?"

She shrugged. "Probably. Good one for a meditation instructor, don't you think? Meet you in the parking lot."

Piper stopped by her office for her purse and to freshen up, and when she exited the building, he was waiting for her by his Mercedes. When she approached, he walked to the passenger's side and opened the door for her. She slid into the supple leather seat and felt butterflies taking flight in her stomach again. She hadn't been this attracted to someone since Matthew. Her eyes were drawn to his hands on the steering wheel, his long and elegant fingers, and she found herself imagining what they would feel like on her body. *Stop it*, she scolded herself.

They sat at an outside table, under the orange awnings. Piper looked at the menu, but her stomach was in such a flutter she wasn't sure she could eat anything. "I think I'll just have one of the small plates," she said.

"Really? I'm starving. All that meditating made me work up an appetite." They both laughed.

"I'm sorry you didn't like the class," she said after they'd ordered. "Have you ever done meditation on your own?"

"No. I have to say I don't see the point of it."

She nodded. "I think many people feel that way until they try it. I'm sorry this wasn't a good experience for you today. What were you hoping for?"

He looked away for a moment and then turned his eyes back

to her. "I guess I was hoping for some relief." He paused. "I've gone through a rough patch the last few months. But I'm feeling hopeful again."

"I'm glad. Fred is lucky to have you as his attorney."

"I'm going to do everything in my power to live up to his faith in me."

She wanted to offer him a word of encouragement but didn't want to seem condescending. Instead, she said, "I'm a great listener. If you ever need someone to talk to, I'm just a phone call away."

Leo smiled at her. "Thank you."

The waiter brought their lunches, the roasted eggplant for Piper and a Reuben for Leo.

"I feel bad that you wasted your money on the workshop lunch. You must let me pay for this to make up for it," Piper said.

"Absolutely not," Leo said. "I invited *you*."

Piper took a taste of eggplant and watched Leo take a big bite of his sandwich. "How is it?"

He nodded his head. "Delicious."

She leaned back in her chair. "I know you practice law, and you don't like meditation," she said, "but what are some things you *do* like? What's your favorite book?"

"That's easy. *The Count of Monte Cristo*. Yours?"

"*The Alchemist*," she said without hesitation. "Your favorite song?"

"Hmm, that's a little tougher. Let's see. Hard to pick one, but if I have to, I guess it would be 'Black' by Pearl Jam."

"Oh, that's a great one. Mine would be 'Moon River,'" Piper said. He looked a little taken aback, and she laughed. "What can I say? I was born in the wrong decade."

"A classic," Leo said. "Movie?"

"I'm a big fan of old movies. I've probably seen every black-and-white film there is, and love them all, but if I had to pick a favorite, it'd be *Brief Encounter*."

Leo frowned. "I don't think I've ever seen that."

"It's about two married strangers who meet in a train station and fall in love. Very passionate and very sad. And the music! I still get goose bumps every time I hear Rachmaninoff's Piano Concerto Number Two."

He was staring at her with those dark eyes, and she shifted in her chair. "You?"

"Me?" he said.

"Your movie."

"*The Godfather*, without question."

They sat that way, chatting, for over an hour, long after they'd finished eating, and she'd perked up even further when Leo mentioned that he'd become involved with the Save the Sound Foundation in Westport. The organization was now lobbying for a bill that would prevent people from using pesticides on their lawns if they lived within a thousand feet of any waterway.

"It's infuriating when I'm walking in the beach neighborhoods and I see those little yellow signs on lawns. Don't they realize that poison runs right into the water? The same water my children swim in." He shook his head.

"I completely agree. Pesticides are one of the reasons I buy only organic produce. And I never use that poison on my lawn, *especially* since I'm near the water."

"A local business owner *and* a waterfront property holder? We could use another voice like yours at our meetings."

"When's the next one?"

"It's in two weeks. Thursday at seven at the Town Hall."

She smiled at him. "I'll be there." She was thrilled to have another excuse to see him, not that these meetings did any good. It was usually just a bunch of bureaucratic blowhards who loved the sound of their own voices. But she would put up with that if it was a chance to spend more time with Leo. The more she learned about him, the more she saw that he was definitely her type. And she intended to make sure she was his.

| 6 |

JOANNA

The kids and I had been at Compo Beach since midmorning. Though it was still a week before Memorial Day, the sun was shining brightly, and we had camped out near the water's edge so I could keep a close eye on the children as they played in the water. Even though there were barely any waves in the Sound, they were drifting on their boogie boards back and forth in the shallows, laughing and splashing each other.

"Can we go to Joey's and get burgers and more fries?" Stelli asked. We'd feasted on the famous French fries and hot dogs at the restaurant next to the pavilion a few hours ago, but they were getting hungry again as three o'clock approached.

"Maybe just some fries. We don't want to spoil your dinner," I told him, then held out my hand. "Come on, Evie, we're going to get a snack."

I gave Stelli a quarter for the gumball machine and he stood, transfixed as always, as a brightly colored orb journeyed down the spiraled tunnels and landed in his hand.

I turned to Evie. "Do you want one, too, sweetie?"

She shook her head. "No, they're gross. They've been sitting in that thing for who knows how long. Probably since last summer."

I laughed. "I certainly hope not."

We got fries for Stelli and an ice-cream cone for Evie, and then found an open picnic table under the pavilion. I shooed a seagull away as we sat. The kids dug in, and I tried hard not to snatch a fry from Stelli's basket. No matter what I did, I couldn't seem to get rid of the extra twenty pounds that had been plaguing me for as long as I could remember.

Evie pointed. "Look, there's Daddy!"

"Where?"

"Right there!" She stood and ran to him. His face broke into a smile when he saw her. Holding hands, they walked over to us.

"What are you doing here? I thought the retreat didn't end until early evening." I was happy to have him here, but I had been hoping the workshop would have been useful to him.

He took a seat across from me at the picnic table and shook his head. "If I had to endure another minute of that baloney, I would have gone crazy. I appreciate the thought, but that scene is definitely not my cup of tea."

But the funny thing was, he looked happier. Maybe he hadn't realized that it had been a little helpful. I tried to press him gently. "You were there half the day; did you get *anything* from it?"

"I had a nice chat with Piper, the owner, who, unlike Zodiac, the leader—how's that for a crazy name?—seems pretty grounded. One thing that did resonate was a quote from Rilke that she wrote down for me," he said, pulling a card from his pocket. "'Live the question now. Perhaps you will then gradually, without noticing it, live along some distant day into the answer.'"

I stared at him. I almost said, *And by then you'll have forgotten the question*, but I could tell he was serious. Maybe you had to have heard it in some kind of context. And if inspirational quotes gave him a foothold on the ladder to health, I sure wasn't going to question them. "That's great," I said, giving him a big smile. "I'm glad you got something good out of it. So, are you hungry?"

He shook his head. "No. I grabbed lunch after I skipped out." He turned to the children. "Are you little stinkers having fun?"

"Yes!" they answered in unison.

"Are you going to swim with us, Daddy?" Stelli asked.

"You bet, buddy. I'll go change now."

The kids finished their snacks and we went back to the beach, where Leo and Stelli splashed around while Evie and I stayed in our beach chairs with our books.

It was good to see Leo laughing and actually enjoying himself. After a while, he swam back to shore and motioned to Evie. "Your brother wants you to go in the water."

Evie looked at her father over her book. "Okay."

"Thank you, Evie. You do such a good job of looking after your little brother," I told her.

Leo ran a hand through his wet hair as he picked up a towel. Beads of water glistened on his toned body, and I had the urge to reach out and touch him. I knew he wasn't ready for intimacy, though—I'm familiar enough with depression to know it kills sexual appetite along with everything else. I did feel some hope today—his cheery mood was a small glimmer of light breaking through the clouds.

He took the beach chair next to mine, and I handed him a Coke from the cooler. He grabbed the can and took a long swallow. "Thanks, Jo." Looking straight ahead and keeping an eye on the children, he continued. "I'm going to have to go into the office tomorrow. I hate to work on a Sunday, but you know there's never enough time to prepare for a trial, and—"

"You don't have to apologize. I've got everything covered. The kids and I will be fine."

"Are you sure?"

"Of course. How are you feeling about the case at this point?"

He sighed. "Well, the deposition from the psychologist at the Phoenix Recovery Center will help to show Fred's commitment to sobriety. I'm rallying the troops tomorrow to give out marching orders. There's just so much still to do."

"You always get it done."

He nodded. "I suppose so." He leaned farther forward in the beach chair, his elbows resting on his knees and his hands clasped together. Without looking at me, he said, "I'm thinking maybe we should cancel the Memorial Day party."

"What? No, you can't," I objected. It was a tradition he'd started years ago, before we'd even met. The party would be a time for him to reconnect with friends and colleagues. Calling it off felt like a step backward in his recovery.

"I'm not in much of a festive mood, and I've got so much on my plate with this case."

"But everyone loves the party," I said gently. "And besides, you'll enjoy it once it's here. You shouldn't make a rash decision that you'll regret later."

He was quiet. After a moment he sat back, and when he looked at me, I saw resignation in his eyes. "Maybe you're right. But you've got a lot on *your* plate. Especially since Rebecca's not here." The children's nanny had left to care for her father in Michigan after he had had a fall and wouldn't be returning for another couple of weeks.

"Don't worry. I've got this," I assured him. He smiled and nodded.

I knew he would be glad once the day came. He'd be surrounded by people who cared about him—clients, colleagues, and friends, all of whom looked forward to it and most of whom had already RSVP'd. I'd given the caterer the final count this morning. It was the same menu every year—barbecued beef and all the fixings. And yesterday I'd placed an order with the florist for the table centerpieces. This year, they would be red dahlias, white lilies, and blue irises in round white vases. There were still a few tasks left to do—I still needed to get in touch with the face painter and magician the kids and their friends had loved last year—but I knew I'd be able to pull it all off.

I looked over at Leo, who had a faint smile on his face as he watched Evie and Stelli splashing around. We were going to come out of this on the other side. I just knew it.

7

PIPER

Piper lay in bed, eyes open, wide awake. She turned to look at the clock on the bedside table—two a.m. This had been happening to her every night recently—actually, ever since she'd met Leo.

Moving to Westport had been the right decision. At first, she'd been skittish, looking over her shoulder, afraid she'd be found. But after a few months, she'd fallen into a comfortable routine of working at Phoenix all day, then coming home to a quiet house to cook, read, and center herself until the next day. She had promised herself that she would take a year to be alone; that, no matter what, no matter how perfect a man seemed, this time she'd resist.

As soon as she'd met Leo, she'd known it was a promise she wouldn't keep. But the thought of getting involved with a new man brought up memories of the last one, and thinking of Matthew brought back her nightmares. Dark dreams in which Matthew's ex-wife chased her, yelling *Murderer, murderer!*

Throwing back the covers, Piper rose from the bed. There was no way she could go back to sleep now. She made herself some chamomile tea and grabbed her laptop from the counter, though she knew that screen time in the middle of the night was bad for her circadian rhythms. Sinking into the plush sofa cushions, she opened the computer and waited, fingers poised on the keys, for inspiration to strike. She needed to channel her energy into something positive, like a new blog post. Maybe she'd write about starting over.

She'd tried to do just that when she left California after all that blame and finger-pointing. Her mental images of that time still ate at her insides, and she felt a flash of anger burn through her as she looked at the diamond-and-sapphire ring on her right ring finger and remembered how Ava, Matthew's first wife, had actually accused her of stealing it. But Matthew had given her his mother's ring when he proposed, with the understanding that it would one day go to his daughter, Mia, on her own wedding day. But of course, that wasn't going to happen now.

She shook her head as if to sweep the memories away. She didn't want to let Ava steal one more minute of her peace. Suddenly, she had a different idea for the blog post and found her fingers flying across the keyboard.

HOW TO DEAL WITH THE HATERS

You know who they are—those people who seem intent on nothing but stealing the happiness from others. They're the ones who see a negative motive in everything you do. Those folks who blame you for everything from the weather to the sinking of the *Titanic*. They're haters. They have nothing good to say to you or about you. These are toxic people who need to be cut from your life without a backward glance. Maybe it's your mother or your father. A sister or a brother. It doesn't matter. If they're not having a positive influence on your life, they don't belong in it. Find a new sister, a new brother. Blood is not destiny. True connection arises out of mutual respect and benefit. Take a good look around you, identify them, and eliminate these blood-sucking parasites now. Before they ruin your life.

She stopped, her breath coming in short gasps. She couldn't post this. The center's blog—really, its whole image—was all about positivity. But it had made her feel better to put the words on the page. She highlighted the whole paragraph and hit Delete. Thinking of her audience, she began a new post.

MOVING ON AFTER LOSS

Life isn't fair—how many times have you said that to yourself and to others? That simple statement, though true, doesn't begin to plumb the depths of sadness and despair you often experience when something truly terrible happens. After a tragedy, the days are dark, filled with whys and what-ifs: What if you hadn't argued? What if you had pulled up to that intersection five minutes earlier? Why do you feel so guilty? Why *my* husband? Why now?

There are the days when you feel fragile, as if you were made of glass and could shatter at any moment. And finally, when you think you will never smile with pure happiness again, acceptance comes. You will recognize its arrival by the awakening of emotions that you've held at bay for so long. Suddenly, you will find yourself hoping to meet someone with whom to share the rest of your life. And if you're lucky enough to find that person, I say to you, pursue it with all your might. Don't be afraid. Don't let obstacles deter you. If it's worth having, it's worth fighting for. Life is short. Don't let the past keep you from reaching out to grab the future. Believe that it is possible to love with your whole heart again, and to be loved in return. No matter the cost. Peace and Blessings.

That was better. Piper shut down the computer, put her hands behind her neck, and stretched. She'd post it tomorrow. All the blog posts were signed simply with "Phoenix" rather than her name. Let readers make of it what they would.

It was already four o'clock, only an hour before her alarm was set to go off. Even if she managed to fall asleep for the next hour, she knew she'd get up feeling worse. The meeting for Save the

Sound wasn't for two more weeks, and she hated that she had to wait that long to see Leo again. They'd exchanged mobile numbers, so maybe she'd send him a flirty little text in the meantime. She pulled her phone out and swiped to his contact. Thinking a moment, her fingers began to type: Guess what I just picked up at the bookstore. The Count of Monte Cristo. Maybe we can have a little book club meeting when I'm finished. xo. She hit Send and then allowed herself a moment to relive their lunch together, feeling warm inside. Suddenly, images of Matthew and his daughter flashed through her head again.

"Go away!" she shouted.

Matthew was gone, and nothing would bring him back. She stood up straighter and took a deep breath. It was time to put old ghosts to rest.

| 8 |

JOANNA

I had only a few hours to finalize all the details before the guests began to arrive for the party. Pouring a cup of coffee, I sat at the kitchen table and went over the list one more time. I decided to see if perhaps my mother would change her mind and come. At first, she had promised to be there, but then she'd called me two days ago to say she was under the weather. When I took her to the doctor yesterday, he could find nothing wrong, but she still insisted that she was too tired even to attempt a showing. She'd battled chronic fatigue syndrome and depression for as long as I could remember, vacillating between bouts of energy and months when she could barely get out of bed, so I'd learned to become self-sufficient at an early age. I brought her number up on my phone. It rang seven times, and, just as I was about to hang up, she answered.

"Hello?" Her voice was thready.

"Hi, Mom. Just calling to see how you're feeling."

"A little better, hon. Just tired. Ready for the big day?"

"Pretty much. Are you sure you don't want to come for a little bit?" I asked, even though I knew crowds made her anxious and she'd feel out of place. She rarely ventured from her house, and I wished there were a way I could help her to expand her world.

"No, I'm going to take a pass. I'll finish the jigsaw puzzle you got me. I love this kitten one. It's much better than the one you brought over last month with all those skyscrapers."

Why were her compliments always backhanded? I bit back the urge to snap at her; this was one of the things Celeste and I were working on in therapy. "I'm glad you like it, Mom. I'm just sorry you're not up to coming."

"Besides, it's no fun going unescorted. Just another casualty of being left by your husband," she continued, a whine in her voice.

My parents had gotten divorced a lifetime ago, when I was only nineteen, but my mother still played the martyr all these years later.

I suppressed a sigh and forced a cheerful note into my voice. "Okay, then. Get some rest. Feel better." I hung up.

The kids were bursting with excitement, counting down the hours until the fun began. Practically every area of the backyard had been designated for one kind of game or another. There was a face-painting station, a bouncy house, a row of carnival games with stuffed animal prizes, and a snack bar for the kids with all sorts of delicious treats, my favorite being the caramel apples. There was even a photo booth. When they got tired of all of that, the saltwater pool had been filled with floats of all shapes and sizes, and we'd hired two lifeguards to be on duty for the party. Many of the adults would enjoy one of the two hot tubs and the frozen drink bars set up next to them, with bartenders at the ready. Aside from the standard Memorial Day fare of hot dogs and hamburgers, the spread would include pit beef barbecue, corn on the cob, coleslaw, potato salad, baked beans, and watermelon. No one would leave hungry.

I poured myself another cup of coffee and started to review the list one last time, then realized that Stelli and Evie already had their bathing suits on.

"Guys, get over here—let's get some sunscreen on you before we forget."

Evie came right away, but Stelli ran in the other direction. I sighed. I didn't have time for this today, but I knew that Stelli wouldn't respond to my being cross, so I got Evie covered in lotion, then called to her in a stage whisper. "I wonder where Stelli has gone. Did he disappear? I can't see him."

Evie giggled and pointed to where Stelli was partially visible behind a chair.

"I think he must be using his powers of invisibility, Evie. I need to find him and put this magic lotion on him before he disappears forever."

"If you don't do it soon, we'll never see him again," Evie said, playing along.

"That would be so sad. Then I couldn't see him to give him the special Spider-Man comic book I just got him."

"Here I am!" Stelli jumped out from behind the chair.

I pretended to look around. "Where? I can't see you."

He ran to me and threw his arms around my legs. "Here. Put the lotion on so you can see me."

As I rubbed it on, Evie and I pretended to watch him appear one area at a time. By the time I finished, we were all laughing.

"What's so funny?" Leo said as he came into the kitchen.

Stelli ran up to him. "We were putting my magic lotion on." Leo smiled, looking over at me.

"Good thing. I'd hate for you to disappear."

By four o'clock, there were over a hundred guests roaming the property, and I began to make the rounds, greeting everyone and making sure all was going well. I was standing at the bar by the pool, the summer heat making me wilt, and wishing I'd chosen something cooler than linen capris and the long-sleeved cotton shirt I'd picked only because it hid my jiggling upper arms. It was while I was chatting with Annette Morris, one of Leo's partners' assistants, that I noticed a stunning blonde in shorts and a tank top walk over to Leo. She didn't work at the firm, and she wasn't a neighbor, and something about the way they were talking to each other sent alarm signals through me.

"Who's that?" Annette asked.

"I've never seen her before. Maybe she's a guest of someone else from the firm." I tried to sound nonchalant. "Well, have fun. I'm going to mingle a bit."

As I made my way over to Leo and the mystery woman, I was stopped several times by people thanking me and telling me what a wonderful party it was, but Leo and the blonde were still talking when I finally reached them. It took a minute before they seemed to register my presence, and he turned and looked at me.

"Joanna, this is Piper Reynard from the recovery center, the one who tried valiantly to persuade me not to give up on meditation." They both laughed.

"To no avail," Piper said, giving Leo a conspiratorial look, suddenly making me feel as though I'd intruded on a private joke.

Leo went on. "She's new in town, so I thought this would be a good way for her to meet some folks."

I was surprised and a little stung that he hadn't mentioned inviting her to me. She was gorgeous, with chiseled cheekbones, luminous blue eyes, and a fine straight nose. She had a face to rival any actress's. Why had I insisted he go to that damn class? I smiled at her, hoping she couldn't sense how dumpy I felt next to her, and reached out a hand. "Welcome. So nice to meet you. I've been meaning to check out the Phoenix Recovery Center."

"You should come by. I'd love to offer you a complimentary class."

"Thanks. That sounds great," I said, trying to sound sincere, but I wasn't a fan of yoga. And her ease around Leo—not to mention her striking looks—was making me uncomfortable. "How long have you been in Westport?"

"I moved here in January, but I've been so busy with the business, I haven't had time to make many friends."

"Oh, where did you move here from?"

She hesitated for a second. "The West Coast. But I've moved around a lot. It's been hard for me to put down roots. It's so beautiful here that I'm hoping I finally can. Have you always lived in the area?"

"Yes, I was born in Connecticut. Pretty unadventurous, huh?" I said.

"Adventure can take many forms. You can take a journey without traveling a mile."

"That is so true," Leo said, looking at her as though she'd just solved the riddle of the Sphinx. He was normally so pragmatic.

I forced a smile again. "Well, nice to meet you. There's plenty of food and drink, so I hope you'll dig in," I said, even though it looked like she didn't eat at all. She had to be a size two or zero in those little tan shorts, her long legs shapely, without an ounce of cellulite, and arms as buff as they could be. I turned deliberately to Leo.

"Leo, I think Stelli wanted you to see his lion face. He just had it painted." I looked at Piper. "Stelli loves his daddy so much—they're like two peas in a pod."

"Well, I'd better go check on my boy. Enjoy yourself," Leo said as he walked away.

As he moved through the guests, Piper's eyes never left him. I wasn't surprised. Women had always been attracted to Leo, some even making it clear they didn't mind that he was married. There was one thing I knew about Leo, though, and that was that he had integrity. He'd always been a loyal and faithful husband. Still . . . there was something about this woman that made my antennae go up.

The rest of the party went by in a blur. I was continually on the lookout for her and watching Leo, trying to see whether they spoke again, but she didn't seem to have a hard time meeting others. Before she left, she walked up to Leo and put a hand on his arm. They talked for a moment, then he gave her a hug. By the time the last guest drove off, it was after nine. The kids were exhausted, so I put them to bed and then joined Leo in the den.

He sat in the red armchair texting, and when he saw me enter the room, he quickly put his phone away. I bit my tongue and didn't ask who he'd been texting. Leo didn't like to be questioned. "Everyone seemed to enjoy themselves, don't you think?"

"I do. It was another great party. You did a good job."

"Thank you. I hope you're glad we went ahead with it."

He smiled. "I am. You were right."

I cleared my throat. "Piper seemed nice."

"She's very nice. Smart, too."

I felt the heat start at my neck and spread to my face. I had to be careful. If I said anything negative about her, it would only make him come to her defense. "She came alone, so I assume she's not married."

"She's a widow, actually. Her husband died last year." He answered so quickly and with such assurance that I immediately knew that they'd talked about it.

I dropped it, but as soon as Leo went up to bed, I googled "Piper Reynard" on my laptop, but the only hit that came up was the Phoenix Recovery Center, whose main page featured loads of pictures of the space and the programs and none of her. I clicked on the About Us tab on her website, then her name.

Piper Reynard specializes in grief and recovery work. She is the owner of Phoenix Recovery Center, an oasis for all who seek to find mental clarity, spiritual awareness, and emotional healing.

Not much of a bio, and there was no photo of her on that page, which seemed odd. I put her name back into the Google search bar and scanned all the entries. As I scrolled down, I did a double take: Reynard the Trickster. I pulled up a reference page that gave me the background on a medieval character named Reynard the Fox:

Though Reynard is sly, amoral, cowardly, and self-seeking, he is still a sympathetic hero, whose cunning is a necessity for survival.

I sat still, staring at the description. Was Reynard even her real name? Maybe the reason I couldn't find anything from her past is that she'd changed her name. And if she had, had she deliberately chosen "Reynard" because of its disquieting meaning?

But that was crazy. Certainly, it was just a coincidence. I'd just never met a woman so beautiful who didn't have at least a flattering headshot somewhere online these days, especially if she had her own business. Had she found a way to erase herself online? And if so, why? What was she hiding?

| 9 |

PIPER

Piper rushed home after her five o'clock yoga class, grabbed a quick snack of yogurt with fresh blueberries, and went upstairs to shower. She pulled on jeans, slipped into a pair of black sandals, and moved to the full-length mirror. She didn't like the way the jeans looked with the shoes, so she kicked them off, put on her white canvas boat shoes, and checked herself out again. Perfect. She'd been surprised and pleased when Leo had responded to her text with an invitation to his Memorial Day party last week. But to her disappointment, he had been busy with his duties as host most of the time. Then when he'd finally turned his attention to her, Joanna had cut their conversation short.

It was a short drive to the Town Hall, an imposing yellow building with tall white columns, and once inside, Piper was surprised to see how crowded it was—not one empty seat in the first ten rows. She scanned the room but saw no sign of Leo. Her stomach sank, and for a moment, she thought of leaving. Suddenly, she felt someone take the seat next to hers. His lips parted in a wide smile as he met her eyes.

"You made it," he whispered.

She nodded. "I've been looking forward to it."

Before they could talk any further, a man walked to the podium, introduced himself, and reviewed the agenda for the meeting.

That was followed by a series of boring monologues, mostly the reading of minutes from meetings with state officials, which Piper thought would never end. When the meeting finally came to a close, Leo and Piper both rose, and she stood back as several people clustered around him. One woman was going on and on about a petition she wanted to circulate at her country club, all the while fawning over him. It didn't look like he'd be free anytime soon, so Piper picked up her purse and slung it over her shoulder as she headed toward the exit. Before she'd taken more than five steps, though, she stopped. What was she thinking? She'd waited for this all week, and now she was going to just turn and run? No way. She walked back to where he was and put a hand on his arm.

"Just wanted to say good night," she said to him, hoping he'd take the hint and extricate himself from the woman.

He held up a finger to Piper, turned to the country club woman, and handed her a card. "I'm afraid I have to call it a night, but please feel free to call or email me about any other concerns you have, okay?"

As they left, Leo turned back to her. "Thanks for sticking around."

"Well," she said, "it was an interesting meeting. Thanks for inviting me. I'm going to get going."

Leo frowned. "How about a drink? It's only nine thirty, and I promise I won't keep you out too late."

She felt her face flush with pleasure and her stomach seesaw. "Sure. And you can keep me out as late as you like." Piper wanted to retract the words as soon as she said them, fearing she sounded too forward. But when he looked at her with those warm brown eyes and a grateful smile, she felt relieved.

He put a hand on her back as they walked to the door, and she felt a shiver go up her spine at his touch. "Why don't we just walk over to The Pointe?"

"Sounds good."

The night air was cool, and Piper swung her sweater over her shoulders as they walked.

"Cold?" he asked.

"A little." She pulled the sweater more tightly around herself as Leo took his jacket off and put it on her shoulders. It felt romantic, gallant even.

"Here we are," Leo said, as they stopped in front of the restaurant and he opened the door for her.

They sat at the bar and ordered two martinis. By the time they'd ordered their second drinks and discussed the plans for Save the Sound, Piper was feeling pretty uninhibited.

"So," she asked, "what do you do for fun? You know, when you're not crusading for justice or saving the planet."

"I hike and swim with my kids, I travel, and I used to fly."

Piper was surprised. "Fly? As in you were a pilot?"

"Yup. As in I *am* a pilot. I used to have a single-engine Beechcraft Bonanza that I kept at the airfield. My wife gave me such a hard time about it, though, that I ended up selling it."

She deflated a little at the mention of his wife. But he was here, after all, with her. "You're full of surprises."

They stayed for another round, and Leo insisted on picking up the check. It was after eleven when he ordered an Uber for them since they'd been drinking. They could get their cars in the morning. When the car pulled up to her house, Leo asked the driver to wait, and he escorted her to the door. She unlocked it and turned to him. "I had a wonderful time tonight."

"I did, too. Thanks again for coming. It was nice getting to know you better," he said.

She had hoped he might kiss her good night, but he simply smiled and walked back to the car, giving her a wave before the driver pulled away from the curb. She looked forward to the night when his own car would be parked in her driveway until morning.

| 10 |

JOANNA

I had canceled my appointment with Celeste, because I had forgotten that I'd scheduled a dental checkup for Stelli and Evie at the same time, but now I really needed to talk to her. She didn't have an opening but had promised to call me in between sessions. As I paced in the kitchen waiting to hear from her, I was in a panic.

When Leo had casually mentioned last week that he'd invited Piper to the Save the Sound meeting, I'd been concerned. It was after eleven when Leo had gotten home from it, and I was pretty sure he and Piper had gone out afterward, since these meetings never went on that late. I'd pretended to be asleep that evening because I wasn't ready for a confrontation, but now, just a week later, I checked his calendar to see dinner reservations in Greenwich. I called the restaurant to confirm the reservation, to see if maybe it was a surprise for me and the children, but no, he'd made a reservation for two. I had a sneaking suspicion that Piper was on the menu.

"Thanks for calling," I said after picking up on the first ring.

"Of course," Celeste reassured me. "I'm sorry my schedule is so jammed this week. What's going on?"

"I think Leo's improved mood may have something to do with a woman." I quickly told her about his Greenwich dinner tonight.

"Joanna, Leo has never given you any reason to doubt him before. You don't know that he's having dinner with Piper. It could be a business dinner, couldn't it?"

"He never goes all the way to Greenwich for a business dinner.

I think he wants to go somewhere he won't be recognized. Besides, there's something about Piper that worries me. It's not that I think he would do anything wrong, but . . . I don't know . . . I think she's trouble."

"Have you discussed any of this with Leo?"

"I tried, but he got defensive. I saw a text from her on his phone the other day while he was in the pool with the kids. Something about how she was watching *The Godfather* and what a good movie it was. I made the mistake of asking Leo about it when he came back in the house."

"What did he say?"

"He got angry and asked why I was reading his texts. I tried to backpedal, telling him that his phone had been on the counter and I thought it might be an urgent work thing. But he was still irritated. He seems annoyed with me for every little thing lately."

"Maybe you just need to give him some space. He's finding his feet again after a really rough patch. Of course he'd lash out at you, being the person closest to him, someone he can be himself around. You might just find you have nothing to fear after all. Why don't you try to focus on yourself and see what happens?"

She may have been right, but I knew in the pit of my stomach as soon as I'd seen "Oyster House 8:00" in his planner that I had reason to worry. Despite Celeste's advice, I asked Leo about it later that day.

"I didn't know you'd made a reservation at the Oyster House," I said, hoping against hope that he'd tell me it was for the two of us.

He gave me a hard look. "Are you checking up on me?"

"Of course not," I lied. "They called here to confirm the reservation."

"It's a business dinner."

"For Fred Grainger's case?"

"Yes. I'm meeting Piper there."

My stomach was churning. "I thought you said you'd gotten everything you needed from Fred's counselor. Why do you need to have dinner with Piper?"

"I just want some more background on the center."

"Do you think that's a good idea? It won't look good if anyone recognizes you. You shouldn't be seen in public with anyone associated with the witnesses you're calling for his defense."

His mouth was set in a hard line. "I've told you, Joanna, I don't need you to monitor my every move. I need my space. I appreciate how much you've done to support me and everything you've had to take on these past few months, but I'm better now. Stop hovering and checking up on me all the time. And you don't need to lecture me on legal protocol: I'm the lawyer."

"I'm not trying to lecture you. I'm just trying to help." His reminding me that I didn't have a law degree was a cheap shot. He knew how much I regretted not finishing school. And besides, we'd always talked about work, until recently.

He shook his head. "It would be helpful if you would drop it." I didn't understand what he was getting so defensive about if he had nothing to hide, but Celeste had warned me that people coming out of a depressive episode can get easily irritated, as they were suddenly dealing with an influx of more emotion. I worried that I was beginning to sound like my mother—her suspicion and constant questioning. That hadn't done her any good with my father, and it certainly wouldn't endear me to Leo.

I put my hands up in supplication. "Consider it dropped."

But of course, I couldn't drop it. I hired a sitter and borrowed my mother's car, confident he wouldn't recognize it, then drove to the restaurant and found a spot on the street. Watching the entrance in the rearview mirror, I waited. At precisely eight, I saw two people walking toward the door and felt a knot in my stomach when Piper came into view. She was dressed in a body-hugging navy-blue dress, her shiny blond hair looking as though it had just been professionally blown out. Given my dark hair and brown eyes, Piper and I were polar opposites, I realized, and I wondered if that's what had attracted Leo to her.

He put his hand on her back and guided her in. I felt my cheeks burn, my hands clench into fists. Breathing in and out, I forced myself to calm down. He was either lying right to my face, or he was lying to himself—if they talked about the case at all, I'd be shocked. But this all seemed so outside of his personality—at least, his old personality. I was worried that this was more the doing of Piper, this stranger with no Internet history, than his.

My next move needed to be calculated. I sat there for a long while, trying to decide what to do. Finally, I realized that I wanted to be with the children, to remind myself of everything I had at home. But first I had to return my mother's car.

When I pulled into her driveway, I saw that the lights were still on. She was sitting at the card table working on her jigsaw puzzle while a rerun of *The Golden Girls* blared from the large television in the corner. Her hearing was getting worse, I realized, and made a mental note to make an appointment for her with the audiologist. She clicked the remote, and the TV went silent.

"Those girls have the right idea. Everything would be so much better if I lived in a nice house in Florida with some good friends. Look at all the fun they have. My life is the pits," she grumbled, taking a long swallow from the glass of wine on the table next to her. I sighed. Mom wasn't supposed to drink with her condition.

"Thanks for lending me your car," I said as I put her keys on the table.

"You're welcome. What's wrong with your car? Couldn't that

big shot Leo let you use his?" She'd never thought much of Leo. She didn't think much of any man, really, not after what my father had done. There was no way I was going to tell her about his dinner. I knew what she'd say. *All men are liars. You can't trust any of them.*

"I'm low on oil," I lied. "I had an appointment and didn't have time to stop. I'll swing by a gas station now."

"Make sure you do. You don't want your engine to burn out."

I nodded absently. "How are you feeling today?"

She shrugged. "Not great. I think I need to go back to the doctor this week, see if he can give me something for these headaches. Can you take me if I get an appointment?" She gave me a pitiful look. "I'm sorry to be such a burden."

I walked over to her and put my hands on her shoulders. "You're not a burden, Mom. Of course I'll take you. But . . . the doctor did tell you that alcohol can exacerbate the headaches." I looked at the glass of wine again.

She gave me a sheepish look. "I only have it sometimes. I'm lonely, and you're always so busy. If your father hadn't up and left—"

"It's okay." I didn't want to hear her rage against my father right now. He'd left years ago, as in over twenty of them, and I had other things on my mind. "I understand. Just let me know, and I'll be happy to take you. I'll stop by and check on you tomorrow."

"Thanks, dear." She unmuted the TV and went back to her show.

• • •

He got home before the sun rose but not *much* before. I was waiting for him when he walked in, and he was clearly startled to see me there, pacing in the hallway. I didn't wait for him to speak.

"I was worried. Do you realize how late it is?" My voice was shaking. "I couldn't sleep."

He put a hand up, looking at me as though I'd lost my mind. "Whoa. I got a call while I was at dinner. One of the firm's clients was arrested, and they lost his paperwork. I've been at the jail all night. His attorney's in the hospital, so I had to go. It's been a hell of a night."

Then I noticed his disheveled appearance, the tie askew, his usually perfect, thick, black hair out of place. He did look like he'd been up with a client all night, and certainly he had been many times before. This whole thing with Piper was making me overreact. "I'm sorry. You know how I worry." I took a deep breath. "Why don't you try and get some sleep? I could certainly use some."

He shook his head. "I need to get to the office early today. I'm just going to take a shower and get going."

In spite of my restless night, the morning went off like any other. I got the kids ready for the day, made coffee, gave instructions to the maid service, and took care of all the little minutiae that comprised my life—our lives. As I did so, I told myself that I had nothing to worry about. After all, Leo had been a loyal and devoted family man for years. But was I underestimating how his depression might have changed him? He may not have been looking for anything, but I had a feeling she was.

I went to the computer and pulled up his Outlook. When I saw her name in the sender line, I clicked on it. I suppose it didn't occur to her that I'd have access to his work in-box. The message was from a few days ago.

> You're never going to believe what happened today. I was at the dentist, in the waiting room, flipping through a *People*, when I came

across an article about YOU! It was about the case you won two years ago, the woman accused of killing her in-laws. A whole spread. The woman sitting next to me glanced over (a bit nosily) at the picture of you and said, "Oh, my, he's a handsome one." I told her you were even better-looking in person.

Even when I try not to think of you . . . it's impossible.

Have a wonderful day and do remember to take a break from your desk. Use the app I showed you and remember the quote from Anatole France: "If the path be beautiful, let us not ask where it leads." Xo P

I felt like my entire body was on fire.

One thing was for sure: Piper was interested in much more than court cases and conservation, whether Leo realized it or not.

| 11 |

PIPER

Piper opened the door, and Leo stepped into the foyer, bringing in the steamy July humidity with him. He kissed her lightly on the cheek, and she tried to restrain herself from letting him see how much she wanted him already.

"You look beautiful," he said, giving her an appreciative smile.

"Thank you," she said, grabbing her clutch from the table and pulling the door shut behind her. They were seated as soon as they arrived at the restaurant, and Leo scanned the menu. "What looks good to you?"

"I'm thinking about the swordfish," she answered, putting her menu down.

"Shall we order a Chardonnay then?"

She nodded, and he ordered a bottle of DuMOL. As they raised their glasses, smiling and looking into each other's eyes, she could almost feel the heat coming from his side of the table.

"I was a little surprised to get your call," she said. She wanted to lay her cards on the table before the evening went too far.

"You were? Why?"

She straightened up in her chair a bit and softened her voice just so as she said, "I didn't think you were ready for a new relationship. You told me that you still loved your wife."

He leaned back in his chair and was quiet a moment. "There will always be a place in my heart for her, but I know I have to move forward. I've been struggling for months, and I'm tired of being sad. I have to move forward. You've helped me to see that."

She felt encouraged by his words but wanted to be sure. "I've never been a big believer in games, so I hope you'll forgive my frankness. I've been attracted to you since the day I met you, but I didn't think you were available. Are you really sure you are?"

He reached out and grabbed her hand, and a thrill ran through her. "I'm certain. Don't you remember the quote you sent me about the beautiful path? If I've learned anything in my life, it's that you have to reach out and grab happiness with both hands. You make me happy." He tilted his head. "Can I be honest, too?"

She nodded.

"I knew there was something special between us from the start, too. I think, Ms. Piper Reynard, that you are my destiny."

She took a sip of her wine, trying to temper her elation. Her past was littered with starts and stops. Things had too often gone badly, but this time would be different. This time, she would make sure that nothing got in her way.

"I like the sound of that." She squeezed his hand. "If I'm your destiny, I want to know all about you. You've told me a little about your family, but what was young Leo Drakos like?" she teased.

"I had the best childhood in the world. I'm the youngest of three sons. Wonderful parents—hardworking, honest, loving—I think I told you that my dad owned a restaurant in Astoria, down the street from where we lived." He talked with great passion about his family—their fierce love and loyalty to one another, their pride in Leo's accomplishments, the raucous and fun dinners around their dining room table, and their family trips to Greece. He made it all sound magical, and so different from her sterile and lonely upbringing that as she looked across the table at him, she felt a longing to be part of this warm and devoted family.

"Did your mother work in the restaurant, too?" Piper asked.

"Sometimes on the weekend, but never when we were small. She was at home every day after school, and she made dinner for us every night. She's an amazing cook."

Piper filed that tidbit away. Their love of cooking would be something that she and his mother would have in common. She'd been able to forge a good connection with Matthew's mother, and Ethan's, too, for that matter. Now, she'd get another chance with Leo's.

"How did your brothers feel about you not working in the family business?"

"There was no issue—Gus and George always wanted to work at the restaurant. They loved it. They were happy for me because they knew I was doing something I loved. My father insisted on paying for my undergrad, but when I went to NYU Law, I waited tables to help cover my tuition. My family's always been very supportive of me."

"They do sound wonderful," Piper said.

"When you meet them, you can see for yourself."

"I look forward to it." And she meant it. She *was* looking forward to it and hoped they would like her. She was reticent to ask her next question but went ahead—forewarned was forearmed and all that. "Did they always get along with your wife?"

"Yes. She was good to my family from day one. A devoted daughter-in-law. My mother and father adored her—they never stopped. But they don't know the whole story."

"The whole story?"

He shrugged. "I'm sorry, I know we're being open and honest, but to say more wouldn't be fair to her. Suffice it to say that things are not always what they look like on the outside."

She didn't press him.

He put his hand over hers and gave her a small smile. "Since I've met you, Piper, I feel lighter, like a heavy load has been lifted from my shoulders. I can't remember the last time I felt so happy."

They talked until the restaurant closed then went back to her house. He seemed hesitant when she invited him in, but he followed her into the living room, and they sat beside each other on the sofa, the soft glow of moonlight spilling into the quiet darkness. After their conversation had been exhausted, he put his arm around her and she laid her head on his shoulder. He leaned forward and, putting his hand on her cheek, gently turned her face to his. Their lips met in a deep and passionate kiss. She wanted to whisk him upstairs to the bedroom and make love to him all night, but she could tell he was a traditional man, the kind who wanted to make the first move, so she held back.

He looked at his watch. "It's late. I need to get home."

She did her best to hide her disappointment as they stood and kissed again, this time longer and more slowly. Desire burned within her. She didn't know how much longer she could wait, but she was in it for the long game and didn't want to scare him off.

His voice was husky as he whispered in her ear. "You are a hard woman to resist."

"You don't have to," she teased.

He cupped her face in his hands. "As much as I hate to leave, I do have to get home. Can I see you again this weekend?"

She nodded. "Yes."

"I'll call you tomorrow," he said.

Later that night, she lay in bed and thought about the days ahead and all they had to look forward to. The only cloud on the horizon was the inevitable day when she would meet Leo's kids. She'd never wanted children of her own, something about which she and Ethan had been of one mind, so it'd been easy when she was with him. Stelli and Evie would probably be wary of her at first, and she thought about ways she might get them to like and accept her. She needed to be careful and not come on too strong. She knew it was a delicate thing, introducing one's children to the new girlfriend. The children would have to be part of any future she'd have with Leo, but they were young and malleable. Maybe that would make the difference this time.

| 12 |

JOANNA

The morning after the clearly-not-business dinner, I knew I had to take some kind of action, but I was having trouble coming up with a next step that didn't make me seem like a jealous shrew. Finally, it came to me in a flash. I would email Piper and tell her I'd like to take her up on her offer of a free class at her "recovery and healing center," to get a look at her in her own element. I knew that yoga was going to be a stretch for me—pun intended. I've never been much of a gym person; at most, I hop on the treadmill for half an hour or so, and much prefer walking or swimming. I guess that's why I don't wear a single-digit size. I figured I'd stick to the back of the class and hopefully nobody, especially Piper, would notice my ineptitude.

I'd gone online to google some basic moves so that I'd know my Downward-Facing Dog from my Tree, which, if you ask me, are ridiculous names. The Warrior poses, however, I can get behind—at least they make you sound like you're kicking some ass. Clad in black Lycra and carrying a newly purchased yoga mat, I took a spot in the crowded studio. I was relieved to see the low lighting and had to admit the music coming from the speakers—which had been designed to look like stones—was soothing. *How hard could it be?* I thought. It was yoga. But then I paid closer attention to the women surrounding me. Women who looked like they could bounce a quarter off their bicep muscles. Tanned, blond, boasting diamond rings on their left hands that could have served as brass knuckles, all of them—every single one—looked as though they hadn't eaten in weeks. *Tank-Top Girls*, I call them. You didn't get into that kind of shape by just breathing and stretching. Even though this was billed as a beginner's class, it was clear to me these women had done yoga before.

Two minutes before the hour, Piper walked in dressed in sky-blue yoga pants and a sports bra that showed off her six-pack. Everyone stood at attention, staring at her as if she were royalty. Her long blond hair was pulled back into a slick ponytail, her perfect complexion devoid of makeup. Even bare-faced, she was stunning.

"Hello, everyone! It's a beautiful evening to get healthy! Any newcomers today?"

I wasn't about to raise my hand since she'd already acknowledged me with a nod when I first walked into the center. A woman in the front raised hers, fortunately, and Piper focused her attention there.

"Welcome! Go at your own speed. Remember, we're all running our own race."

I groaned inwardly. It was like she'd memorized a book of platitudes. I tried to keep my eyes on her, but it was difficult in some of the positions my body had to endure. I might have been wrong about loving the Warrior poses—my legs trembled as I tried to hold Warrior Two. From the glances I was able to steal, Piper was an unquestioned star at yoga. Her body did amazing things. I'd already known my figure was no match for hers, but with her agility? Forget it. Men probably wanted to tumble into bed with her the first time they saw her. My face burned at the thought of Leo thinking that about her.

At the end of the class, we lay on our mats, relaxing our bodies. My muscles were already sore. Piper dimmed the lights, and in a soft voice, she read a poem about staying connected to nature and the Earth. Then she walked slowly around the room with aromatic oil and asked us to take a moment of appreciation for our time in class. *Gratitude is restorative*, she said. And then from the front of the room, facing us as we sat up on our mats, she put her hands together in Prayer pose and uttered the word *Namaste*, to which the class responded, "Namaste." I had looked it up earlier and knew it meant "the divine in me bows to the divine in you."

I was eager to get out of there before the women dispersed, and luckily so many of them were crowded around Piper, vying for her attention, that she didn't notice me leave. As I stood outside by my car, fishing in my bag for the keys, I spied the gorgeous redhead with a killer body who'd been a few mats over from me.

"Hi, there." I approached her and put on my brightest smile. "This was my first yoga class, and I just have some beginner questions. Do you mind if I ask how long you've been coming here?"

"A while now. I usually go to Piper's barre class, but my work schedule is a little crazy this week. She's a super yoga teacher, not to mention she's a great person."

A Piper groupie, I thought. "Yeah, she seems very nice," I said, nodding, hoping she'd go on.

"Oh, she is. We've become friends."

"How nice. I heard somewhere that she's new in town."

"Yeah," she said, looking off as if in thought. "Somewhere out west, Oregon or California? I can't remember which." She looked at her watch, then back at me. "Well, I've got to run. It was nice to meet you."

"You, too," I said, and went back to my car. Vague. That's the vibe I was picking up from Piper. There was definitely a vagueness surrounding her.

Just as I opened the car door, I saw Piper come out of the center.

Quickly shutting it, I walked over to her, figuring I might as well take the opportunity.

Her eyes widened when she saw me. "Joanna, hi! I was wondering where you'd gone. How did you like the class?"

"It was a bit difficult, to be honest. I'm not sure yoga is for me."

She looked uncomfortable, her hands fingering her keys. "The first time can be hard, but if you keep it up, you might find you like it."

I nodded and maintained eye contact. "Leo tells me that the preliminary work on the case is proceeding well and that you've been a big help."

She just stared at me.

I went on. "He and I were talking about the timing after your meeting the other night. At the Oyster House."

I watched her carefully and saw the slightest flicker of a tic in her cheek. She took a step back, her face now a mask. She wasn't going to give anything away. I could see that.

"Well," she said, backing up even more, "I need to get going. Nice to see you, and thanks for trying us out."

"One thing," I called as she was walking away. She turned, giving me an impatient look. "It could put Leo in jeopardy, being seen with a potential witness."

"I don't know what you're talking about. I have to go," she said in a huff and walked quickly to her convertible. Figures it was one of those expensive imports.

I stood alone in the parking lot, thinking about our exchange and berating myself for having handled it so clumsily. I shouldn't have been so impulsive, should have thought more before I spoke. She worried me, though. Leo was a good judge of character; you hone those skills as a criminal lawyer. But I was seeing something in her that he was missing. When she looked at me with those cold eyes and unyielding expression, I'd felt a chill in my spine. She hadn't reacted at all to my words of caution, and even if she didn't care about me—and that seemed relatively certain—shouldn't she care about her new "friend" Leo? But it got me an answer: Piper Reynard was not the kind, feeling soul she pretended to be. Of that I was sure.

13

PIPER

Piper couldn't stop thinking about her evening with Leo. She found herself smiling as she replayed it over and over, and couldn't wait to finish her classes and get home and talk to him. She'd barely been able to concentrate all day, checking her phone for the texts he was sending her, telling her he couldn't wait to see her, how she made him feel alive again, even trivial tidbits about how his day was going. It reminded her of her high school days, the notes she and Ethan had sent to each other, how much in love they'd been.

The one sour note had been when Joanna showed up at the yoga class. It felt like her eyes would burn holes through Piper, and it had been all she could do to concentrate while she taught. And then afterward, when Joanna had confronted Piper in the parking lot, she'd just wanted to tell her to go away and get a life—and flashed right back to Ava screaming at her in public. Instead, she'd walked away, but as she strode to her car, she was already formulating the conversation she'd need to have with Leo.

When she got home, she called him, ready to get to the heart of the matter.

"Hey there. How are you?" His voice was warm.

"Well, actually, I've been better. I've just had a visit from Joanna. She came to the center and took a class, then approached me in the parking lot."

She heard a tsk of disapproval on the other end of the line. "What did she say?"

"It was what she didn't say—a warning to stay away from you."

"What do you mean?"

"Leo, listen. You told me you're ready to move on. She doesn't seem to understand that. I have very strong feelings for you, too, but I can't let myself get in the middle of this."

She heard a loud sigh before Leo spoke again. "She's having a hard time coming to grips with the situation. I'm trying to be kind. But you have to believe me—I want to look ahead, not back. And when I look ahead, I see you." He paused, as if to let that sink in. "I hope you feel the same. And I hope you'll stick around while I sort everything out."

"I want to, but . . ." She trailed off, certain he'd prompt her to finish her thought.

"But what?" he asked softly.

She smiled—he wanted to know, wanted to make things right with *her.* "I . . . I hate thinking of her living there still."

Leo cleared his throat. "I'm working on that. She's going to be gone soon. I promise."

Piper didn't answer right away, letting him sweat it out, then finally spoke. "Please don't make me wait too long."

| 14 |

JOANNA

After my terrible yoga class and awkward conversation with Piper, I needed to wind down. I checked on a sleeping Evie and Stelli, whom the sitter had put to bed, then poured myself a large glass of merlot. Whatever was going on or not going on between them, it was clear to me that she was uncomfortable seeing me, a flesh-and-blood reminder that Leo wasn't actually on the market. Though I'd intended only to make that clear to her, I worried that my confronting her might have forced his hand. What I didn't realize then was that I was about to take too many false steps and make too many mistakes.

I wanted to look my best when he got home, so I headed to the closet and looked through the dresses hanging there. Each time I'd seen Piper, she'd looked like she'd stepped off the pages of some kind of glossy magazine, and I didn't want him to compare my more casual style with hers and find me lacking.

My eyes were drawn to a red cocktail dress, which I pulled off the rail, unzipped, and stepped into. It was tight, but if I dimmed the lights, maybe he wouldn't notice. After squeezing out of it and laying it carefully on the bed, I went to the dresser, found some Spanx, and pulled them on. I squeezed into the dress a second time—it fit better now—and applied some red Chanel lipstick, smoothed my hair, and went downstairs to wait. I was sitting in the corner of the living room, sipping my wine, when my phone rang.

My mother's name flashed on the screen.

"Hi, Mom."

A voice I didn't recognize came over the line. "Hello, is this Mrs. Doyle's daughter?"

I felt my stomach drop. "Yes?"

"I'm calling from Norwalk Hospital. Your mother fell and broke her leg. She's going into surgery shortly, but she asked us to call you before she was taken in."

"Oh my gosh! I'll be right there." As I rushed back into the hallway, Leo walked in the front door and we almost collided.

His eyes widened when he saw me. "What are you wearing?"

"I . . . I just wanted to look nice. Please, Leo," I said, running up the stairs, "I wanted to talk tonight, but my mom's in the hospital. I have to change and get over there."

"What happened?" He followed me to the second floor.

"She broke her leg. That's all I know. I have to get to the hospital."

"Yes, of course. I'm so sorry to hear it. Call and let us know how she is, okay?"

I left the house, touched by Leo's concern.

When I got home late the next afternoon, I was exhausted. I'd spent the night at the hospital in a chair next to my mother's bed. She looked so frail and vulnerable, and I wished there was something I could do to help her as she moaned in agony, despite the painkillers the doctor had prescribed. It was a displaced fracture, but it could have been worse. She could have broken a hip and been sent to a rehab facility. She did, however, need someone to take care of her at home. I'd asked her to come stay at the house, but she refused, saying she wanted to be in her own space, not to have to worry about Leo looking down on her, thinking she was not up to his so-called social standards. She'd always felt insecure around him, and no amount of reassurance on my part could change that.

Leo got home early for a change. I'd already filled him in on Mom's condition by text, but I had to tell him what I'd decided in the meantime. As soon as he came into the kitchen, I cleared my throat. "I need to go and stay with her until she's back on her feet, or at least until I can find someone to help her."

He nodded. "Of course, you should do whatever you have to do. I can arrange for a sitter for the rest of the week. And Rebecca's coming back on Monday anyway, so there's nothing to worry about."

"Maybe I could take Stelli and Evie with me?" The thought of leaving them behind was more than upsetting.

But Leo shook his head. "We can't disrupt their routines like that. Besides, your mother only has two bedrooms. Joanna, you should focus on her right now. We'll be fine, I promise."

I packed myself a bag of clothes with a heavy heart. And then I thought that maybe it would be good to give him a chance to miss me. Perhaps a little space would do us both some good.

The children were upset when I hugged them goodbye, but I promised that I'd be back as soon as I could and that we'd talk every day. And of course, they could come and see me, only briefly on the days when they had after-school activities, but at least it was something.

I followed Leo down the front steps as he carried my bag to the car. I spotted the gardener in the distance, trimming the tall hedges along the perimeter, and took one last look around the property before leaving. The garden beds were meticulously cared for, and they were a riot of color, lush with blooms of red, purple, and yellow. I caught the exquisite scent of roses as I neared my car, and turned, standing still to look again at the house I was leaving, feeling a vague sense of foreboding. The sound of the trunk slamming startled me, and then Leo walked around to the driver's side, opening the door for me. I looked at him before getting into the car, waiting for him to say he would miss me, but he simply patted me on the shoulder and said, "Give your mother my best. It's good that you'll be there for her."

And that was it. I drove the twenty minutes to my mother's, tears blurring my vision the entire way. I'd brought her home earlier that morning and had asked a neighbor to stay with her while I ran out. The medical supply company had set up a hospital bed in the living room, where Mom would sleep, so she didn't have to try to navigate stairs with her cast and crutches, and so that I could stay close by to wait on her.

The week went by in a blur. The only bright spot each day was when the sitter brought the kids over. They were so sweet to Mom, and she seemed a little cheered by their presence, although I could tell she was happy to have my undivided attention when it came time for them to leave. As they pouted, I explained why I couldn't go home with them, but Stelli cried for the first few days.

It about killed me. I couldn't do this much longer. I had to find a nurse or someone to stay the night so I could go back and be with my family. One day, just after the kids had left, I broached the subject with my mother, and she looked at me with fury in her eyes.

"I took care of you for your whole life, and you can't sacrifice a few weeks of yours for me?"

"Mom, it's not that," I said, trying to keep my voice even. "The kids need me, too. I asked you to come stay with us, but you insisted on being here. Please try to understand."

"I understand—you care more about that hotshot lawyer than

your mother. The children have sitters and their father. They'll be fine."

"I know, Mom. But they're young. It's too hard for them to come here and then go home without me."

"Fine, Joanna. Abandon your mother. Just remember that I gave up my career for you. I stayed home with you when you had mono. Remember? For six months I couldn't work, and they gave my promotion to someone else. Who knows what direction my life would have taken if I'd been made a manager at my company? Instead, I lost my job. Your father left us for that woman and her daughter. And I took care of you after he was gone, even though you were already eighteen. I could have kicked you out like a lot of parents do when their kids come of age."

I threw my hands up. What was the use? She always won. "I'll stay, I'll stay."

That was my first mistake.

The next week, we were just finishing breakfast when a van pulled up to the house and a man knocked on the door to ask me where to put *all* my belongings—boxes, bags, and suitcases full of my stuff. The boxes looked like they'd been packed hurriedly, the clothing barely folded and overflowing out of the tops, my toiletries in a mixed jumble. My journals and books were thrown together in bags along with some framed photographs. I felt shocked and violated.

Thunderstruck, I called Leo. "What's going on? Did you just have my things sent to my mother's house?"

He sighed loudly. "Damn! I'm so sorry, Joanna. They weren't supposed to come until tomorrow. I wanted to talk to you first." He took a deep breath as my heart hammered in my chest. "Listen, I've been thinking about this for a while now. It's not healthy anymore, living together."

"How can you do this? How can you end it like this? Leo . . . I—"

"Joanna, I've got a client in the waiting room. I *am* sorry, but I have to go for now." He hung up.

Was he serious? How dare he use my mother's accident to get me out of the house? I'd have to go talk to him in person.

I barely made it through the rest of the day, but as soon as the clock hit six, I asked Mom's next-door neighbor to come over and stay with her again, and she kindly agreed. I got to the house before Leo got home from work and let myself in. Rebecca looked surprised to see me when I walked into the kitchen but said nothing. I spent some time reading to the children, then asked Rebecca to take them out to dinner in town. I didn't want them to overhear my conversation with Leo.

While I waited for him, I looked around the room and did a double-take when I spotted a new espresso machine. I'd never known Leo to drink espresso.

I braced myself when I heard his car pull up and the garage door open.

He seemed startled to see me when he came into the house. "What are you doing here?"

"I came to talk to you." My heart was beating so fast I thought I would pass out. It was ridiculous that I was feeling this shaky and nervous, given that this was where I belonged.

He gave me a sympathetic look. "Let's sit down and talk about this calmly." He put his hand on my back and led me gently to the couch in the living room, then turned to me. "Joanna, I'm sorry. I know this isn't what you want, but I just can't give you what you want. I'd like for us to part as friends, especially for the sake of the children."

Tears sprang to my eyes. "*Friends?* I don't understand. I've helped you get through this horrible time, and now you want to get rid of me? How can you just . . . dispose of me after all these years? I've been the one by your side as you've built your practice. I've taken care of the house. Devoted myself to the children. I've always handled everything so you didn't have to worry about anything. And now, you want to replace me and go on with your life?" The pain of his betrayal ripped through me as if I were being torn in two.

He put his head in his hands for a moment, then looked at me again. "I do appreciate everything you've done over the years, but I can't help my feelings. Life is short. I'm in love with someone else, and I need to be happy."

I stood up, my face hot. "Piper Reynard? How long have you known her—three weeks, a month?" My voice rose. "She's just using you. Why can't you see that?" I was losing it, and I knew I sounded crazy, but there was too much emotion boiling up inside me. Later I'd wonder if I had stayed calm, if I had told him about my concerns about Piper's lack of a past and what she might be hiding, would it have gone better? But my heart was shattering, and there was no way to hold it in.

His eyes were filled with pity. This wasn't my Leo in front of me. It was as though he'd been replaced by a look-alike, an imposter. He shook his head. "You're wrong. Piper loves me, and I love her. We're going to be together, and you need to accept that. You'll find someone yourself. You just need to let go."

His words were like a physical blow. I actually staggered backward, trying to catch my breath. "How can you say that?"

"Because it's true. And I want the best for you. You need to get on with your life. I'll be more than generous. You won't have to worry about money."

"You think you can just buy me off? I don't want your money. I want you! I want us!"

"There *is* no us. You need to let go."

"How can you be so cruel? I love you. We're a family. Don't do this."

"Please, Joanna. Don't make this harder than it has to be. You need to go." He rose and stood, looking down at me, waiting. "Come on. I'll walk you to your car."

I followed him to the front door, my mind churning. How could I be losing everything that mattered to me?

| 15 |

PIPER

As soon as Piper had awakened, Leo had called to confirm their plans for that afternoon. After they said goodbye, she poured a second cup of tea, and almost immediately, her phone pinged with a text message. Counting the hours until I see you. Hated having to leave you last night. Xo. Piper smiled. She couldn't wait either. They talked every day now, usually first thing in the morning and the last thing at night, bookending their days. They even managed to see each other three nights a week. She'd been afraid at first that it would be hard for him to get away, but now that Joanna was gone, and the nanny, Rebecca, was living there again, it had become easier. The only thing that frustrated her was that Leo had been taking things very slowly, and had told her that he wanted everything to be perfect when they finally became intimate with each other. Piper still hadn't met the children, and a part of her wondered if that was some sort of a test, if perhaps Leo wanted to make sure that his children approved of her before taking the relationship to the next level. But she was tired of waiting and intended to speed things up tonight.

Piper lifted the tea bag and placed it on the small porcelain dish, smiling to herself. She and Leo had never spent a weekend day together, but this Saturday was going to be different. Stelli and Evie were spending all day Saturday and Sunday morning with Leo's parents. That meant that Leo and Piper had the entire day and night to themselves, and she planned to make the most of their time.

She rose and walked to the conservatory, where a wall of glass faced out across the Long Island Sound, sat in an armchair, and closed her eyes. Her mind had been wandering lately when she meditated, and so she tried to keep herself focused on her breath, in and out. When she looked at her watch, she was pleased to see that a half hour had passed. Pulling out her yoga mat, she did some stretches and a short routine. Her body felt supple and limber.

Everything was good. Even the weather was cooperating—it was a gorgeous July morning, with no rain in the forecast, and winds were from the southwest at ten knots. An ideal day for sailing. She had made arrangements with the club to pack a lunch basket and a bottle of wine for them to take on the sailboat. Leo would meet her on the dock at noon.

With one last look at the calm waters, she went upstairs to dress, pulling on a pair of white shorts and a navy T-shirt, and taking a light sweater from the closet shelf in case it got cooler toward evening. On the way out, she grabbed a tube of sunscreen, since she couldn't remember how much was left in the one on the boat. She'd been so busy at work and her mind occupied with Leo that she hadn't taken it out since the beginning of June, and she'd missed it. Being on the water, controlling the sails and rigging—that was a time when she was alone with the elements and had to concentrate fully. It cleared her head, stopped her ghosts from haunting her. Out on the water, she could be herself, unencumbered and pure.

She walked along the boards and felt a swell of exhilaration as she neared the forty-one-foot Jeanneau she kept docked at the pier. It was a beauty and often a challenge to skipper alone, but Piper loved a challenge. She stepped on board and went below. A small basket of fruit sat on the table, and she opened the refrigerator door to find a variety of cheeses along with a bottle of white wine inside.

"Permission to come aboard, Captain?" Leo's deep voice called to her.

"Permission granted," she said, laughing, as she climbed the stairs to the upper deck.

"What a great boat," he said, running a hand along the shiny railing. "You handle this all by yourself?"

"I do, but it can be a lot, especially docking and tying up. It'll be good to have your help. But we're lucky—the water's like glass. It'll be so peaceful out there today."

They worked the lines together, and Piper maneuvered out of the slip, setting sail. They sailed the Sound in silence, and she noticed Leo's shoulders relaxing as he leaned reflexively into the gentle motion of the boat. After an hour, she tacked closer to shore, set the anchor, and joined him.

"Enjoying yourself?" she asked him.

"I can't think of any place I'd rather be than on this little bit of heaven with you." He reached his hand out to hers and pulled her gently onto his lap. "You make me happy," he said, and his lips touched hers.

The kiss was long and deep, and Piper felt a stirring inside of her that was almost painful.

"Let's go below." His lips were now against her ear, his voice low and husky.

Together, they hurried to the stateroom. Piper turned to him as she reached the bed and paused, waiting for him to undress her. He understood, lifted the T-shirt over her head, and immediately his hands were unfastening her bra, freeing her breasts. He caressed them, first with his hands, then his mouth. Piper let out a moan and lay back on the bed. She had never felt such intense desire. They made love as if starved—urgently and passionately. After a second, more languorous time, they fell asleep to the soft rocking of the boat.

They awoke hungry, and Piper wrapped a leg over his. "How about some food and a glass of wine?"

"I don't know. Can't we just stay in bed forever?" He kissed her, pulling her body closer to his.

"You can come up for air, Mr. Drakos. We have all day." She ran a hand across his belly, nestling her head against his chest.

"I want to know everything about you," he said. "What your dreams are, what's most important to you, all the things you care about."

"Ah, let's see . . . I want to make a difference in people's lives. I know that sounds like a cliché, but I really mean it. I believe in the basic goodness and decency of most people. Sometimes you just have to help them connect to that part of themselves. It's very gratifying."

Leo kissed the top of her head as she lay against him. "You're a wonderful woman, Piper. I feel like I could face anything with you by my side." After a while they got up and dressed, then devoured the cheese and fruit. Piper poured a glass of wine for each of them and took a long swallow of hers.

"We should probably pull up anchor," she said. "It's getting late, and I want to get back while it's still light."

"All right. But first . . ." He took her hand and pulled her back toward the bed, lifted her T-shirt over her head once more, and pressed his body against hers. They fell onto the bed together, locked in each other's arms; his mouth hungrily found hers. She could feel the flush of heat surge through her entire body, as they made wild love.

They sailed back in companionable silence, speaking only when she needed help with the lines. After they had docked the boat and disembarked, they left Piper's car at the club and took his car to her house.

"I'll run upstairs and change for dinner. I won't be long." She rose onto tiptoes and kissed him as they stood in the entrance hall. "There's a bottle of red in the kitchen. Go pour yourself a glass while I change."

"I think I'd rather follow you."

"Down, boy," she said with a laugh.

True to her word, she was back downstairs in ten minutes, her shorts replaced with a long, white slip dress. She'd released her hair from its ponytail, and it hung loose and straight to her shoulders.

"Beautiful," he said appreciatively as she descended the stairs. "You are absolutely glowing."

She smiled at him. "A certain gentleman is the reason for that."

They left the house hand in hand, and as she settled back into the passenger's seat of his car, she replayed their lovemaking in her mind. Things had changed on the boat this afternoon. The relationship was at a completely different level now—intimate and private. They had the whole evening ahead of them, and she knew beyond a doubt that he would stay until morning. It would be perfect . . . and she couldn't wait to have him all to herself all night.

| 16 |

JOANNA

The week after the moving van had showed up, I called Leo every day, but he wouldn't listen to reason. Celeste advised me to give him some space, a chance to see what he was missing. She told me she'd had clients whose husbands had acted the same way when they were in the thrall of an affair, but that after a while they'd come to realize what they had in their wives. But I couldn't afford to wait any longer, with someone as aggressive as Piper inserting herself, and planned to go to the house to confront him. Before I could, late one afternoon the doorbell rang, and I opened it to see a woman standing there. She asked me my name then handed me an envelope. I realized too late that she was a process server. My hands shook as I read the document that announced the end of my life with Leo. He was severing our relationship with the ruthlessness of a shark. No call to warn me, nothing to let me know that he was making it official.

I wasn't even aware I was shrieking until my mother yelled to me from her bed.

"Joanna! What's wrong?"

I stumbled into the living room, my chest heaving with sobs, and thrust the paper toward her. "He's done with me. And I apparently made it easier on him by being the one to leave."

She threw the paper at me and scowled. "Are you trying to blame me? I can't help it if I fell. That bastard was through with you before you ever packed up and left. He's probably shacking up with that blond bimbo right now."

"Stop, Mom. That's enough!" I regretted ever saying a word to her about Piper. I ran to my bedroom and called his cell.

"Joanna?"

"How could you do this to me?" I choked out.

"You got the papers, then?" His voice was flat, devoid of emotion.

"You can't do this. I won't let you. Please, Leo."

"I've told you, Joanna, you've forced my hand. This is the only way that you'll realize I'm not going to change my mind. It's best for all parties involved if we all move forward."

All parties involved? Did he think I was stupid? "I won't sign the papers. I'll fight you!"

"If you do, I'll keep this thing hung up in court until you don't have a penny left. I've been very generous with the settlement, and I was happy to do it. But if you don't sign, I'll make sure you end up with nothing."

"Stelli and Evie will be devastated. How can you do this to them?"

"This is just about you and me. You'll still see the children. I would never try to keep you from them." His voice softened as he spoke, but I knew that once he moved Piper in, he'd try to edge me out. If I signed the papers, I'd have nothing to tie him to me anymore, no leverage to keep him from making a life with her.

I hung up and called Janice, a friend from my book club who was a family law attorney. We spoke for a long time, me railing against Leo and her trying to talk me down. She encouraged me to take the settlement, convincing me that a long, drawn-out fight was good for no one. He was offering me a lot of money, money I needed. I had given up my dreams of becoming an attorney and had spent the years supporting Leo. Now I found myself with no job, and no real prospects, given my responsibilities to my mother. I'd heard of so many women who'd been screwed over by the men in their lives, women who'd been married for years and ended up broke after all their legal fees, while their ex-husbands drove around in luxury cars and took expensive vacations. I had to think of my future. And I had to think of what was best for the children. So I took Janice's advice and signed them. Sobbing, I texted Celeste to see if she could fit me in, but she couldn't see me until the following day.

My mind was racing the next day as I drove over and waited outside Celeste's office. I looked up as her door opened and she beckoned me in, her shiny blond bob swinging back and forth, and looking younger than the thirty-four years my googling had informed me of. She was one of those people who looked perpetually content. Maybe it was because she realized her life was pretty good compared to her patients' crappy existences.

"Hello, Joanna. Please come in."

Her office was modern, all sharp corners and clean edges. A boxy gray sofa with stiff and unyielding cushions was where I spent my time, while she sat in a sleek red chair that looked just as uncomfortable. The walls were the one soothing element in the office, a warm burnt orange that made you want to curl up with a blanket and a good book.

"You sounded upset in your message. Has something happened?" she asked, settling into her chair, pad on her lap and pen in hand.

"Leo served me with divorce papers yesterday. He's making it look like *I* abandoned *him* by moving out, even though he's the one who encouraged me to go and take care of my mother."

She looked perplexed. "How can he do that?"

"He's a lawyer, and a damn good one. He knows practically

every judge in the state. He wants a fast divorce, uncontested, and offered me a lot of money to sign."

She leaned back in her chair and waited for me to go on.

I wiped a tear from my cheek and grabbed a tissue from the box in front of me. "I refused when I first saw the papers, but he threatened me. Said he'd get everything held up in court and I wouldn't see a dime."

"Couldn't your attorney do anything?"

I shook my head. "I don't have one, but I spoke to a lawyer friend who told me Leo could do that if he wanted. She offered to help me. She'd seen women married to millionaires who couldn't afford groceries because the men had tied the money up until the final settlement. I have to take care of my mother. I don't have a job. All the bank accounts are in his name . . ."

"What are you going to do?"

I shrugged my shoulders. "I signed them. I'm hoping he'll come to his senses and realize that this crazy affair with Piper is nothing more than a midlife crisis, an antidote to his depression. What else can I do?"

"What about the children?"

"I could have fought to have them with me, but I don't want them around my mother. I've told you what my childhood was like, all the negativity and manipulation. I won't let her do that to Stelli and Evie. Besides, there are only two bedrooms at her house. The custody can be reassessed once I have my own place, which I can't get until my mother's recovered, anyway."

"Joanna, I understand that your mother's vulnerable right now, but so are your children. Can you hire someone to stay with your mother so you can get a new place where the children can be with you?"

"I guess I could, but I'm honestly just . . . in a bit of shock. Of course I want to be with them, but I also want what's best for them. To move them out of the house they're used to, their neighborhood friends and school—it's not fair to them."

"They're used to the house, but children adapt."

What did she know about children? "If I recall correctly, you're not a mother, right?"

A frown crossed her face quickly. "Well, no—"

"Then you don't get it. When you're a parent, you put your children first, not yourself. Evie and Stelli don't need to be dragged all over the place. They need stability. It's bad enough they're having to deal with problems between Leo and me. I won't allow them to be the sacrificial lambs."

Celeste put a hand out. "Okay, okay. I'm not suggesting that at all. I suppose you know what's best for your own children. I'm just saying that they need their mother more than they need a nice house." She arched an eyebrow.

I was getting exasperated. "Of course they need me. But this is only temporary. Leo has to come to his senses. If I go and buy a new house and get it ready for the kids, he'll think I've given up on him."

And there it was again. The look of pity on her face. She took a minute before answering. "We've discussed Leo's distance these past few months and your suspicions that he was seeing another woman. And now he's admitted that he loves someone else. You've even signed divorce papers. Don't you think it's time you *did* give up on him? I'm concerned, Joanna, that you're holding on to an illusion that you can magically make things right again."

I shook my head, my face hot. "It's not magic. It's love. It's believing in the power of love and the power of our years together. Yes, I signed the divorce papers, but only because I want him to come back to me of his own accord, not because I'm holding a piece of paper over his head. And besides, Piper has bewitched him and turned him against me. I know she's hiding something, and I'm going to find out exactly who she is and what she's done."

She cocked her head. "Forgive me, Joanna, but you're talking out of both sides of your mouth. On the one hand, you say Leo is a wonderful judge of character, yet he chose Piper. If he's such a smart and savvy lawyer, don't you think he'd be able to see through her if she really were hiding some kind of nefarious past?"

I shook my head.

"I think you need to work on acceptance," she continued, her voice gentle. "You need to start a new life without him. I know this is probably bringing back all the abandonment issues from your father, but it's not healthy to delude yourself."

I could feel the vein in my neck pulsating and had to clench my hands together to keep from screaming at her. "You're wrong! My mother *drove* my father away. I've been nothing but wonderful to Leo. He's going to realize what he's throwing away."

She pursed her lips and clicked her pen a few times. "Let's pick this up in two days, during our regular appointment on Friday. I'd like you to really think about what's happened and what it is that you need, Joanna. Try not to focus so much on Leo and saving him from Piper, but on how you're going to build a life as a divorced mom."

I didn't bother reiterating that I had no such plans. It didn't matter what Celeste thought. I knew Leo, and I knew he'd come to his senses eventually. I just had to do whatever I could to make sure it was sooner rather than later.

| 17 |

PIPER

Piper unpacked her grocery bag, where a jar of Jif peanut butter sat on top—Leo had been very specific about the brand Stelli liked. She unscrewed the lid and, bringing the jar to her nose, sniffed and made a face. Even the smell said *unhealthy*. Then a can of tuna for Evie—Piper shook her head. All that mercury. She wondered why Joanna hadn't tried to improve their food choices. She continued unpacking, finding more of the items she'd chosen, like a box of organic granola bars and a fresh pineapple.

Leo was bringing the children to her house for lunch. They had agreed that it might be better and less upsetting for them to meet her here for the first time. It would seem more casual, like dropping in on a friend, rather than having her come into their home. And even though she and Leo had talked it through at length, trying to foresee any hiccups, she was still nervous. What if they hated her on sight? Their mother hadn't been gone that long. Piper would have to make them believe that she and their father were just good friends. Maybe they'd come to see her as a friend, too, and then, when things progressed, they would be more likely to accept the changes.

It was ridiculous to feel so apprehensive, but what kept running through her mind was the night Mia had discovered that her father and Piper were dating. The ensuing confrontation had gone very badly, with the girl either snarling at Piper or not speaking to her, making it plain that she had no intention of accepting Piper. Her responses to Piper's polite questions were curt and snide, unless she was ignoring her completely, which was usually the case. Piper breathed in and out, trying to settle her nerves and her thumping heart. It would be different this time, she told herself. Stelli and Evie were young. They would adapt.

When the doorbell rang, it jarred her, and she felt her pulse quicken once again as she opened the door. Leo stood between the children, each of them with a hand in his.

"Hello," Piper said brightly. "I'm so glad you're here. Come in."

Evie smiled up at her shyly, but Stelli's face remained impassive. Piper swallowed and took a step back as they entered, searching Leo's face for some sign of reassurance. He winked at her as he ushered the children in, and she felt better.

"Piper," Leo began, as they stood in the foyer. "I'd like you to meet Stelli and Evie." He placed one hand on Evie's shoulder and his other on Piper's, nudging them closer to each other.

Piper reminded herself that she needed to be careful. Even though they were young, the children would pick up on any physical affection between her and Leo. It would be hard to keep her hands to herself after the delicious intimacy they now shared, but it was necessary at this point. She bent down so that she was eye level with them. "Your father and I are good friends, and I'm really happy to meet his two favorite people."

Evie's smile grew wider, but Stelli gave her a sullen look, one that reminded her of Mia.

She stood up straight and beseeched Leo with her eyes. "Well," she said, turning to the kids, "I've made some lunch for us, and I thought we could eat on the back porch by the water. What do you think?"

"I love the water," Evie said politely.

"Sounds good. Do you need some help in the kitchen?" Leo asked.

"No. I'm fine. Why don't you take the children outside? I'll bring everything out. We can sit and talk and get to know each other."

The three of them were down at the water's edge when Piper placed the lunch tray on the table she'd set earlier, and she walked along the stone path leading to the pebbly sand to join them. Leo was showing Stelli how to skip stones, but the boy wasn't having much luck. Piper picked up a pebble, bent her wrist back, let it go, and watched the pebble bounce across the water three times.

"Hey, girl. You're pretty good," Leo said.

"Lots of practice. I grew up on the water."

Evie looked up at her with a shy smile, but Stelli glared at her.

"Can I show you how?" she asked him, hoping to get on his good side.

He shook his head. "I don't want to throw anymore," he said, and walked away from them toward the house.

She felt herself deflate, and Leo put a hand on her shoulder. "Don't worry, he'll come around. Give it time."

They walked up the slight hill together, and the three of them took their seats at the table while Piper filled their plates.

Stelli picked up his sandwich, examined it, and took a bite. "Peanut butter and jelly is my favorite," he said as he chewed. Then he made a face and put the sandwich down, pushing the plate away from himself. "The jelly's too lumpy. Yuck!"

"I'm sorry, Stelli. I can make you another," Piper said, swallowing the urge to correct his poor manners. She took his plate and stood.

But he shook his head. "That's okay. I don't like your bread either. Do you have any cookies?"

"I'm afraid I don't. How about a banana?" She held one out to him.

"I guess."

Leo gave Piper a sheepish look and shrugged. "Picky eater."

Piper smiled at him, pretending to sympathize. "How's your tuna, Evie?"

"Good. Thank you, Piper."

At least she was a sweet child, seemingly without a care in the world, her bare legs swinging back and forth under the glass table.

"So, guys," Leo said, "did I tell you that Piper has a really big sailboat? And she told me she would take you for a ride on it if you'd like."

"Cool!" Evie said. "Can we go now?"

Before Piper could answer, Stelli spoke up. "I don't like sailboats. They go slow. I like our boat."

The rest of their lunch was more of the same, with Leo trying to lighten the mood, Evie responding positively, and Stelli squelching all attempts at connection. Piper was becoming more annoyed by the minute and was counting the seconds until this visit was over.

"We'll help clear everything," Leo said when they'd finished.

As they walked through the kitchen to the living room, Piper's collection of blown-glass African animals caught Stelli's attention. He walked over to the shelf, and Piper followed him. "They're terrific, aren't they? I got them in South Africa."

He continued to stand there, transfixed by the figures, and Evie came over to see them, too.

"Which do you like the best?" she asked.

"The rhinoceros," Stelli said without hesitating.

She looked over at Leo and smiled. "Here," she said, taking the plate with his uneaten sandwich from Stelli. "Your father and I will put the dishes away. You stay here and look at the animals."

As she and Leo walked to the kitchen, he whispered, "See? I told you he'd come around. Nothing to worry about."

"You're right. I just want them to like me."

He kissed her on the nose. "They're going to love you just as much as I do when they get to know you better."

She nodded but felt a gnawing doubt.

When they left shortly afterward, Evie said a nice thank-you, but Stelli simply ran out the door without a backward glance. The boy was going to take some work, Piper reflected, but Leo Drakos was worth it. She cleaned up and was about to go upstairs and read when she noticed a bare space on the shelf displaying the animals. She'd bought a collection of the big five: elephant, buffalo, leopard, lion, and rhino. The rhino was gone. *That little . . .*

She stood there, staring straight ahead, trying to think. Obviously, he'd taken it, but she didn't want to upset Leo by accusing his son of stealing. She told herself to practice pausing and breathing deeply. She was too angry right now—she'd wait at least an hour and then give Leo a call.

Making herself a cup of peppermint tea, she took her book of affirmations and sat outside on the porch. By the time she'd finished reading and reciting a few to herself, she felt much better. Maybe Stelli hadn't meant to steal the rhino. He could have just put it in his pocket absentmindedly.

She punched in Leo's number, and he answered on the first ring.

"Missing me already?"

She chuckled. "You know it. Just wanted to say what a pleasure it was meeting your adorable children. I hope they had a nice time."

"They did. Thank you for going out of your way for them."

"Um . . . I was wondering, by any chance, did my glass rhinoceros end up at your house?"

"What do you mean?" His tone became serious.

She laughed nervously. "The kids were looking at the animals, and I can't find the rhino. Maybe one of them put it down somewhere, and I just can't find it? Would you mind asking?"

"Sure, hold on."

She paced while she waited, hoping Stelli would come clean.

"No, sorry. Neither of them knows what happened to it. Stelli said he put it back next to the lion."

She forced a casual tone in her voice. "No worries. It probably fell behind the shelf. I'll find it."

They chatted amiably for a few more minutes, but Piper's heart was beating furiously. The kid was a little liar, and Leo was blind to his flaws. She intended to clear his vision.

| 18 |

JOANNA

Even though it had been a month since I'd signed the papers, I still held out hope that the children might be the vehicle to getting us back together. Of course I never said anything to them about it, but I knew that if I made their visits special, they'd go home and tell Leo how much they wanted me to come back. We'd walk to the beach playground a few blocks away, and I'd push the tire swing as we talked about their day. Some days, we'd go over to the little store and get candy. I did whatever I could to make them happy in the few hours before Rebecca came back to pick them up, and I forced myself to put on a brave face so they wouldn't be too upset.

I knew that Leo was still seeing Piper; I'd seen his car at her house on a few occasions when I'd driven by. But he never seemed to spend the night, and that gave me hope that this was just a mad fling. The children had also mentioned their visit to her house a few weeks ago. I kept my voice casual and asked what the occasion was. They both shrugged and said it had been boring. But I knew if Leo had introduced the children to her, that meant it was getting serious.

The only thing that helped the time pass was the unrelenting pressure of taking care of Mom all day, after which I'd fall into bed exhausted every night. She needed help to get to the bathroom, to get into the shower, and to get dressed. She was terrified of falling and breaking another bone. Over the past weeks, I'd barely had any time to myself. Between visiting with the kids and taking care of her, everything had gone by in a blur. Mom was getting better, and I was hoping that by the time her leg was fully healed, Piper would be out of Leo's system and he'd realize he wanted me back.

I was waiting outside their art camp one afternoon, having told Rebecca I'd pick them up and take them for ice cream. My heart lifted, and I opened my arms as they came down the sidewalk toward me. Stelli came crashing into me first, burying his head in my shoulder.

"Hi, sweetheart. I've missed you!"

"Me, too," he said, his eyes filling with tears.

I held my hand out to Evie. "Come on. Let's make this a fun day. We're going to get ice cream and then we'll go to the playground."

We drove to Carvel and I ordered them each a cone and then one for myself. *Why not*, I thought. We sat in chairs outside the small building, and they both looked contented as the vanilla ice cream with chocolate sprinkles dripped onto their hands.

"So, how was camp today?"

Evie's eyes brightened. "We finished our collages."

I smiled. "Wonderful! I can't wait to see them."

"Piper says she's going to frame them when we bring them home," Evie said, her voice quiet.

My stomach dropped, and I tried to make my voice sound neutral even though I was furious. "Oh, really? Have you seen much of Piper lately?"

Stelli's face scrunched into a frown. "She comes over a lot. I hate her."

Evie looked at her brother. "She's not that bad. She always brings us presents."

I felt my stomach knot up. "What kind of presents?"

Evie shrugged. "She gave me a book on meditation for kids. It has cool pictures in it, too. And remember, Stelli, she gave you that crystal necklace that helps you calm down."

Stelli kicked the ground. "I told her boys don't wear necklaces."

What the hell? "Helps you calm down? What do you mean?"

Evie looked up, thinking. "She said that Stelli is a little overactive and that she might have ways to help him be more calm. I heard her talking to Daddy about it. She said she has some stuff he can take."

Now my heart was racing as anger surged through me. Who the hell did she think she was? How dare she have the gall to suggest such things? These were not her children. And what was wrong with Leo that he would let her?

I kept my voice even. I didn't want to upset them. "Evie, darling, has she given Stelli any kind of medicine? You know, like pills or something to drink?"

Evie licked her ice cream as she thought. "No. I don't think so."

"I would spit it in her face," Stelli said, his face red.

I leaned in closer to both of them. "Now you listen to me. If Piper gives you any kind of medicine—and remember, she might not call it medicine, so any kind of pills or funny things to drink—I want you to tell me right away. Do you understand?"

They both nodded, their faces solemn.

Later, after I drove them home, I repeated what I'd said. "Don't forget what I said. You tell me right away. I love you."

"Love you, too," they said in unison, and I thought my heart would break. I'd call Leo and straighten this out. After they went inside, I drove downtown, where I had some things to return to the Loft. I had just gotten out of my car when I spotted Piper walking down the crowded sidewalk, looking at her phone, oblivious to everything around her. Before I could think it through,

I hurried in her direction, compelled to follow her. I made sure to leave a few people in between us, as the last thing I wanted was for her to see me and report back to Leo that I was following her or something. When she walked into Lululemon, I lingered outside, picturing her grabbing another pair of size zero leggings. I sucked my stomach in, suddenly aware of the pinch of fat over my jeans. Probably shouldn't have had that ice-cream cone, especially since I'd been too busy and too down to drag myself to the gym. She came back out, a shopping bag in hand, and started walking again. She crossed the street, and as she was about to go into Brooks Brothers, a well-dressed man coming out of the store stopped to talk to her. He was clean-cut, in his mid-forties, and had a friendly face. I walked closer, trying to hear what they were saying while still keeping a few people between us so that she couldn't see me. I strained to hear their conversation.

"No, you must be mistaking me for someone else."

"I'm sorry. You're not Pamela D—"

"No. If you'll excuse me." Piper sounded distressed, and she walked away from him quickly, toward the municipal parking lot behind the shops.

The man stood still, watching her as she went, shaking his head.

I followed him to the center of the parking lot, where he stopped in front of a blue BMW. Looking behind me to be sure Piper was out of sight, I approached him. "Excuse me, sir?"

He turned. "Yes?"

"I couldn't help overhearing you a few minutes ago. Do you know that woman?"

He shook his head. "I thought I did. She looks an awful lot like someone I knew back home."

"Home?"

"San Diego."

I came up with a story fast. "Forgive me for prying, but I work for a detective who's been looking into her. He believes she's lying about her identity. I'd really appreciate anything you can tell me."

His eyes widened. "Oh . . . wow. I thought she was Pamela Dunn. She was married to an old friend of mine."

"D-U-N-N-E?" I asked, spelling it out.

"No *E*. I wonder if it *was* her. Her hair used to be dark, but her face looked the same."

"Do you mind giving me your name and number in case my boss wants to call you?"

"Of course not," he said, reaching into his wallet and handing me a business card. "Really strange."

I glanced at the card. Brent McDonald. He was an investment broker. "You said she *was* married. Were they divorced?"

He shook his head. "No. Matthew died. It was a real tragedy. An accident. Things got pretty awful for Pamela afterward. His ex-wife wouldn't leave her alone. Blamed her for all of it."

"What kind of an accident?"

"Sailing. Matthew and his daughter both drowned. Pamela was the only one who survived. It was just terrible."

My blood ran cold. "Could you tell me his ex-wife's name?"

"Ava. Ava Dunn. What does your detective think she's done?"

I'd aroused his curiosity now. "I'm not at liberty to say too much . . . but he thinks she's got a history of swindling men."

"Well, she *was* quite a bit younger than Matthew, but I thought they were in love. I'd see her at the club occasionally, but we didn't really socialize that much—he told me she wasn't a big drinker and didn't care too much for his friends. Ava never trusted her. Maybe she was right. At the time, I thought she was just jealous."

"I'd really like to talk to Ava. If you're still in touch, do you think you could get my number to her? Ask her to call me?"

"Sure. I'm heading home this afternoon, so I'll give her a call."

I wrote my number down for him. "Thank you so much. If you do happen to run into Pamela in the future, please don't mention our conversation. I wouldn't want her to take off again."

He gave me a somber look. "Of course. I understand."

Though I felt vindicated—I *knew* there was something off about her—I was also panicked. If she was this Pamela Dunn, then Leo and the kids could be in danger. Why would you change your name and move thousands of miles away unless you had something to hide? I couldn't wait to get home and google Pamela Dunn. There was no way this woman was going to do anything to hurt Leo or the kids while I had breath in my body.

| 19 |

PIPER

Though she'd only been seeing him for two months, Piper felt like she'd known Leo for much longer. Their nights of lovemaking were amazing, but equally wonderful were the long hours of conversation that brought them closer. Even Stelli had become a trifle less antagonistic. Their outings on her boat had helped with that, because even though he had scoffed that first day at the idea of sailing, he had actually come to like it. The first time she and Leo had taken the kids out, Stelli had given her a look as he stood on the pier near the stern.

"Coming aboard?" she called to him as Evie scrambled on.

Stelli looked from her to the transom and then reached for his father, who helped him on.

"What does it mean?" he asked. "The name of your boat?"

"Ah," she said, clutching the line in her hand. "*Eos.* It's the name of a Greek goddess." At this, she smiled at Leo. They'd already talked about how fated it felt, that she had a connection to Greek mythology before she'd even met him. "Eos is the goddess of dawn."

When he didn't say anything, Piper continued. "And she is the sister of Helios, the sun god, and Selene, the moon goddess. She's a good goddess for sailors." Piper didn't think Stelli would be interested, so she didn't add that Eos was also the goddess of new beginnings or that she was believed to have an insatiable lust for love and adventure.

And so continued their summer weekends of alternating between

Leo's boat and hers, relaxing by his backyard pool, and kayaking on the Sound. The children were getting used to her, although Stelli still kept his distance most of the time. She was doing her best to wean both of them from the food she believed unhealthy, but whenever she replaced their usual food with nutritious substitutes, Stelli complained of stomachaches. He could really be a pill sometimes.

Today, they'd spent the day swimming in the pool at Leo's, and now Piper was putting dinner together while Rebecca helped the children with their baths. She was more than grateful for Rebecca's presence, although the idea of a live-in nanny had given her pause. After all, Rebecca was only thirty-seven, not much older than Piper. But as soon as Piper had met the nanny, her worries dissolved. *Efficient.* Rebecca was nothing if not efficient. Minimal makeup, short hair, plain kid-friendly attire, and sturdy shoes. And her manner was to the point, firm but kind—and utterly boring to any red-blooded male. And Leo was nothing if not a red-blooded man.

She pulled the roasted chicken from the oven and began preparing their plates just as Stelli and Evie came into the kitchen with sun-kissed faces and shiny hair. Leo was a meat eater, and though Piper planned to introduce some healthier vegetarian alternatives slowly, in the meantime, she felt that chicken was at least somewhat better than beef. Though she'd made herself quickly at home in Leo's kitchen, she had not yet ventured to the second floor of the house. It would not be in her best interest for the children to see her walking out of their father's bedroom. She knew that all too well. And besides, she wasn't ready to be confronted with more family photographs, which might be sitting on Leo's nightstand. She'd already seen too many of them in the downstairs living space.

"You two look so clean and shiny," Piper said as the children sat down and she set their plates in front of them. "I made chicken with mashed potatoes and peas. Your dad said you like peas. Is that right?"

"I love peas," Stelli said with a sly grin on his face. "They're good for shooting," he said, picking up one and flicking it across the table at his sister.

"Hey," Evie yelled at him. But the barrage had started, with one pea after another flying in different directions.

Piper stood over them with her hands on her hips. "Okay, that's enough."

He launched another pea at his sister and then one that hit Piper on the cheek.

"Stelli!" Piper's voice rose. "We don't throw food. That is not acceptable."

He stuck his tongue out at her, then slumped down in his chair. "You're no fun. I don't want you here."

Piper closed her eyes, knowing that if she didn't calm down, she would say something she'd regret. "You need to clean the peas up from the floor, Stelli," she said, then walked out and down the hall to Leo's office, poking her head in. "Hey. The kids are having dinner. I'm going to go home and change. Do you want to keep working?"

"No, I'm finishing up now. How about I come over a little after eight?"

"Okay." She started to leave and then reconsidered. "Leo?"

He looked up from the file in front of him. "Yes?"

"Nothing. Never mind. I'll see you later on." She'd talk to him about the nonsense with the peas when he came to her house later. She couldn't stop thinking about it on the drive home and as she showered and slipped into a light silk shift. She really thought

Stelli had begun to warm to her a little, but his scene at dinner tonight showed her just how mistaken she was.

She brushed on a light dusting of blush, a swath of mascara, and some lip gloss, and then put on a pair of gold hoop earrings. She took one last look in the mirror and saw her reflection—tall and bronzed, her hair a silky champagne-gold.

She heard the door open and close as Leo let himself in with the key she'd given him a few weeks before.

"I'm in the kitchen," she called to him.

He came striding in and enveloped Piper in his strong arms. She breathed in the scent of him, feeling the hard tautness of his powerful body against hers. "I've missed you," he said, nuzzling her neck.

She pulled away, chuckling. "It's been two hours."

"Do you have any idea how hard it was to watch you all day in that little bikini and keep my hands off you?"

"I know that patience is not one of your virtues," she said in a teasing tone.

"I'm not sure it *is* a virtue."

"Sit." She pointed to the island stool and poured them each a glass of Sauvignon Blanc. "We're going to have a simple dinner—cold duck and fresh tomatoes direct from my garden."

"Sounds perfect." He picked up the glass of wine and drank.

"Leo," she began, as she served them, "something happened today that we need to talk about."

His brow furrowed. "You sound upset. What is it?"

She pressed her lips together. "It's Stelli." She recounted what had happened at dinner with the peas.

"That's what's worrying you? He was just being a boy. I don't think it's anything to get upset about. I mean, granted, it's not great table manners, but—"

"No, Leo. You're missing the point. I think he does these things to deliberately upset me."

"Now wait a—"

She put her hand up. "Let me finish, Leo. It's apparent that he doesn't want me around. Surely you see that, too, don't you? He doesn't like me. And it worries me. I care about him and don't like to see him upset." She knew she'd get further couching her complaints in concern for the child.

"It's not that he doesn't like you. It's just that he's missing his mother. I guess it can seem like he's doing things on purpose, but he's just a kid. He's not plotting or manipulating. He's acting out because his mother's gone. It has nothing to do with you."

She deflated slightly. "It feels like he will never accept me as part of your life."

"Piper, listen. We need to give him time. He'll come around eventually. But right now, we have to give him the benefit of the doubt. Do you think you can do that?"

Could she? Hadn't Matthew said the same thing about Mia? Time and patience hadn't helped at all.

"He's young. He's hurting," Leo said. "Please. Give him some time."

"Of course I will," she answered, wanting to reassure him.

They finished their meal in silence, and by the time she cleared their plates, Piper had made up her mind to commit to patience. She wasn't about to lose Leo over the antics of his overindulged son.

After dinner, they strolled down to the shoreline. The night air was still, and the light of the full moon shone on the Sound like a Monet. With their arms around each other, they stood, looking at the calm sea.

"So beautiful out here," Leo said.

"Mmm. I love it here. The moment I saw the house, I knew I had to have it."

He dropped his arm from her waist and turned to face her. "Do you think you could be happy somewhere else?"

"Happiness comes from inside, Leo. It's not a place."

"What I meant was, could you leave this house?"

"What do you mean?" she asked, a slow smile spreading across her face.

"I love you, and I want to spend the rest of my life with you." He went down on one knee and took her hands in his. "Will you marry me, Piper Reynard?"

She was overwhelmed at how quickly it had all happened. She gently tugged his hand, and he stood, so they were face-to-face. "Yes," she whispered. She put her arms around his neck, pulled him to her, and kissed him.

He pulled away and caressed her cheek. "I don't want you to worry. Everything is going to work out. Believe me. We *will* become a happy, united family. And I will love you forever."

"I believe you, Leo," she said, and buried her head against his shoulder. "And I'll love you forever, too."

| 20 |

JOANNA

When I got home from downtown, my mother was sitting in her favorite chair, her leg propped up, while her aide Molly served her a sandwich. Mom's insurance paid for this nursing help, but I was so grateful for the break it gave me, I would have gladly paid out of pocket. I gave Molly an apologetic smile as Mom talked nonstop at her, recounting every last detail of her fall and her time in the hospital.

"You were very lucky, Mrs. Doyle. It could have been much worse," Molly said.

"Humph. I wouldn't exactly call a broken leg lucky." Mom took a bite of her sandwich and made a face. "This has mustard. I asked for turkey with mayonnaise, not mustard." She dropped it onto the plate and pushed it away from her.

"I'll take care of it," I said, picking up the offending dish before Molly could. "Are you feeling any better today?"

She nodded. "A little. The pain is better, but my leg swells up if I stand for too long. Getting old is not for the faint of heart, I'll tell you that." She sighed loudly. "I don't know why I can't ever seem to catch a break. The only silver lining is that now you spend more time with me."

It took everything I had to keep from losing it with her. I knew she was selfish, but her unwillingness to see that her accident had cost me everything was beyond comprehension.

"Well, Molly is still here for a few hours, so I'm going to go do some work on my computer for a while."

"What work?"

"Just updating my résumé," I lied.

"I hope you realize that you can't take a job yet. I'm not ready to be on my own."

I left her there without answering and went into the kitchen to make a cup of coffee. As it brewed, I typed "Pamela and Matthew Dunn San Diego" into the search bar of my laptop. The page filled with item after item on Matthew: a 5K run on the Bay to fund-raise for literacy, real estate transactions, a father-daughter dance. Then I saw a page with both their names for the Red Cross Ball in Palm Beach. I enlarged one of the photos. They were on the dance floor, and though the woman in the picture had dark brown hair, not blond, her figure looked like Piper's, and from the little I could see of her face, it could definitely be her.

I searched for his obituary next and clicked on it. Matthew Dunn was society with a capital *S*. He'd come from a pedigreed family with generations of wealth and standing. I studied the picture of him. He was good-looking in a bland sort of way—watery blue eyes, sandy-colored hair, tall, and thin. He had his arm around a beautiful young girl. According to the article, both he and his daughter, Mia, had drowned while sailing in Mission Bay. There wasn't much detail about the accident, though, as the article focused more on his philanthropy and contributions to his community.

I tried to find a number for Ava Dunn, but not surprisingly, it was unlisted. She had no Facebook or Instagram presence, either. I still hoped that Brent would give Ava my phone number and she'd get in touch, but if I didn't hear anything tomorrow, I'd call him. In the meantime, I decided to see if Matthew's daughter had

had a Facebook account and typed in "Mia Dunn." I felt a pinch in my heart at all the messages of condolence on what had been turned into a memorial page, post after post saying how much they'd miss her, filled with little teddy bear emojis and hearts and angels. I clicked through to look at her photos. She looked like a lovely girl. She'd sailed, played tennis and chess, and also played the violin. I pressed Play on a video of her giving a school concert, and realized that she'd been good. Very good. What a tragedy that her life had been cut so short. There were also pictures of a younger Mia with Matthew and a woman I assumed to be Ava, her mother. They looked happy. How had Piper managed to lure him away?

There were hundreds of photos to go through, mostly of Mia with friends and a number with her dad, but I didn't see any of her stepmother. Just when I was about to give up, I came across a photo that had been taken in a parking lot, perhaps after another school concert. Mia was standing between Matthew and Pamela but leaning toward her father, so it looked more like a picture of the two of them with Pamela awkwardly standing on the other side. Matthew was looking at his daughter adoringly, but large sunglasses hid Pamela's eyes. Again, it was hard to be certain, but she looked an awful lot like Piper. I examined it again and realized I'd almost missed a telling detail—Pamela's hands were clenched into tight fists.

I sat there, staring at the screen for a long while, before taking a few screenshots and emailing them to myself.

Walking back into the living room, I pulled Molly aside. "Is it possible for you to stay a few more hours? I can pay you for the extra time."

She nodded. "Yes, how long do you need me?"

"Just until around six?"

"Okay."

"Mom, I'll be back," I told her. "I have another errand to run. But Molly will be here."

My mother shook her head. "You just got home. Fine, pick me up some Oreos while you're out, will you?"

The half-hour drive to Leo's office gave me time to think about my phone call with Stelli yesterday. Crying, he'd told me that Piper was now having dinner with them every night. She'd even started cooking for them, giving Rebecca some evenings off. Leo was doing everything possible to cut me out of his life and "move on," as he put it, but as far as I was concerned, as long as the children were affected, then it was still my business. And until I knew what Piper was up to and why she'd hidden who she was, I couldn't be sure any of them were going to be okay.

My thoughts were churning, and I became more certain with each passing minute that Piper was indeed the mysterious Pamela. But why? Why would she have needed to lie about her past or change her name after an accident? It didn't add up . . . unless it wasn't an accident.

When I got off the elevator on his floor, I strode quickly down the hall and stopped at the desk where his assistant sat.

"Hi, Missy. Is Leo alone? I really need to speak with him."

She smiled at me. "Hi, Joanna. How are you?"

"I'm okay, thanks."

"Go on in, he's not in a meeting."

He looked up as the door opened, and his expression soured. "What are you doing here?"

"I need to speak with you. It's important."

He shook his head. “Shut the door, and sit down.”

I took a seat in front of his desk. “Has Piper moved in with you and the kids?”

“What business is that of yours?”

“If they’re upset enough to tell me about it, it’s my business. Stelli told me she’s there every night. He doesn’t like it.”

Leo’s face darkened. “He’ll adjust.” He leaned back in his chair, seeming to consider something, then exhaled. “Look, I may as well tell you, though the children don’t even know yet. I’ve asked her to marry me, and she’s said yes.”

My mouth dropped open, and I broke out into a cold sweat. “You can’t marry her. You just met her.”

He shrugged. “Sometimes you just know.”

How had she fooled him so completely? “No. Listen. I learned something. She’s not who she says she is.”

“What are you talking about?”

I told him about the man I’d seen downtown. “I can show you.” I fumbled as I tried to pick up my phone, tapping on the first of the two screenshots I’d taken. I handed the phone to Leo. “See? Her name is Pamela Dunn, and she was married before. Her husband and her stepdaughter died under suspicious circumstances. Stelli and Evie are not safe. You’re not safe!”

He looked at me as though I’d lost my mind. “Joanna, you need to get some help. I’m not interested in your crazy conspiracy theories.”

“She’s lying about her background. Do you even know where she’s from?”

He stood up. “I know everything about her background, and I don’t intend to discuss it with you. I want you to leave.”

“I won’t allow you to put Stelli and Evie in danger.”

His face turned bright red. “I want you out of here now. If you come here again, I’ll file a harassment complaint. You won’t like the consequences.”

Tears blinded my eyes as I rose and ran from the office, grateful that Missy wasn’t at her desk to witness my humiliation. I knew how ruthless Leo could be when there was any obstacle in his way—and right now, that’s how he saw me.

21

PIPER

Piper walked along the short finger pier that jutted out from the main deck to Leo's boat, a trickle of perspiration running down her back. It was a hot and muggy August day, the air heavy and still, without even the slightest hint of a breeze. She had forgotten how oppressive the summers were on the East Coast. California weather had spoiled her.

"Good morning! We're all set to go," Leo called from the deck.

Evie stood next to him and waved at her. "Hi, Piper. I have my bathing suit on. Look." Evie unzipped her terry-cloth cover-up to reveal a turquoise bathing suit with a mermaid on the front.

"Evie! What a pretty suit. I have mine on, too, underneath my shorts. We'll go swimming together later." Piper held out the bag in which she'd packed food for them to Leo. "Lunch," she said, as she stepped on board.

Leo put his arm around her, kissing her lightly on the cheek. "I missed you last night," he whispered.

Piper had stayed late at the center the night before, overseeing another mindfulness retreat. By the time she'd left the office, she'd decided to go home and try to get a good night's sleep in preparation for their outing with the children. Today was the day they were going to tell Evie and Stelli that she and Leo were getting married.

Stelli sat in the swivel seat at the helm, moving the wheel back and forth and making *vroom* noises.

Piper walked over to him. "Hi, Stelli. Are you the captain today?" She ruffled his hair, and he jerked his head away from her. She counted to ten, determined to remain calm. Why couldn't he be more like Evie?

"Okay, time to cast off," Leo called out. "I'm going to need that seat after we're untied, buddy." He gave Stelli a tap on his knee. "You can sit on my lap, okay?"

"I'm your mate, right?"

"Right. My number-one helper."

Stelli's lips parted into a wide grin. "No girls allowed, right?"

"Well . . ."

"You promised."

"Just for now. Evie will be my mate on the way back. And then Piper the next time."

"No fair," the boy whined.

"Completely fair, buddy," Leo said as they pulled away from the dock.

Piper took Evie's hand. "Let's go sit on the sundeck together."

As they passed the no-wake zone and were able to pick up speed, the air felt cooler. Piper and Evie sat side by side as the wind whipped through their hair. She still hadn't gotten used to the noise, and even though the Sabre boasted a quiet ride, it couldn't compare to the silence of a sailboat gliding sleekly through the water. Piper turned to the young girl. "Are you looking forward to going back to school?"

Evie was silent for a minute, her lips pursed. "I guess." She looked down and made invisible designs on the deck with her finger. "I don't know who's going to take my picture on the first day," she said, continuing to trace a shape.

Piper wasn't sure what to tell her. Before she could, Evie spoke again. "On the first day of school, Mom takes a picture . . ."

Piper could tell that Evie was trying not to cry. "I bet your dad will take your picture, honey. And it will go with all the other first-day-of-school pictures. Will you show it to me afterward?"

"Sure." Evie gave her a tentative smile, and Piper put her arm around the child's shoulders. She was so easy to like. She didn't know how many times she'd wished that Evie were Leo's only child. It would make things so much easier.

As the boat came to a stop, they sat up straight and looked around.

"How about we anchor here and have some lunch?" Leo called to them.

"Sounds good," she said, rising along with Evie and heading to the galley for plates and cold drinks.

"I'll help you." Evie followed and stood behind her, taking the cans Piper handed to her.

Piper spread a red-and-blue-paisley cloth on the deck and emptied the canvas bag. "Come sit, everyone. Peanut butter and jelly for the first mate," she said, handing a sandwich to Stelli. "This time, no lumps in the jelly."

He took it from her wordlessly.

"Thank you?" Leo reminded him.

"Thank you," Stelli repeated.

"Do I have turkey?" Evie asked.

"You do indeed." Piper handed one of the wrapped sandwiches to Evie and the other one to Leo. "Turkey and Swiss on rye for the captain," she said, then picked up a plastic container of salad and removed the lid. She took a forkful as Stelli watched her.

"How come you always eat salad?" he asked, taking a bite of his food.

"Because I like salad. And it's good for you."

He shrugged, taking another bite. "I don't like salad."

"Well, that's okay. We all like different things."

"Can we go swimming when we finish eating?" Evie asked her father.

"Absolutely. Can't have a boat ride without a swim. But we'll wait a little before we go in the water. How about if I read a story before we do?" Leo reached a hand under her life vest, tickling her, and Evie squealed with delight.

When they finished lunch, Stelli scrambled into Leo's lap. "Story, Daddy."

Piper leaned back against the cushions, looking at the cozy family picture—Leo's arms around Stelli and, as he held *The Swiss Family Robinson*, Evie next to him, leaning against his arm. She closed her eyes as Leo read, listening to the sonorous voice that she had come to love so much.

Afterward, they swam for over an hour, the children jumping from the steps into the water over and over again, until both of them were exhausted. Piper took them below, and Stelli nodded off instantly. Evie didn't take much longer, and once they were both sleeping soundly, she took two beers from the refrigerator and went back on deck to join Leo.

"They both went out like a light," she said, handing him the can of Dale's Pale Ale.

"Thanks." He flipped the top. "Nothing like the sea and the salt air to tire them out."

"How do you think they're going to react when we tell them?"

"It might take a little while for them to get used to the idea, but they'll be fine. I'm sure of it."

"I hope so. Stelli still doesn't seem to be too happy to have me at the house."

"Don't worry. He'll come around."

By the time they were ready for dinner, it was still light, but this time the four of them ate at the table. Leo made a big to-do about the apple pie Piper had made, and she dished out vanilla ice cream to go on top of it.

"Yum," Stelli said, as he spooned it into his mouth.

Leo smiled across the table at Piper and gave her a reassuring smile. "So," he began, "Piper and I have some wonderful news to tell you."

Evie and Stelli looked up from their desserts.

"Piper and I have been good friends for a while now. And I know you've liked having her as your friend, too. I really like it when she's with us, and I'd like her to be with us all the time. I think you'd like that, too. So . . . I asked her if she would marry me." He reached across the table and took Piper's hand. "And she said yes."

No one said anything. Piper looked from Stelli to Evie, whose eyes were as big as saucers.

Still, neither of the children spoke.

Leo cleared his throat. "I hope you'll tell Piper that you want her to be part of our family. And we want you both to be in the wedding. Evie, you and Piper can pick out a special bridesmaid dress, and I'll take you to get your first suit, buddy," he said, turning to Stelli.

"I don't want a dumb suit," Stelli said, pouting.

"Come on, you'll look so sharp. And Yiayia and Papou will come and stay with you when we go on our honeymoon."

"Where are you going?" Evie asked in a quiet voice.

"Paris," Leo told her.

"We'll bring you back lots of presents," Piper said.

"Why can't we go with you?" Stelli asked.

Leo looked at Piper and smiled. "Next time, Stel."

Stelli jumped up from the table and ran up on deck. Leo started to follow, but Piper put a hand up to stop him. "No, let me," she said, and went up after Stelli.

He sat huddled on one of the cushioned benches, his head in his hands. Piper sat down next to him, and from the corner of her eye, she saw Leo standing in the doorway. "I'm sorry you're upset, Stelli. I know that your mom hasn't been gone for very long and that you miss her. I'm not going to try to be your mother, but do you think we could be friends?"

There was no answer.

"Please? Could we try? I love your daddy very much, and I want all of us to be happy."

He lifted his head slowly and looked at her with sad eyes. "Do you know there are tiger sharks in the Sound?"

"No, I didn't know that."

"I wish one ate you."

Piper didn't say anything for a minute, just looked at the small figure next to her, with his head down again, huddled as if he wanted to disappear into himself.

"It's okay, Stelli. I understand you're upset." She spoke so Leo could hear her, but then she leaned in and whispered to the boy. "But be careful what you wish for. Often, when we wish others harm, it comes back onto us."

| 22 |

JOANNA

I needed to prove that Piper was the mysterious Pamela, but I still hadn't heard from Ava Dunn. When I'd called Brent this morning, he told me he'd found out from a mutual friend that Ava was traveling over the Labor Day weekend but would be returning in four days, on Monday. I impressed my urgency upon him, and he relented and gave me her cell phone number. There was no way I could verify that the woman in those photos was Piper until I could ask Ava for some clearer pictures.

My Google search had revealed that Ava Dunn was very rich—her maiden name was Forrester, which was one of San Diego's oldest families and worth a few hundreds of millions. Their name was all over California—hospital wings, university libraries and classroom buildings, concert halls, art museums, charitable foundations. They had the kind of money most of us only dream about. She was educated, too. She'd gone to the best private schools in California and then to Wellesley, spending her junior year abroad at Oxford. When she married Matthew Dunn, her fortunes increased even more. From what I could find, she'd never worked at a real job, but, judging by the articles and pictures, she seemed to be involved in every charity that existed in Southern California.

My phone rang, and I saw that someone was calling me from the house.

I picked up immediately, concerned. "Hello?"

"Daddy's getting married!"

It was Stelli. I broke out in a cold sweat. Married?

"Stelli, sweetheart. Calm down. When is it happening?"

Sobs came over the line. "Saturday. I hate her!"

They were getting married in two days? Leo hadn't told me that they'd set a date, and now it was obvious that he wanted to hurry and get it done without my knowledge. I was so furious, I couldn't move. How had she managed to oust me so fast? I needed to stall him until I spoke with Ava, but she wouldn't be back until Monday. I couldn't let Piper become his wife and Evie and Stelli's stepmother.

"Calm down, sweetie. I'm going to think of something. Where's Evie?"

"She's out shopping with Piper."

"Okay, have her call me when she gets home, but don't let Piper know she's doing it. Don't worry. I'm going to find a way to fix this."

After we hung up, I racked my brain. I wasn't about to show up at the wedding and make a scene. I'd already been humiliated enough. I wondered if Leo's mother might intervene, though. She was always so good at seeing through people, and surely she could tell that Piper wasn't good for him. I started to dial, but put the phone down. It wasn't fair to put her in that position. I dialed Leo's cell instead, pacing as the phone rang.

"Hi, Joanna." The frustration in his voice was apparent before I'd even said a word. "What's up?"

"Shouldn't you be telling me? I've just had a call from a very upset Stelli. You're getting married Saturday?"

He sighed loudly. "I was going to call you."

I'll bet he was. "What's the rush, Leo?"

"We thought it best to do it before the children start back at school. This way things are settled before the school year begins."

"But you hardly know her! And she's not who she says she is. As a matter of fact—"

"Stop it, Joanna," he interrupted me. "I'll hang up if you say another word. I know you're not happy, but it's my life."

I bit back an angry reply. I had to think of the children. "Look, Leo, it's going be a stressful day for the children, watching their father marry someone else. Why don't you let me take them out in the morning for a little while, to the beach and for some ice cream?"

"I don't know if that's a great idea."

"Regardless of what's going on between you and me, we both love the children and want what's best for them. I promise not to say anything negative. I just want to make the day a little easier for them."

"All right, but only if you promise: not one bad word about Piper."

I rolled my eyes. "Of course not. I'll pick them up around ten and have them back in plenty of time. What time does the ceremony start?" I couldn't bring myself to say the word *wedding*.

"It's five o'clock, but they need to be back here well before that."

"I'll have them back by two," I said, meaning it.

When Saturday arrived, I drove over to the house a few minutes early and watched from the street as flowers were delivered, tables and chairs were brought in, and a flurry of activity unfolded. I was surprised to see that the kids' croquet set was still up, that she hadn't cleared it away for the big day. I waited until ten o'clock on the dot, just like I'd arranged with Leo, and pulled up to the front of the house. The children ran down the hill and jumped into the car, and once they were settled in their seats, I pulled away.

"Hi, my darlings. It's a beautiful day. All ready to go to the beach?" I looked in the rearview mirror and saw that Stelli was pouting and his arms were crossed.

"You said you were going to do something. They're still getting married. I checked."

I took a deep breath. "Sweetheart, there's nothing I can do about that. But Daddy loves you, and I'm sure it will all be fine. I wanted to try to cheer you up before Daddy's wedding."

Then Evie, in a small voice, said, "She's making me be a bridesmaid, and Stelli is the ring bearer."

I swallowed the lump in my throat.

"I hate her, and I'm too old to be a stupid ring bearer!" Stelli piped up. "She's always telling me to be quiet. And she hogs Daddy. Why can't you come home?"

My heart sank. Stelli was a spirited child, full of joy and energy, but to someone who wasn't used to children, he could be a handful. And Piper struck me as someone who didn't have the first clue about kids. "I'm trying to. I love you so much."

Stelli kicked the seat. "You said you were just going to be gone for a little while. You lied."

"Oh, my darling. I wanted to come back, but your daddy wanted Piper instead of me." I knew I'd promised Leo I wouldn't say anything negative, but I couldn't let Stelli think I had willingly abandoned him.

"It's not fair," he said.

Evie spoke then. "Daddy wants us to call her 'Mommy Piper.' She's nice, but I don't want to call her that."

It took everything I had not to scream. I gripped the steering wheel harder. "You do *not* have to call her that. I'll speak to Daddy."

"I don't want Daddy and Piper to be mad at me for telling you," Evie said.

"They won't be mad, honey. I promise," I assured her. I was going to let Leo have it. How could he be so thoughtless? Poor Evie always wanted to make everyone happy, and Leo was putting her in an impossible situation. *Mommy Piper?* That woman would never be their Mommy.

When we arrived at Compo Beach, I let the children pick out where to set up our little camp. They chose a spot right by the shimmering water, where we laid down the towels and pulled out the toys, and I sat on the sand with them as we built our sandcastle. After about twenty minutes, Stelli looked up. "I want ice cream."

"How about lunch first?"

He shook his head. "Later. You promised us ice cream, remember?"

"Okay, let's walk over to Joey's."

"Can't you go? Let Evie and me finish our sandcastle."

I looked behind me to Joey's, a hundred feet or so away. "I don't know, honey."

"Please! Someone might wreck it if we leave," he pleaded.

I stood. "You have to promise not to go in the water." I looked at Evie. "Promise you won't let him out of your sight?"

She nodded.

Grabbing my purse from the beach chair, I hurried inside and ordered them each a cone. Vanilla for Evie, chocolate for Stelli. I turned around every few seconds, craning my neck to see out the door and check on them. They were fine. As the boy behind the counter handed the cones to me, one of them fell. He turned back around to make another. When I looked again, I saw only Evie sitting on the sand. My heart jumped into my throat. Where was Stelli? Frantic, I stood on tiptoes, looking all around her, but still there was no sight of him.

I ran from the stand back to the beach.

"Where's Stelli?"

Evie was deep in concentration rounding out the edge of the castle and looked up, distracted. "What?"

"Stelli? He's not here!"

I ran up to the lifeguard stand in a panic. "Have you seen my little boy? Around this high?" I held my hand up. "He was right here, but now I can't find him."

He put his binoculars up to his eyes and scanned the water.

It must have been less than a minute, but it felt like hours before I saw Stelli playing with another little boy farther down the beach.

I ran to him. "Stelli, you scared me! I thought you were lost."

He looked up. "I just wanted to play with the dump truck."

I took his hand. "Come on, let's go back to your sister."

The three of us went to Joey's together for new ice cream, and then an hour later, we had lunch and spent a little time at the playground. The rest of the day passed in a pleasant blur. By a quarter to two, I decided I should probably get them back. We gathered up our things, my arms full with towels and beach toys, and I couldn't hold Stelli's hand.

"Stay right next to me, sweetie. It's a busy parking lot."

Before I could step down from the curb, Stelli ran into the road ahead of me. "Look, a dollar!"

"Stelli, no," I screamed, watching as if in slow motion when a pickup truck slammed on its brakes, narrowly missing him.

In a panic, I dropped everything and ran, helping him up. I reached out and swatted him on the behind. "Stelli. You have to listen!"

He started crying, and I picked him up and took him back to the curb, where Evie was waiting, her face white.

"You hit me!" he wailed, his voice loud.

"I'm sorry, honey. You just scared me."

A woman about my age in a black bikini stomped over to us, a look of outrage on her face. "I saw you hit your little boy. What's the matter with you?"

Before I could answer, she called to a police officer standing a few feet away. "Sir, sir—this woman just *hit* her child."

My knees buckled. This couldn't be happening! I'd never laid a hand on either of the children before. And besides, it was just a swat, barely anything, in reaction to a terrifying moment. Surely everyone had had a moment like this?

But the next thing I knew, we were in the backseat of a police car heading to the Westport Police Station. The children were terrified, and I did my best to calm them.

"It's going to be okay, guys. They're calling Daddy."

"You'll have to wait here until DCF arrives," the officer told me as he showed the three of us to a windowless room. He brought in water for the children but nothing for me, looking at me like I was some sort of hardened criminal. Stelli sat on my lap, and I stroked his head while we waited, my other hand holding Evie's. It wasn't long before Leo and Piper burst into the room.

The children jumped up and ran into their father's embrace. "Thank God you're okay." He hugged them close, tears rolling down his face. He stood up and glared at me, fury in his eyes, his voice a low growl. "What happened, Joanna? The police said there was a suspicion of"—he lowered his voice so the children couldn't hear—"child abuse."

Piper jumped in then, her tearstained face red with anger. "I told you not to let her take them today. We're supposed to be getting married right now, not standing in a police station!"

Before I could say anything, Leo cut in. "We need to take this discussion elsewhere," he said, inclining his head toward the children. "Piper, take them to the detective's office while we wait for DCF. I want to talk to Joanna alone."

After the door closed, he looked at me and spoke in the tone he used for witnesses. "They told me that you hit Stelli. Have you ever done that before?"

"Of course not. You know I love him, and I would never hurt either of them. It was just a heat-of-the-moment reaction to his running out into the street in front of a truck. It happened before I even realized it."

He gave me a skeptical look. "I'll see what the children have to say about that. If I find out you've been hurting them in any way . . ." He balled his hands into fists. "And did you know that now DCF is going to investigate *me*, make sure that *I'm* a fit parent?" He shook his head. "Do you know how easy it is for parents to lose their rights?"

I started to cry. "I'm sorry. I just got so scared when he ran into the road. You have to know I would never ever, ever hurt them." I looked at him and suddenly felt very tired, every emotion draining out of me.

"This is the final straw. You stay away from us. I'm going to fix it so that you'll never be able to come near any of us again."

And just like that, I was newly full of anger. I was on my feet before I even realized it. "You can't do that. They need me."

He started to speak, then just shook his head and stalked out of the room. I sat there alone for another half hour, until the police officer returned and gave me a citation for child abuse and a court date.

The children had left with Leo without even saying goodbye.

| 23 |

PIPER

Piper took the dress from the hanger and unzipped it, glancing briefly at the pale-blue Valentino she'd bought for the wedding that never happened. She'd told Leo it was a bad idea for the children to be with Joanna that morning, but he wouldn't listen. If she didn't know better, she might think that Joanna had gotten herself arrested on purpose just to stop the wedding, but even she couldn't be that desperate. It had been humiliating, having to explain to the guests that the wedding wasn't going to happen. After they'd gotten the call from the police, they sent everyone home. By the time DCF had finally arrived and then finished interviewing all of them, including the children, it had been close to six o'clock. They were all too drained even to talk about rescheduling the wedding.

The only positive thing that had come out of it was that Leo had been enraged with Joanna. Piper had never seen him so angry. Maybe he'd finally listen to her and cut off all communication with that woman.

When they'd gotten home from the police station with the children, his family was still there, waiting for them. Evangelia, Leo's mother, a serious look on her face, had pulled Piper aside before the Drakos family all left to drive back to Astoria.

"I understand the children are not happy that you and Leo are marrying. It is a big responsibility, having children. You are not just marrying my son, you know, but my grandchildren as well.

You have to consider their feelings, too." She walked away before Piper had the chance to respond, which was just as well since she might have said something to her soon-to-be mother-in-law that she would later regret.

The kids were still crying and asking for Joanna. Stelli ran up to his father and beat his fists against Leo's chest, yelling at him to bring her back. Leo's face had gone white, and Piper could see that Stelli's pain was killing him. And poor Evie had looked so small and lost, crying into the beach towel she was holding.

The next morning, the first thing Stelli said to Piper was "At least now I don't have to be a stupid ring bearer. I'm glad I went to jail instead."

A few days before the wedding, Piper's things had been moved into the house. She had spent every day since the aborted ceremony wishing she were still in her old house, which she was now preparing to list, instead of in the middle of a three-ring circus. She could only hope that things would improve once she and Leo were married. One thing was for sure: her suspicions about Joanna had been legitimate. She reminded Piper of Ava, when she'd tried to ruin Matthew and Piper's wedding six years ago. That day, none of the flowers had arrived—either at the church or the country club. When she'd called the florist in a panic, they'd told her that they'd received a call canceling the order the week before.

Matthew's mother had stepped in and found a florist to pinch-hit. But it wasn't the same. Ava had achieved her goal of disrupting everything. And now Joanna had done the same thing, only worse.

She thought about her first wedding. It seemed a lifetime ago. Maybe she and Ethan had done it the right way—a simple ceremony with the two of them standing hand in hand under a full moon on the beach in California, a commitment to love each other forever and into eternity. They had been so young. Too young to know that forever was an impossible promise.

She looked at the dress she was holding. Sighing deeply, she wiped her eyes and stepped into it, then sat at the vanity and took her time to finish her makeup. She sat back, satisfied, and then went down to join Leo.

"You look beautiful," he said as she reached the bottom of the stairs.

"Thank you." They had decided to go alone, with only Leo's brother George as a witness. She took his hand in hers as they walked to the car together.

Piper settled into the passenger's seat and clicked her seat belt into place as Leo pulled out of the garage. "I wish I could make everything up to you. I know getting married at the courthouse is not the kind of wedding you wanted."

"Oh, Leo. It's not your fault. We have to use this experience as a transformative one."

"How do you mean?"

"As we heal, we are reborn. Nothing happens in a vacuum. As terrible as that day was, we've overcome it together. And it will help our relationship deepen."

He looked confused. "Still . . . you didn't deserve what happened last week. I'm so sorry."

"Don't nourish your myth."

His expression turned to one of bemusement. "I'm sorry, Piper, but I have no idea what you're talking about."

She smiled at him and squeezed his hand. "I'm sorry. I get a little carried away when I'm upset. It helps to center me to try and reframe things in a more palatable light. What I mean is that the delusion that you are responsible for what happened . . . that's a myth, and you don't have to atone for something that isn't your fault."

She was, however, still blaming him for canceling their honeymoon to Paris, a move that had seemed unnecessary. No amount of persuading on her part had convinced him, and she was afraid to push too hard. So now they were stuck here because Leo was afraid to leave the children, even though he'd gotten the courts to agree that Joanna was a risk to the kids and couldn't come near them. But just in case Joanna still tried to see them, he'd told Rebecca not to answer the door for anyone, no matter who, if he wasn't at home. The worst part was that Stelli and Evie were still moping around. Stelli, especially, was a problem, talking back to Piper and refusing to listen to her. Something had to be done.

"Leo, I've been thinking."

"Yes?" He glanced at her then back at the road.

"I know Joanna is legally required to stay away now, but the children still hope they'll get to spend time with her. We both know that she's unstable. What if she had done something worse? I really don't believe that that was the first time she hit Stelli. I just saw a bruise on his arm that looks like it's a few weeks old."

His hands tightened on the steering wheel. "I could kill her."

She thought back to one of her clients in California, when she'd had her counseling practice. "I know a man who suspected his ex-wife was hurting their kids. The children would never admit it—they rarely do—but it was going on for years, and finally he was able to prove it when the daughter broke down and admitted it. It was subtle abuse, pinching and grabbing, but it wreaked havoc on their emotions, and the kids suffered for a long time." She was exaggerating slightly, but the story was based in fact.

"That's horrible."

"Yes, it is. Joanna's been acting so erratically since I met you.

She's not willing to accept that we're together. And what if she decides to take the children and disappear forever? We really need to make sure her access to them is permanently severed. You need to use all your connections in the legal community to make sure that happens."

"It's in the works. What happened at the beach is now on the record, which helps, of course. But we don't need to talk about this now, my love, on our way to get married."

"It's just been weighing on me that the kids need to accept that they won't see her anymore. For their own good, we need to make it clear to the children that she's never coming back. And that will make it that much easier for me to adopt them."

He looked over at her, surprised. "Really, you'd want to do that?"

"Of course. I'm going to be your wife, and I very much want to be their mother." If that was what it would take for them to be a real family, she could put aside her reservations about motherhood.

Piper said no more, but she was glad he was pleased with her idea.

One thing was for certain: come hell or high water, she needed to get Joanna out of their lives for good.

24

JOANNA

I sat in my car, where I'd been parked since dawn, fighting the urge to run up to the house, bang on the door, and insist that they let me see the children. I knew that would be a huge mistake. I haven't been able to sleep at night, and I can't stop crying. I don't remember ever crying so hard. How could Leo be so heartless to take Evie and Stelli away from me? Five days ago, the three of us were playing in the sand together, and now there's a court order against me. I have no idea when I'll see their sweet faces or hold them in my arms again.

I looked at my watch. Almost eight o'clock. They would be leaving for school soon. I knew I should start the engine and pull away, but I desperately wanted just a glimpse of them. When I saw the front door open, my heart began to race. I couldn't catch my breath, and I told myself again that this was a very bad idea—if they saw me, it would only give Leo more ammunition—but I was rooted to the spot and couldn't move. Before I could think, Piper emerged with the children. Stelli's backpack fell from his shoulder, and she ran over to pick it up, shooing them both into the SUV. I started the car and hurriedly drove away before they could see me, cursing Piper for stealing my life, and headed to my appointment with Celeste. By the time I reached her office, my heartbeat had slowed to normal and I felt a new resolve come over me. She would help me figure out a way to fix this.

As soon as I sat down, I blurted out, "They've gotten a protective order against me, and now Leo is trying to get sole custody permanently. They're launching a full-scale investigation."

Celeste leaned forward. "So, for the immediate future, Leo has sole custody? Are you able to visit the children?"

"No! They're painting me as a child abuser. I can't go near them. And she's trying to cut me out of their lives entirely. They've changed the number to the house phone, so I can't call the children, and if I try to go anywhere near them, I risk losing them permanently. Leo's cell phone number gives me a recording—I think he must have changed his number, too. They've even turned Rebecca, the nanny, against me. We used to be so close, but when I text her now, she tells me she can't be caught in the middle. Leo's the one who signs her paychecks, after all."

She shook her head. "I hope you have a good attorney who can help you navigate this."

I nodded. "My friend Janice, the lawyer I told you about, is helping me, but Leo's connected in the legal community. Don't forget that. I'm sure Piper is whispering in his ear at night. She's Lady Macbeth." I sighed heavily, the emotion settling in my chest. "I didn't mean to hit Stelli. I barely tapped him. I was already so wound up that day about the wedding and then got so rattled when that truck almost hit him." I took a breath, trying to keep from crying.

"Don't believe anyone who tells you family court is fair. It takes weeks to get a court date, and if you get the wrong judge, you're screwed. Leo is a brilliant litigator, and Janice is no match for him, but at least I know she's on my side. I'd be afraid to hire anyone he knows in case they were biased toward him, even subconsciously."

"I see," Celeste said, and then was quiet for a moment, as if considering what I'd just told her. "So have you thought any further about what your next steps might be?"

"I have to find character witnesses to testify that I've never done anything like this before. The irony is, I'm worried that Piper is the one who's a danger to the children."

Celeste frowned. "I understand that you're upset and looking for a way out, but that's fantastical thinking. You have no basis for that."

"Actually, I do."

Her eyebrows rose. "Which is?"

"I finally spoke to Ava Dunn. She sent me pictures of her husband's wife, Pamela." I pulled out my phone and handed it to Celeste. On the screen was a photograph of a slender woman standing on the beach and dressed in white shorts and a cropped black T-shirt. "Look—it's Piper, only with black hair. I'm flying out to California and meeting with Ava tomorrow."

"What do you hope to gain by that, Joanna? So what if she was married before—lots of people have been. It has nothing to do with her marriage to Leo."

"But it does, it does. Ava's ex-husband and daughter died in a sailing accident. Piper was with them, and she was unharmed. Ava thinks she was responsible for both of their deaths."

I leaned back and waited for Celeste to digest this.

"I understand that the fact that Piper must have changed her name is alarming," she said with a sigh. "But I think you need to tread carefully, Joanna. You don't know anything about this woman or what happened. Accidents happen every day. It's a big leap to assume that Piper is a murderer."

I was becoming exasperated with Celeste's inability to grasp the obvious. "But if she is, I can't just sit back and wait until she hurts my children. I need to find out what happened to her husband and stepdaughter."

"Joanna"—her voice held a warning tone—"if you're not supposed to be around the children, and you are, you could lose them forever. Don't give up what you really want just to prove a point."

I clenched my jaw. "That's not it at all. Call it mother's intuition, but something's off about that woman, and I won't let her hurt my babies."

"I understand." She paused, and I swear, I could see her figuring out how to change the subject. "What about your mother? How are you going to do this while taking care of her?"

"Mom's walking now and almost healed," I told her. "She wasn't happy about my trip, but nothing is going to get in the way of my doing whatever is necessary to protect my family."

| 25 |

PIPER

Piper leaned in closer to the bathroom mirror. *Damn it.* Where had that spot come from? There was a big red blotch on her beige linen blouse. She thought back to the last time she'd worn it—picking the kids up from a birthday party—and remembered the sticky lollipop Stelli had been holding as he got into the car. It must have somehow rubbed against her as she helped buckle him in. She took a deep breath and told herself that it was okay to feel annoyance, that it would pass. She was new to this mothering thing, and she needed to be kind to herself, to give herself time to figure it all out. Wasn't that what she told her clients? Piper pulled out a different top from the master bedroom closet, relieved again that Leo had cleared it out for her before she'd moved in. She'd take the beige blouse to the dry cleaner's later.

It was pajama day at school, and she'd volunteered to take the kids, but Stelli had looked less than thrilled at the prospect. Leo and Piper had been married for two weeks, so it was natural that the children still hadn't fully accepted her. Of course, they still wanted their mother, not her. And despite Leo's long talks with the children about how the four of them were a family now, she could see the skepticism in both their eyes.

She went to the kitchen to make them breakfast, but Rebecca had beaten her to it. A sumptuous feast of homemade waffles and whipped cream, bacon, and coffee cake was displayed on platters. She resisted the urge to point out that these weren't the healthiest of foods with which to start the day, and she said good morning and made herself a cup of coffee instead. She'd be making changes to their diet soon enough.

"Are you sure you wouldn't prefer it if I took the children to school?" Rebecca asked her.

Piper gave her what she hoped was a sweet smile. "I appreciate that, but I've cleared my calendar for this morning. I wasn't planning on doing pickup, though." If this woman was worried she'd be out of a job, she needn't be. Piper had no intention of giving up the center. "Can you gather their backpacks and get them ready?"

The nanny pushed a strand of hair behind her ear and returned the smile. "Certainly." Why was she always so formal?

"Earrrrrrrrr! Kerplash! Watch out!"

Piper jumped as a remote-controlled miniature Land Rover crashed into her ankle.

"Stelli! What the he—" She stopped herself.

Rebecca gave her a sharp look then ran over to the child. "Stelli, you know better. Not in the house. Apologize at once to Piper."

He gave her a goofy smile. "Sorry!"

"It's okay," she said, rubbing her ankle. "Have a bite to eat, and then we'll go to school." Evie joined her brother at the table, putting some bacon on her plate. She looked at Piper. "Can you take our picture before we go, Piper? Like you did on our first day? Mommy always took our pictures for special school days, too . . ." Her eyes filled, and she took a bite of her bacon.

Piper gave her a sympathetic smile. "Of course. We'll do one of you together and one of each of you alone. Okay?" It was obvious that Evie was missing her mom even more than usual today.

Evie nodded and bit her lip, while Stelli stared at his sister, his lip trembling. "I want Mommy!"

Piper gave Rebecca a helpless look, but Rebecca pointedly

ignored her. She probably wanted to see how Piper planned to handle this.

She got up and crouched down by Stelli's chair. "I know you want your mommy, Stelli. But remember what we were just talking about, how your dad told you that she's in heaven? Mommy is watching you from up there, I promise. She'll always be with you." Piper looked at her watch. "Can you finish up now? We have to leave in ten minutes, and we need time for the pictures."

Stelli pushed his plate away, his bacon untouched and only three bites taken from his waffle. "I'm not hungry anyway."

"How about some green drink?" She took it out of the refrigerator.

"Yuck. It has grass in it."

She poured it into a glass and held it out to him. "Here, taste it. There's no grass, Stelli. It has yummy fruit like bananas and blueberries."

He looked at her with suspicion. "I saw you put grass in it."

"No. You saw me put in kale and spinach."

"Gross." He slid his chair out and picked up his backpack. "I bet you put awful stuff in my lunch," he mumbled as he walked out of the room and into the foyer.

"Stelli doesn't mean it, Piper. He's just sad," Evie said.

All of the anger drained out of her. "I know, sweetie. I know. Come on. Let's go take some pictures."

Evie nodded.

"Where shall we do it? Here in the hallway?" Piper asked her.

"Outside on the steps. That's where we always take them," Evie directed.

"All right. Let's go," Piper said, and they trooped out the door together and stopped at the bottom of the stairs, where Stelli was waiting. Piper straightened his pajama top and moved back, focusing on them with her iPhone camera. "Okay. Say 'platypus.'" She took several pictures and then moved next to them, holding the camera for a selfie. "Let's take one all together." And she clicked the camera button again.

As they drove to school, Piper felt better. Breakfast hadn't been great, but the pictures hadn't gone badly. It wasn't until she'd dropped them off and swiped through the photos that she saw Stelli's face in the selfie. His eyes were scrunched up, and he'd stuck out his tongue. So much for progress. She'd have to be a little more creative going forward, or maybe a little more forceful.

| 26 |

JOANNA

I landed at San Diego International Airport at eleven in the morning and had a few hours to rent a car, check into my hotel, freshen up, and grab a bite before I met Ava at her home at three. I had hoped to connect with her in person before Leo married Piper, but that hadn't worked with her schedule. But when I spoke to Leo's mother, she told me that they had gotten married three weeks ago. I unpacked my suitcase, changed into a linen pantsuit, and pulled out of the Hyatt on Park Boulevard after punching in Ava's address in Del Mar Mesa, thirty minutes away. When I arrived, I saw that her house sat on a slight rise with a wide stone-paved driveway leading up to it. It was a long and meandering Spanish-looking home, imposing and grand. Back in Connecticut, I'd looked up the address and seen the value of the house—$4.6 million. Almost reasonable, when you compared it to the $20 million to $50 million homes dotting the landscape.

I parked in front of the house and walked through a lovely courtyard with exotic trees and beautiful landscaping to the front door, noticing the graceful arches and ornamental ironwork on the windows and lanterns. Ava answered the door herself, and I was a bit taken aback. I'd seen attractive photographs of her online, but in person, she looked like she was made of plastic, with the skin on her face taut, her eyes squinty from too much filler, and her lips a little too large. Trying to hide my reaction, I smiled and said, "Hello, Ava. I'm Joanna. Thank you so much for making the time to see me."

"I wouldn't have missed this," she said, shaking my hand and opening the door wide. "Please, come in."

It felt like I had entered a foreign world as I followed her through the house. The arched hallway with wooden ceiling beams and earthy terra-cotta tile was so very different from the formal East Coast aesthetic I was used to. We passed a wide, curving stairway with hand-painted tiles on the stair risers and Ava turned to me. "I thought we'd sit outside by the pool. Unless you'd rather be inside?"

"That sounds lovely," I said.

As we went by the kitchen, Ava stuck her head in. "Juliet, will you bring us out some cold drinks?" We continued through the sunken living room, whose wall-to-wall glass doors were opened wide to the outdoors.

I gasped as we stepped outside to a private paradise of waterfalls gliding over stonework into a huge swimming pool of the brightest turquoise blue. Luscious tropical plants and trees surrounded the entire patio area, and giant ceramic pots held flowers of purple, blood red, and periwinkle. The effect was enchanting.

"Have a seat." Ava indicated a lounge chair with a soft orange cushion, and just as we sat, Juliet arrived with a pitcher of lemonade and two crystal glasses. She placed the tray on the round mosaic table between us, poured the drinks, and retreated.

I took a long swallow, but Ava ignored her lemonade. "So . . . tell me more about this new identity Pamela has created for herself."

"As I told you on the phone, she moved to Westport earlier this year. She bought a big house on the water and a small business that was . . . I guess what could be described as a cross between a meditation and health center. She expanded it and added all kinds of alternative therapies. My husband met her because of a client, but then I stupidly encouraged him to take one of her classes, which was how she got her hooks into him." I knew she'd gone through something similar, but nonetheless I was embarrassed to talk about it with a stranger. "I wasn't even out of the house. I don't know how she did it, but it's been less than six months, and they're already married."

Ava was nodding as I spoke. "She's a calculating bitch. And she's dangerous." Her eyes filled with tears. "I can't lay all of the blame for my marriage problems at her feet, because I was the one who screwed up first. Matthew was always so busy with work that it was almost as if I were a single mom, and I was very lonely. I had a short fling with a younger man, but it meant nothing." She took a deep breath and waved her hand dismissively. "As I said, Matthew was so involved at his investment firm, not paying attention to me and traveling all the time. We separated, but I realized after I left that I'd made a huge mistake. I told him I wanted to come back and give our marriage another chance, for the sake of all the years we'd been together and for Mia." At this she began to weep.

My heart broke for her, and I waited silently as she composed herself and went on. "He had just begun seeing Pamela. Or Piper, as you know her." Her lip curled into a sneer. "She did everything she could to keep us apart. We weren't divorced. He was still a married man even though we were separated."

"How long was it before they were married?"

"Oh, it wasn't long. She was pushing him to get a quickie divorce. Matthew threatened to expose my affair, to tell Mia. I couldn't have that, and besides, as the months went on, I knew he was never coming back. She had him in her thrall. He was bewitched."

I sat up straight. "Yes, that's exactly the word. She *bewitched* Leo."

Ava closed her eyes and nodded. "When he was awarded shared custody, it nearly killed me. I didn't want my daughter near that woman, but I had no choice. Mia hated going to their house on weekends, but I felt there was nothing I could do. I should have insisted. She would be alive now if I had." She was crying again, deep choking sobs.

My heart began to beat faster. On the phone, she hadn't provided much detail about the accident, saying she'd prefer to speak in person. I was about to ask her more, but she went on, seeming to need to get it off her chest.

"Mia would come home from there, and it would take all week just to get her out of her funk. Pamela would be overly affectionate with Matthew in front of her, flaunting their relationship. And she began to exert more control at the house, even forcing Mia to drink her horrible green smoothies, which gave her stomachaches. I told her to pretend to drink them and then flush them down the toilet."

I sighed sympathetically. "How awful. Your poor daughter."

"I should have done more to keep her from my child, but I couldn't prove anything to the courts, and Matthew wouldn't relent. He kept telling me that I needed to give her a chance, that she cared about Mia. I still can't believe that I was the one who brought that creature into our lives."

"What do you mean?" I asked.

"I'd hired her to give Mia sailing lessons. At first Mia didn't want to learn, but Pamela won her over. Mia loved her when she was her teacher, thought she was the coolest thing. Of course, Mia had no idea, and neither did I, that Pamela was only trying to get close to her dad. Once they were married, she couldn't have cared less about my daughter."

"She was a sailing instructor?"

Ava nodded. "Yes, at our country club. Just on the weekends. I think she did it to meet a rich husband. I guess she saw all the money that was being thrown around and decided she wanted to be elevated from the help to the helped. You know, after she married Matthew, he gave her the money to leave the practice where she worked and start her own counseling office. But she had no interest in helping anyone but herself. She's a master manipulator."

I nodded. "I've come to the same conclusion."

Ava's eyes were smoldering, and she spoke with bitter resentment. "That sailing accident was no accident. Matthew and Mia were expert swimmers, and they both knew how to sail . . . but somehow they both drowned, and she got out alive. She killed my daughter. And she got away with it."

Her words made me tremble. "I'm so sorry for your loss, Ava," I said. "And I'm sorry to bring this up, but I'm worried that my children are in danger, too. She takes them out on her sailboat most weekends, and I'm terrified that something bad is going to happen to them."

She leaned forward now, getting closer to me. "You're right to be concerned. She's evil, and she's smart. She knew how to make sure that nothing could be pinned on her."

"How did she get away with it?" I asked.

"Pamela's story was that a squall came up suddenly. Something broke and the boom hit Mia, who went overboard. Pamela said she'd tried to get her to wear a life vest earlier, but she refused. Of course, no one can corroborate that."

"What happened to Mia's dad?"

"Matthew went right in after her, but they got caught in the sail and drowned. Pamela said she threw the life preservers out, did everything she could, but lost sight of them in the high seas." Her eyes were now filled with rage. "I know she orchestrated the whole thing, sabotaged the boat."

"Was there no way to prove that? Wasn't there an investigation?" I asked.

Ava's fists convulsed with suppressed rage. "Yes, but the police concluded that it was an accident." She twisted her hands together. "Matthew had changed his will in her favor. There was a large trust fund for Mia, but since she died, too, the bulk of his estate—over twenty million dollars—went to Pamela. She stayed in the house for a while, but this is a tight-knit community, and I made sure everyone knew what she had done. No one wanted her at the country club, or anywhere else, for that matter. She finally sold the house and moved away."

"And that's when she became a new person," I said. "She came east to find another target. But I don't understand. Doesn't she have all the money she needs now? Why does she need another rich husband?"

"I don't know. Maybe it's not the money. Maybe it's something else."

I felt a terrible chill go up my spine, despite the warmth of the sun on my face.

"What was her maiden name? Maybe I can find something out about her past that would help me convince my ex-husband she's dangerous."

She shook her head. "It's Rayfield, and she comes from Annapolis, Maryland. Just a small-town girl looking to strike it rich."

I left Ava's feeling shaken, and though it was nearly six o'clock by the time I returned to the hotel, I wasn't hungry. The only thing I felt was a sick ball of fear in my stomach. Ava was a broken woman. Though I'd been in awe of her house and everything she had, all the money in the world couldn't make up for losing a child. It made me more determined than ever to keep digging and stop Piper before she could do the same thing to Evie and Stelli—and Leo.

I had a terrible night, restless and hovering between wakefulness and a half sleep. I know I dreamed awful dreams, but when I awoke in the morning, they were all hazy. As I showered and dressed, an image would come to me and then fade just as quickly. Still lacking an appetite, I sat at the small desk in my room and dialed the number for the California Department of Health and Vital Records I'd found on their website. I knew it was a long shot, but I thought that maybe if I got a copy of Pamela and Matthew Dunn's marriage license, it might reveal something more about her background.

I was prepared to reroute my trip home, fly to Sacramento, and go to their offices, but when I spoke to a clerk in the office, I was told the only way to obtain records was by mail. Disappointed, I downloaded the necessary request form and asked the hotel's business office to print it for me. I got down a cup of bitter coffee and half an English muffin as I filled out the form, put it and a check into an envelope, and asked the front desk to mail it for me. I hoped my efforts would produce some useful information, but having to wait for almost a month would be agony. What if that turned out to be too long? It occurred to me then that Ava might have a copy of Matthew and Pamela's marriage certificate. I could have kicked myself for not asking her yesterday and punched her number into my phone.

After three rings she picked up. "Hello?"

"Ava, it's Joanna. Do you have a copy of Matthew's marriage

certificate? I've requested a copy from the state, but it could take weeks."

"I don't have one on hand, but let me see what I can do. I might be able to pull some strings and have it sent to you sooner."

"Thank you. I'm sorry to bring up things that are so painful for you, Ava. I—"

"No, not at all," she interrupted before I could continue. "I'll do anything I can to help you expose her. I want her to pay for what she's done. The justice system has failed me, but I won't rest until she suffers for what she did."

"And I will do my best to make sure that happens. Thank you so much for seeing me. I'll stay in touch and let you know anything I discover. Thank you again."

I quickly checked out and drove to the airport. I couldn't wait to get home and to spend some time looking into Pamela Rayfield.

| 27 |

PIPER

With the children back in school and settling into the routine of their days and early bedtimes, Piper was spending more time at the center again, and she cherished her only opportunity to recharge. Their new setup was taking getting used to on all of their parts, she admitted to herself. The first time she'd made tofu stew with quinoa for dinner, Stelli refused to eat it. If it had been up to her, he would have gone to bed hungry, but Leo thought differently.

"It's all right. You don't have to eat it, buddy. You'll try it another time," Leo had said, getting up to make Stelli a sandwich.

Stelli had picked up his bowl of stew, taken it to the trash can, and dumped it out, giving her a victorious look.

Piper pressed her lips together, furiously tapping her foot under the table. "Leo, that's not right. Stelli needs to know that it's wrong to waste food."

Leo looked over at his son, who stood in front of the trash can with his arms folded across his chest. "Piper's right, Stel. There are lots of children who don't have enough to eat. We're really lucky that we do. We shouldn't waste it."

"It tasted awful," Stelli said.

She could tell that Leo was trying not to laugh. "It was just different. That's all. Look"—he'd pointed to Evie—"Evie's eaten all of hers."

"I liked it," she said. "I think Stelli's being a brat."

Piper had raised her eyebrows at Leo as if to say, *See? I told you he's acting out. Even his sister sees it.*

She had to give Leo credit. From then on, he stayed firmly on her side when Stelli was being picky about food. *At least try it*, he would say to him, and Piper was satisfied that it was a good compromise. One Friday night, she had something else she wanted to introduce, so she made spaghetti for dinner, one of Stelli's favorites.

When she brought it to the table, his eyes grew wide and so did his smile. "Oh, goody. Spaghetti!"

"Garlic bread, too," Piper said, setting the bread plate on the table. It had been hard for her to serve bread with pasta, but she knew both Leo and Stelli would love it, and she wanted everyone in a good mood.

"So," she said, after they'd been eating awhile, "I thought we'd play a little game while we're at the table, before we watch a movie."

They stopped eating for a moment and looked at her. "What kind of game?" Evie asked, putting her fork down.

"I want all of you to think of something you were thankful for today. It can be something that happened or someone you know or even just a thing."

Evie raised her hand.

"Yes, Evie?" Piper said, smiling at the girl's manners.

"I'm thankful that my friend Jennifer is back in school and not sick anymore."

"That's really lovely, Evie. What about you?" Piper looked at Leo, wanting to give Stelli more time to ponder.

"Easy. I'm thankful for you little rascals," he said, ruffling Stelli's hair. "Your turn, Stel."

Stelli tapped his fork against the plate and looked up at the ceiling for a few seconds. "I'm thankful for my Lego Explorer."

"Okay, good. My turn. I'm grateful for my new family." Her smile froze when she saw that Stelli had rolled his eyes. Ignoring him, she continued. "Now, this is a little harder. I want you to sit and be very quiet. It will help if you close your eyes." Piper let her words sink in and closed her own eyes. "Everyone's eyes closed?"

There was a murmur of yeses around the table. "Okay. Now pay attention to what you're feeling right now. And remember, there are no right or wrong feelings. Just whatever you're feeling right this moment."

She heard Leo clear his throat, but otherwise, there was only silence. After a minute, Piper opened her eyes. "Okay, now open your eyes and let's talk about what we felt."

"Piper—" Leo said, but he was interrupted by Evie.

"I felt really sad. Today when Jennifer came back to school, some of the kids were really mean to her and they made fun of her 'cause the medicine made all her hair fall out. I wanted to yell at them and tell them to leave her alone, but I didn't say anything. I was scared."

Leo and Piper exchanged looks. She'd had no idea that Evie's friend was seriously ill.

"Come here and sit on my lap, pumpkin," Leo said to his daughter.

She rose from the table and went to sit on his knee, and he put his arm around her. "Sometimes it's very hard to stand up to kids who are being mean and nasty. If that happens again, I want you to talk to your teacher. It's not your job to stop them. It's hers. Your job is to be Jennifer's friend."

Piper smiled and nodded her head at him. "What about you, Stelli? How were you feeling?"

"This is stupid."

"Stelli, tell Piper you're sorry."

Stelli threw his fork across the table and flipped his plate over, spilling spaghetti all over the place mat. "Why do I always have to tell her I'm sorry? Why is she such a big baby?" He jumped up from his chair.

"That's enough, young man." Leo gently pushed Evie from his lap, rose to his feet, and stood over Stelli. "You will not be disrespectful." Taking the boy's hand, Leo led Stelli from the room.

Piper watched this little drama, exasperated, and wondered how Leo was going to handle it. "Would you help me clean up, Evie? Then we can have our pudding while we watch the movie."

"Okay," Evie said, and began to clear the dishes.

They were halfway through *Wonder Woman* when Leo finally came downstairs alone and joined them in the family room. Piper was dying to know what had transpired, but she didn't want to disappoint Evie by interrupting the film. Finally, after Leo had tucked Evie into bed and returned, she asked him.

Leo shook his head. "He ranted for a while. He was so angry. I've never seen him so angry. I finally settled him down, and we talked about old times." He pulled Piper closer to him on the sofa. "This has been a much harder adjustment for him than for Evie. Stelli was so close to his mother. Not that Evie wasn't, but it was different with Stelli." He sighed. "Anyway, he was pretty exhausted after all the histrionics. I lay down with him, and we both fell asleep for a bit. Sorry it took me so long to come back."

"You did the right thing. He needs to talk about it." She paused, letting that sink in. "In fact, I've been thinking a lot about ways we might help him. There are natural remedies, you know, things that are completely safe and effective. And lots of alternative therapies that could work, too. Why don't you let me try some of these with him?"

"I don't know. I don't want him taking any kind of psychotropic drugs."

"No, of course not. I would never suggest that. The things I'm talking about are completely natural and benign. But they might ease his anxiety and anger."

"You think so?"

Piper nodded. "I do."

"I don't want him to feel like there's anything wrong with him," Leo added.

"I understand. I can just add a little something to his smoothies. He'll never know."

"All right. Let's talk more about it tomorrow."

She snuggled closer to him, satisfied. She'd cleared the way. Now it was time to get to work.

28

JOANNA

My restless night really hit me after takeoff, and I slept for almost the entire five-and-a-half-hour flight, which is saying a lot when you're flying coach. It was midnight when we landed at JFK, and I was still an hour from home. As I took the shuttle to the parking garage to retrieve my car, I felt a second wind and couldn't wait to get home, power up my computer, and resume the search.

The house was dark when I pulled up, as were the others on the street. The last thing I wanted to do was wake my mother, so I shut the car door quietly and tiptoed to the front door, pushing it gently shut, then turned on a lamp. The drabness of the small living room overwhelmed me after being in Ava's house. Hers had been so full of light and color, and now I was back in this tiny space that seemed even more dark and depressing than before.

But it was time to brush aside my feelings of resentment or self-pity and get to work. After brewing a pot of coffee, I sat down at the kitchen table and typed "Pamela Rayfield" into Google. A bunch of Facebook profiles came up first, but none of them were hers, of course. I scrolled down farther, but still nothing. Then I had an idea. Ava said that Piper had been a sailing instructor. I typed "Pamela Rayfield sailing." Voilà! An article in the *Capital Gazette* came up: "AYC High School Senior Wins Another Major Title." The article chronicled the third award Pamela had won that year at the Annapolis Yacht Club. A photo of her on the sailboat showed a younger, dark-haired Piper with a smile as wide as the boat. How was it that someone so accomplished at sailing had been unable to keep her second husband and her stepdaughter safe at sea? There were no other hits that seemed to be about her, so I tried "Pam Rayfield" and the first thing that came up was an obituary.

> *Pam Rayfield, 93, died peacefully in her home. She is survived by one sister, Margo Spencer, and a daughter, Sheila Sherman.*

That certainly wasn't her. I thought about poor Sheila. Had she ever married? Had she spent her entire life taking care of her mother, never having a life of her own? She was probably in her seventies by now, finally free but too old to start her own family. I looked through the rest of the page to see if there was anything else of interest. Some Facebook profiles of other Pam Rayfields, but they resulted in nothing. On a whim I logged in to my Facebook account and typed "Pamela Dunn" into the search bar. Nothing. "Pamela Rayfield Dunn." Others came up, but none were her. Finally, I tried "Pamela R. Dunn." It was her! I clicked on the page and a picture of Piper filled the screen. There were only two posts. One was a picture of the beach and under it she'd written *California is as beautiful as they say.* The other post was of her on a sailboat with Matthew Dunn. The name of the boat was *The Pamela.* He must have bought it for her. How ironic that it's what killed him. The most recent posts were from four years ago—it seemed she hadn't been active on Facebook since. I looked through to see her friends. There were only a handful.

I knew sleep would be impossible after all the coffee and now this discovery, so I pulled up the children's birthday video on my phone. They were born on the same day—March 14—but two years apart. Stelli's and Evie's smiling faces filled the screen as I sat watching the video I'd filmed just a few months ago. Stelli sat on the floor, his smile huge, revealing the adorable gap where his two bottom front baby teeth were missing. He was opening the package and squealed with excitement.

"Yes! A stomp rocket."

Leo got on the floor with Stelli, and together they took it out of the box and set it up. Evie was exclaiming over the American Girl Crafting Kit, and I felt like my heart would burst from love as I watched. I'd been so determined that Stelli and Evie would never know the disappointment I'd had as a child, feeling unheard and uncared for. I made sure that they'd gotten every item on their list. I'd done the shopping on my own, of course. Leo was always far too busy.

There was a pause in the video and then it picked up again. In the afternoon, we had taken the kids to the Beardsley Zoo, where Stelli had been especially entranced by the tigers, but Evie's favorites had been the adorable little prairie dogs. We sat outside eating ice cream at one of the picnic tables, and as I filmed the three of them, they stuck their tongues out and made funny faces at me.

Looking back, I would say it was one of the happiest days of my life. So different from the birthdays of my own childhood, when my mother was usually sick in bed and my father was out of town on business. Now, watching the video and seeing how happy we were together, I couldn't wrap my head around what happened, how quickly I'd lost them. I decided I would call Janice later today.

Maybe I could ask her to call Leo as my attorney and get him to let me see the children. She could explain to him how important it was for their well-being and get him to make the courts change their mind. I knew there was still a good man inside him somewhere. He'd have to see the light, wouldn't he?

| 29 |

PIPER

The incessant ringing wouldn't stop, and when Piper finally picked up, it was with a sigh. She held her hand up and motioned for Joshua to stop the recording of her latest podcast. Now they'd have to start over again from the beginning.

"Pam . . . er. Piper Drakos." Damn. She had to be more careful. It was one thing to mess up the last name, but she had to remember she was Piper now. Leo had been so happy when she readily acquiesced to his request that she take his last name. She didn't care since she'd made up *Reynard* anyway. And she liked the idea of sharing the same last name with her husband and the children. It made them seem more like a family.

There was a sound of throat clearing. "Mrs. Drakos? Don't worry, Stelli is fine, but we need you to come to the school. There's been . . . an incident."

She looked at her watch. "What sort of an incident?"

"We'd rather discuss it in person. Can you come now?"

She stifled a groan. "Yes, of course. Did you try to reach Mr. Drakos?" she asked.

"Apparently he's in court. See you shortly?" *Of course he was*, she thought, her annoyance growing.

Pressing End, she rushed from the studio to her office to grab her purse. Her thoughts raced as she drove the few miles to the elementary school. This kid was going to be the death of her. High-spirited didn't begin to cover it, though she understood that he was going through a tough time. With Joanna gone, he'd clung even tighter to Leo. Piper had tried, was still trying, to win him over, but nothing seemed to be working.

Slowing the car, she pulled into the parking lot and took a deep breath before getting out. Stelli was sitting outside of the principal's office, where the receptionist was reading him a story. She looked up as Piper came in.

"You can go on in—Dr. Parker is waiting for you," she said. Piper couldn't read her tone.

"Hi, Stelli," she said before going in, aware of the other woman's eyes on her, but he didn't look up.

Dr. Parker, a striking sixtyish woman with silver hair pulled loosely into a stylish chignon, rose from behind her desk and reached her hand out as soon as Piper entered.

"Thank you for coming right away. Please have a seat."

"What's happened?" Piper wanted to get it over with.

Dr. Parker leaned back in her chair, and appraised Piper with cool, green eyes. "I'm concerned about Stelios's frame of mind," she said, using his formal name. "The mother of one of his classmates is in the hospital. She just had a baby. Stelios told the little girl that her mother would probably die, and she'd never see her again."

It felt like all the air had left her lungs. Piper opened her mouth to speak, but nothing came out. She stared at the woman across from her for what felt like an eternity before she finally spoke. "It's been a hard year for Stelli. I'm not sure what to say."

Dr. Parker raised an eyebrow. "Well, what I would hope you would say is that you'll have him speak to someone. Clearly, he is very confused about what happened with his mother and still needs closure."

Piper saw a good opportunity. "I completely agree with you, Dr. Parker. He has had some anger issues at home, and you're right—he is confused. His father and I have talked about getting him help, but Mr. Drakos thinks it may resolve by itself if given time."

"I'm very encouraged by your concern and desire to get some help for Stelios. Perhaps if I had a word with Mr. Drakos, it might help to get the ball rolling."

Piper gave her a grateful smile, seeing she had made an ally. "Yes, I think that would be extremely helpful. I don't know if you're aware, but my center has a specialist in grief recovery."

The principal's stern demeanor had softened, and she looked at Piper with renewed interest. "No, I wasn't aware of that. Stelios is fortunate to have you in his life. I'll send a note to your husband urging him to take your advice."

Piper stood and reached her hand across the desk. "Thank you so much. I can't tell you how much I appreciate your support."

"Thank you for coming in, Mrs. Drakos. It was a pleasure to meet you."

Piper turned and left the room, pulling the door shut behind her. Stelli looked up from his book, his eyes wary as Piper crouched down next to him.

"Hi, sweetie. Would you like to come home now or stay for the rest of the day?"

"I want to go back and play with my friends."

"Okay. Rebecca will pick you up at two then." She leaned in to give him a peck on the cheek, but he pulled away. She felt her face flush in embarrassment, and she stood up. "I'll be going now."

She was humming as she drove away.

Stelli had barely glanced at her when she got home from the center that afternoon, clinging instead to Rebecca. Evie, on the other hand, had been a darling. She'd joined Piper at the pool, reading her Nancy Drew book while Piper tried to concentrate on her own book, *The Happy Stepmother*.

"Excuse me, Piper. There's a delivery truck here. Did you order some furniture?" Rebecca called from just inside the sliding doors. Piper had, but she'd completely forgotten, and she jumped up, threw on her cover-up, and walked inside and upstairs to the front hall, Evie following behind her.

The decor in Leo's house was traditional and, in her mind, boring. The house itself had good bones, wonderfully high ceilings, and great light, but the floral fabrics and heavy wood furniture did nothing for it. She liked a modern look, with vibrant colors and cleaner lines. Besides, she wasn't about to live with furniture another woman had chosen.

As soon as Piper instructed the moving men to remove the existing furniture from the living room before bringing in the new items, Evie turned to her, her eyes wet with tears. "Where are they taking our sofas?"

"They're going to donate them to charity. We've got brand-new furniture coming right away to replace them. Won't it be nice to freshen things up?"

Evie ran into the room and threw herself on the sofa. "No. Mommy picked these out!"

Piper felt a pit in her stomach. She hadn't considered that the children might be upset. They never even sat in the living room. She crouched down so that she was eye level with her stepdaughter.

"I'm so sorry you're upset, Evie. I was just trying to make the house more cheerful. I really think if you give the new furniture a chance, you'll like it."

"What are you doing?" Stelli came running in, with Rebecca behind him.

Piper looked at Rebecca helplessly. "I didn't think—"

"Clearly," Rebecca interrupted her. "Children, come with me." She led them from the room with a disapproving backward glance.

The blood pounded in Piper's ears, and she wanted to scream. She looked at the men, who were standing around, waiting for instruction. "I'm afraid there's been a mistake. Please take the new pieces back. I'll call the store and straighten it out."

She sat for a moment and took a few deep breaths, trying to calm down before she went to speak to the children. Was she really supposed to get their approval before she made any changes in the house? It was her house now, too. But obviously they still regarded her as nothing more than a guest. She looked up as she heard footsteps approaching. Rebecca stood in the doorway.

"I canceled the delivery."

Rebecca nodded. "A wise decision. The children are going through a lot, and you just can't do things like that with no warning."

"Pardon me?" Piper raised her eyebrows, ready to tell Rebecca what she could do with her opinion, but Rebecca put up a hand.

"I know I'm not family, but I've known the children since they were babies. I love them and want only what's best for them."

"And you're implying that I don't?" Piper asked, incensed.

"Of course not. I'm only suggesting that you be a little more sensitive to the fact that they're still grieving. They miss their mother. I know you're eager to make this your home, but you have to think of them first."

Piper stood up. She was not going to sit here and be lectured by the help. "You're right, Rebecca. You're not family. And if you ever try to tell me how to behave again, you won't be taking care of them any longer." She walked out before Rebecca could respond.

She would speak to Leo tonight. How hard could it be to find a new nanny?

At a little past five Leo phoned to tell her not to hold dinner, as he'd be working late again. He'd warned her before they got married that he worked long hours, but she hadn't counted on his practically living at the office. The three of them—Piper, Evie, and Stelli—sat down to a dinner of chicken curry that Rebecca had made earlier. As Rebecca served, Piper was chilly toward her and told her to take the rest of the evening off. After helping the children with homework and reading a few bedtime stories, Piper tucked them into their beds and went to her office down the hall to work on her blog while she waited for Leo.

Around ten, she heard the chime of the door opening and shut her laptop. She found Leo in the kitchen, rummaging in the refrigerator.

"Didn't you eat?"

He shook his head and walked over to her, pulling her into an embrace.

"I didn't have time. I'm so wiped I don't even know if I have the energy to now."

"Sit down," she commanded him. "I'll make you something. You have to take better care of yourself."

She filled a glass with filtered water and handed it to him. He sat at the kitchen table and looked through the mail while she threw together a veggie omelet and toasted a slice of whole wheat bread. After she put the steaming plate in front of him, he wolfed it down, giving her a grateful smile.

"Thanks. I was hungrier than I thought."

"You have to stay nourished." She cleared her throat and put a hand on his arm. "Listen, I know you're tired, but I need to talk to you about something."

He raised his eyebrows.

"I got a call from the principal today about Stelli."

A concerned look came over his face. "What happened? Is he okay?"

Piper nodded. "He's fine, but I think he's still having a hard time processing what happened. He told a little girl that her mother was never coming home from the hospital, that she would probably die." She arched a brow. "She just had a baby."

Leo's eyes widened. "Oh no. What did you say?"

She shrugged. "Dr. Parker was pretty adamant that he needs help. I told her that you and I have discussed getting help for him and looking into some naturopathic therapies. She thought that was an excellent course of action. In fact, she's probably going to tell you that herself."

Leo stood up, his expression inscrutable. "He's young. We just have to do a better job of making him understand that she's not coming back."

"Leo, it's not enough to talk about heaven. That just confuses him. He doesn't understand why she can't come home."

He ran a hand through his hair, his voice rising. "Okay, I get it."

"There's one more thing."

"What?"

"It's Rebecca." She filled him in on what had happened that afternoon. "She's overstepping. I think we should consider looking for a new nanny."

His expression turned dark. "Aside from me, Rebecca is the one stable force in the children's lives right now. We can't replace her. It's not fair to them. They've lost enough."

"But, Leo, she practically yelled at me and tried to tell me I wasn't being a good mother. I'm trying so hard, and she's making me feel like a failure."

"Of course you're not a failure. But you really shouldn't have decided to redecorate a room without checking with me first."

Her heart began to beat faster. "I wanted to surprise you. I thought you'd be happy. You told me you never liked that furniture."

He sighed. "Yes, but . . . look, you have to understand. The children need time. You can't just spring these changes on them."

She began to cry softly and turned away. "I'm sorry. I was just trying to do something to show you I feel like this is my home now."

He came up behind her and put his arms around her. "Don't cry, darling. Everything will be okay. And you and Rebecca will work things out. It's just going to take time for everyone to adjust and figure out their boundaries."

That hadn't gone the way she'd hoped. Sighing, she trudged up the stairs, her mind working overtime. Although this didn't really qualify as a fight, it was the first time he'd been obviously frustrated with her. It was far too soon in their marriage for this kind of conflict. When she came out of the bathroom after brushing her teeth, she saw he was already in bed, rolled onto his side, eyes closed. Throwing off her robe, she slid in next to him and pressed her body against his. Her lips found his neck, and she gave it some feathery kisses. He rolled toward her, his eyes opening.

"Are you too tired?" she asked, her hand caressing his chest.

"Never too tired for you." He pulled her on top of him, running his hands over her body. "You're in control tonight, baby. Go for it."

That's exactly what I intend to do, she thought.

The next morning, she decided not to go into the center and slept in, letting Rebecca get the kids off to school. It was a little past nine when she finished getting dressed and went to her home office to go through emails and check the blog. A wonderful massage therapist she'd discovered a few weeks ago would be over at eleven, and then she was going to spend the rest of the day reading by the pool. But first, a little admin work had to be done. Piper logged on to the blog and started reviewing comments to approve them before they went live. As soon as she read the comment under the latest blog entry, "Putting Your Own Oxygen Mask On First," her hand froze over the mouse. It was clear whose handiwork it was. Her voice was unmistakable—and clearly recognizable by her choice of words. *Bitter and jealous. It was Joanna.*

> You have some nerve! Life is not an airplane ride. In real life, you have to put the children's needs before your own. That's what I've always done with my children—the ones you stole from me. You don't care at all about anyone but yourself, and you know nothing about parenting. Maybe that's why you don't have children of your own—you only go after ones who belong to other people.

Pulse racing, she hit the Spam button and drew several deep breaths. She could *not* let this get to her. What the hell was it with these women? Didn't they know when to quit? Piper's hand hovered over the mouse while she debated the wisdom of emailing Joanna. But no, it would only fuel the fire. Best to ignore it and move on.

She thought back to the last time she'd seen Ava, about a year ago, right before she'd moved east. Piper had been shopping at Neiman's in San Diego when she turned and saw her late husband's ex watching her, a look of pure hatred on her face.

"Well, if it isn't the black widow!" Ava said with a laugh, then more loudly, "Have you found your next victim yet?"

Piper had spoken in a low whisper, conscious of two women nearby staring at them.

"Ava, please, not here. Why can't you leave me alone?"

Ava had arched a perfect brow. "What, you think I'm following you? I've been shopping here for years. You're the one who doesn't belong." She glanced at the Hermès bag in Piper's hand. "You can buy designer clothes until you're blue in the face, but it won't change who you are inside. They will never cover up the monster you are underneath."

Piper bit her lip. There was no point in arguing with her. Things would only escalate. Ava had never cared if she made a scene; in fact, she thrived on it. So Piper turned and walked away as fast as she could, her face hot. When she opened the door, a screeching alarm sounded, and she realized she'd forgotten to put back the purse. "Shit!" she swore under her breath. Turning around, she walked over to the counter to set the bag down.

Ava called over to her. "Honestly, Piper. You don't need to steal. Oh, but that's right—stealing is what you do best. Other women's husbands . . . children. Until they're no good to you, and then you kill them."

Placing the purse on the counter, Piper strode out as calmly as she could, holding her head up high. She wasn't going to let Ava and her unhinged rants get to her. But she'd known then that, once again, it was time for her to make a fresh start.

| 30 |

JOANNA

I wanted to go over to the house and try to talk reason into Leo, to make him understand that I needed the children and they needed me. But Janice promised me she'd look into some other options and she convinced me that by going over to the house I'd be jeopardizing my chances of ever seeing the children again. And I'm sure that that's exactly what Piper would want me to do. I debated going to Leo with what I'd found out about Piper from Ava, but I worried Piper would just come up with a good story. After all, if the authorities hadn't found enough evidence to charge her with anything, it was unlikely that someone as completely under her spell as Leo would believe it.

Taking a sip of coffee, I heard my mother's footsteps on the stairs and looked at my watch. Ten thirty. She had never been an early riser. I'd always gotten myself off to school, making my own breakfast and packing a lunch before catching the bus. Sometimes she was awake when I got home, but often she'd be napping because of her chronic fatigue. My father and I used to cook in the evenings when he wasn't traveling, and I loved those times with him. He loved seafood and taught me how to butterfly shrimp, make a perfect pot of clam chowder, and fillet a fish. Sometimes, we'd make the fluffiest pancakes on Sunday mornings while Mom stayed in her room sleeping. But those times with him were too few and far between.

"Good morning. How did you sleep?" I asked as she came

into the room wrapped in a brown terry-cloth robe. Her leg was healed, but she still favored the other one.

"Terribly, as usual," she replied. She plopped down opposite me on a leather chair whose stuffing was peeking through its cracks. "I know the doctor said I'm all better, but it still hurts. Stupid doctors. What do they know?"

"I'm sorry. Do you want to take some aspirin? That might help."

She grunted. "Hmph. Nothing helps."

"Can I get you some coffee?"

"Not yet. I just need to sit for a little." She leaned against the back of the chair and eyed me. "So . . . what are your big plans for the day?"

"No plans. I've been feeling so sad this morning. I dreamed about Stelli and Evie last night. I miss them so much it hurts. I miss Leo, too, even though I know I shouldn't."

"I'm sorry that he's keeping you from the kids. It's heartless. But Leo only cares about what he wants. He's selfish, just like all men. Just like your father."

"Leo is *not* like him."

"He doesn't care about you. You need to face it, honey. He left you. Just like your father left us." She rose heavily from the chair, shaking her head, and left me to sit and brood. Her words made me think back to my high school graduation day, when Mom and Dad were both happy, and even seemed to be getting along for a change. Right before we left the house for the ceremony, my father stopped by my room, where I was putting the finishing touches on my hair.

"Jo, let me look at you."

I turned to him and smiled, my lips bright with the new pink gloss I'd bought the day before.

"You're so grown up. My baby's all grown up." He sat down on my bed, looking around the room. "I still remember the day you decided you wanted red walls. Remember?"

I looked at him in the mirror and laughed. "Yeah. Mom had a fit, saying it looked like a bordello."

He shook his head. "I thought you'd get tired of it. But I have to admit, it works."

"Now the room will be mostly empty, except when I'm home from college on breaks," I said, walking over to him and taking his hands in mine. "And you'll come see me at BU, right?"

He gave me a sad look. "Let's not think of being apart. Today is a celebration." Reaching inside his suit pocket, he pulled out a slip of paper and handed it to me. "Here. Don't tell your mother."

It was a check, folded in half. I opened it and gasped. Ten thousand dollars! "Dad! What is this for?"

"A graduation present. I want you to take it and open an account in your name only. It's for a rainy day."

I was flabbergasted. I hugged him, then I took the check and hid it in my dresser drawer.

The rest of the day went by in a blur. My parents smiling and waving from the stands. A celebratory dinner with them before I joined the rest of my friends for an evening of partying, as we stopped by the homes of four different friends.

The next morning, a Sunday, I awoke to my mother's screams. I ran into the kitchen, where she was sitting at the table, a piece of paper in one trembling hand.

"Mom! What's wrong?"

"He's gone," she said, not looking at me but staring straight ahead. "Gone for good." Her fingers opened, and the paper dropped to the floor. I grabbed it and began to read.

Ida,

By the time you read this I will be long gone. Things have been over between the two of us for a long time now, but I made you a promise all those years ago, and I've kept up my end of the bargain. Joanna is an adult now, and just as it's time for her to start her own life, it's time for me to take mine back. You don't have to worry about money—I paid off the house, and I'll continue to support you. But in return, I want an easy divorce. My lawyer will be in touch. You won't see me anymore, and you know why. Tell Joanna that I love her and that I'll get in touch with her when the time is right. I know you'll say I'm a coward for not explaining things to her myself, but I didn't want to ruin her graduation. Maybe I am a coward, but I just couldn't do it. I hope she'll understand one day. Try and be good to her.

Bill

I started to shake, and the words wouldn't come. Sinking down into the kitchen chair, I placed the letter on the table. "What is he talking about?"

She turned to look at me, and the loathing in her eyes was so intense I recoiled. "He's gone to live with *her* full-time now. Her and her child. Got himself a new family."

"Mom. You're not making any sense. Live with who?"

She got up then, started making coffee, putting dishes in the dishwasher. Turning to me, she said, "Eggs?" Her voice shook, and with one hand she wiped from her cheeks the tears that she'd been trying to hide. I stood up and went to her, putting my arm around her frail shoulder. She started to cry then, violent racking sobs that made her body shake. I'd never seen her like that before.

I held her while she cried, and then, as abruptly as it had started, it stopped.

"Sit. I'll make you breakfast."

I wasn't hungry, of course, but I sat and waited, reading through the note again. He was making it sound like I would never see him again. I knew that he and my mother hadn't been happy together, but how could he leave without telling me or saying goodbye? He was my father, and I loved him. I assumed he'd always be there, and the thought that he was gone forever—that now it would be just my mother and me—devastated me.

"He admitted that he's had a mistress for years. He waited until you were grown up to leave. I guess I have to depend on you to take care of me now," she said.

"But I'm moving to Boston in the fall."

She shook her head. "I don't think so. Your worthless father said he can't pay the tuition. Maybe you can take classes at a community college."

I ran from the room, tears blinding my eyes, and up to my bedroom. Shutting and locking the door, I grabbed the phone from my nightstand and dialed my father on his cell phone. She had to be lying. He knew how much going to BU meant to me. My heart raced as the phone rang, then almost stopped when the recording came through. *I'm sorry, but the number you are trying to reach is no longer in service.*

I didn't talk to my father again for years. I found out later that he married the woman he'd been living with part-time since I was eight. Mom's chronic fatigue had gotten worse and worse right after he left, and she became too dizzy to drive. So I'd used the money he'd given me to enroll in the local community college, stayed in my room with the red walls, and took care of my mother.

I didn't want to think about my father anymore. He had made the choice to leave me, so different from the way I'd been torn from Stelli and Evie. Every time I thought about how much I missed them, I felt a knife in my heart. I couldn't bear it if they believed I'd abandoned them. They needed to know I'd fought for them, that it was Piper's fault we were separated. I sat and thought and decided I would write them a letter.

My dear precious Evie and Stelli,

I miss you both more than you know. I think about you every minute of every day, and I want you to know that I am always watching you, even if you don't see me. I watch over you to be sure you are safe, and I want you to know that I will never let anything bad happen to you. Just as your guardian angel protects you, so do I. Never forget that. When I close my eyes, I pretend that we are holding hands and talking to each other. You can do that, too, when you close your eyes. Picture me standing next to you, holding your hand, whispering in your ear, giving you a kiss on the cheek.

I want you to think about all the fun times we had together at the beach, at the house in Maine, at Christmastime. You know where all the photograph albums are. Take them down from the shelf and look at the pictures of us together and remember how happy we were. Look at all the books we used to read together and remember our bedtime hugs and kisses. I promise that we will be happy that way again one day, and I hope that it will be soon. No matter what anyone tells you, I am always with you, and I will always love you. Forever and ever.

xoxoxoxoxoxo

By the time I finished the letter, I was crying uncontrollably, and my mother came into the room.

"What's wrong?" She moved closer to me. "Why are you crying?"

I wiped the tears from my face, holding the letter and looking up at her standing over me. I needed her to tell me it would all be okay.

"What is this?" she asked, taking the piece of paper from my hands. She scanned the page and then dropped it back into my lap. "Get it through your head, Joanna. They're all moving on: Leo, Stelli, Evie. Like *he* did." Her voice rose hysterically as she spoke. "What's a letter going to do? Nothing. You don't think I begged your father to come back? That I didn't try everything I could think of? What did it get me? Nothing. A big fat zero." Her face was pinched with resentment.

Full circle, I thought. I'd come full circle, living again with a mother who was too preoccupied with herself to think of anything or anyone else. All I could do was pray that Leo would come to his senses and return to me. And if I had to do a few things to help that along, so be it.

| 31 |

PIPER

When Piper had gone upstairs to wake Evie for Leo's firm's annual father-daughter lunch and law event at Leo's office, the child was already awake and in her favorite blue dress and patent leather shoes. She'd hardly been able to talk about anything else at the dinner table the night before, and it was apparent that her excitement hadn't dimmed.

"Can you put my hair in a French braid?" Evie asked.

"Sure," Piper said. "Grab your brush."

Evie stood in front of the sink facing the mirror, and Piper stood behind her, braiding the girl's long, thick hair. She'd gotten good at it after watching Mia French-braid her own hair every morning. As Piper's fingers worked, she thought about the young girl who had been her stepdaughter for four years. Mia had been eleven when Matthew and Piper married, and was very unhappy that her father was remarrying. She'd made it clear to Piper that she blamed her for breaking up her parents, though of course that wasn't the full story. Things may have settled down over time if it hadn't been for Ava, who would bring Mia over hours late, intentionally spoiling any plans Piper and Matthew had made. One weekend when they were having a party to introduce Piper to Matthew's friends, Ava had shown up, ostensibly to drop off a book Mia had forgotten, and then ended up staying. She knew all the guests, of course, and she completely stole the show, acting as if she still lived there, playing the hostess. Piper had been mortified, and she pulled Matthew aside to tell him to do something. But he said he couldn't humiliate Ava in front of their daughter, so he did nothing. Piper often wondered if she would have put up with it if she hadn't been so taken with Matthew. But that was all in the past now. She couldn't second-guess herself or dwell on it.

"There," she said, finishing the braid and tapping Evie gently on the shoulder. "All done."

Evie turned her head both ways, looking at Piper's handiwork in the mirror. "Thank you, Piper. It looks pretty."

"You're welcome. Why don't you go downstairs? Your father is waiting for you at breakfast."

Piper watched the girl skip away and headed down the hall to Stelli's room. It was empty, so she went downstairs to find him already dressed for school and knocking at the door to Rebecca's suite off the kitchen area. The door opened, and Rebecca emerged holding a plastic Spider-Man action figure.

"Here you go, sweetie. I glued it back together."

He took her hand, and they walked toward Piper.

"Good morning, Stelli. Glad to see you're all dressed and ready," Piper said.

"Of course," Rebecca said stiffly. "Why wouldn't he be?"

The nanny was still acting prickly. Piper inhaled, trying to keep herself from being short with her. She had to remember to keep her eyes on her own side of the street and not let someone else's bad mood or bad manners affect her or make her say something she'd regret later. The three of them moved in silence into the kitchen, where Leo was pouring milk into Evie's cereal bowl. *So much for a healthy breakfast*, Piper thought.

Leo looked up and smiled at them. "Good morning, Stel. How's my boy?"

Stelli pouted and took a seat next to Evie. "How come Evie gets to go to work with you and I don't?"

"It's a father-daughter event, pal," Leo said.

"Not fair!" Stelli put his elbow on the table and rested his cheek against his hand.

Piper had a thought. "Would you like to come to the center with me?"

Stelli didn't look at her. "No thanks," he mumbled. "I want to go with Dad."

Leo patted his shoulder. "I'll bring you to the office another day. Now eat your breakfast, or you'll be late for school." Leo turned to Evie. "Are you finished? It's almost time for us to go." He rose from his chair and put a hand on Piper's arm. "Would you help me with something?"

Piper frowned and followed him into the foyer. "Is something wrong?" she asked in a low voice.

"No. I was just thinking we could all meet for dinner. Stelli's feeling left out, and I thought maybe you could pick him up from school and take him back to Phoenix with you. That way they'll both have had a 'work' day. Then you can meet Evie and me for dinner at Fat Cat Pie Company. A special treat. What do you think?"

"Sure. But I don't know whether Stelli will really want to, since I just asked him and he wasn't interested in coming with me."

"That's just because he was disappointed that he can't come with me. I think after he's had some time to cool off, it will be good."

"Okay. I'll let Rebecca know that I'll be picking him up. What time shall we meet?"

"Early. Say five thirty?"

She nodded, and Leo leaned in to kiss her just as Evie came into the hall. "I'm ready, Daddy."

He grabbed his briefcase with one hand and Evie's hand with the other. "Let's go, then. We're going to have a great day."

Piper went back to the kitchen to find Stelli looking even more miserable than before.

"I have a great idea." Piper tried to put some excitement in her voice. "How about if I pick you up from school and you can come to work with me for a few hours? You can help me, and then we'll go meet your daddy and Evie for some pizza at Fat Cat's. We can even get some ice cream afterward. What do you think?"

He looked at her with big, sad eyes and shrugged. "I guess."

It wasn't a very enthusiastic response, but at least he hadn't thrown food at her or crashed a toy car into her leg. She kept telling herself that eventually she would win him over, but sometimes it seemed futile—after all, it had never happened with Mia.

She didn't need to pick Stelli up until three, so she went home around noon to meet with the designer she'd hired to redo their bedroom. This time she had cleared it with Leo, who had agreed that it was unreasonable to expect her to sleep in a room his former wife had decorated. When they finished, she saw that Rebecca had brought in the mail and left it on the counter. Things had remained strained between them since their clash, until Rebecca had apologized and Piper had told her it was water under the bridge. Truthfully, though, Rebecca was still on probation in her mind, but for Leo's sake she was willing to try to make things work. Glancing through the mail, she froze when she saw an envelope for Stelli and Evie written in a sprawling handwriting and with no return address. She grabbed it and opened it, her hands shaking. Sinking down on a chair, she read it and felt her heartbeat increase. She folded the letter and put it in her purse. The children were finally coming to accept that Joanna was gone, and Piper intended for it to stay that way. She grabbed her bag and left to pick Stelli up from school.

The line of cars wound around the parking lot, and Piper checked her email while waiting for school dismissal. Soon, the first graders would be marched outside and escorted to their waiting parents or caregivers. She recognized some of the mothers from the back-to-school night she'd attended. They'd been friendly enough, but distant. No one had made an effort to engage her in conversation or get to know her. It had been awkward for her, although she had put on a good show of looking relaxed and as if she belonged. She'd been grateful that at least these mothers were not hostile, like the mothers at the school Mia had attended. There, she had truly felt like an outsider, and she'd known it was a result of Ava's constantly bad-mouthing her to the other moms. Evidently that wasn't happening here.

She caught sight of Stelli and inched the car up slowly as the line moved forward. He ran to the car, jumped into the back, and buckled his seat belt.

Piper turned to look at him before driving off. "Hi, Stelli. Did you have a good day?"

"It was okay." He looked out the window and remained silent all the way to the center.

Piper had cleared her afternoon and had spent part of the morning running around to toy stores for something interesting that would keep him busy, finally opting for a set of sound-activated light blocks. To her utter surprise, she'd hit the jackpot. Stelli loved them and played with them on the floor of her office all afternoon. When it came time to leave for dinner, Piper sensed a definite thaw in him.

"What do you say we clean up the blocks and put them in this special box? I'll keep them in a secret place so no one else will play with them. They'll be only for you whenever you come to the center with me."

His eyes lit up. "You promise you won't let anyone else play with them? Not even Evie?"

Piper made an X on her chest and held her hand up. "Cross my heart." She was encouraged by his change toward her. She wanted Stelli to accept her. More than that—to like her. If his antagonism continued, it would only hurt her relationship with Leo.

Leo and Evie were already seated at the restaurant when Piper and Stelli arrived. It was noisy, and the smell of dough baking in the brick ovens permeated the crowded room.

"Have you been here long?" Piper asked, sliding into the booth after Stelli and facing Evie and Leo.

"Just ten minutes or so. I ordered you a water with lemon." He indicated the glass in front of her. "And a Coke for you, buddy," he said, smiling at Stelli. "Now what does everyone want? I'm thinking maybe a big, big cheese pizza with lots of pepperoni. What do you say?" He looked back and forth from one kid to the other.

"Yeah, a really big one," Stelli said.

"Okay with you, Evie?" Leo asked.

"Yup."

"Are we all set, then?"

Piper picked up the menu and scanned it, hoping there might be something healthier on offer. Lots of pizza combinations, some pasta dishes, and a few salad options. She put the menu down and looked up at Leo. "I'll have a garden salad with oil and vinegar."

"Borrrring," Stelli said, rolling his eyes.

Leo just looked at her and shrugged his shoulders.

"Don't you like pizza?" Evie asked her.

"Well, it's not my favorite. I really love salad, though."

"Mommy always got pizza when we came here. She loved it here, didn't she, Daddy?" Stelli said.

It was as if her happy balloon had been pricked and all the air seeped out. Piper felt her face flush, and when she looked at Leo, his eyes were hard to read.

"Yeah, buddy. She liked it here a lot," he said.

The mention of their mother always caught Piper off guard. It was like walking through an empty field that seemed to have been cleared of mines, and then, bam, having one blow up in her face. She'd believed her time with Stelli this afternoon had brought them a bit closer, but now in a flash she was the interloper again. The three of them all seemed to fit together perfectly. Sitting here, feeling like she was not enough, made her think of all the times she'd felt this way as a child. She'd never felt like she formed a close bond with her own parents.

Her parents were good on paper: accomplished and hardworking. Her father, a mechanical engineer, taught at the Naval Academy, and her microbiologist mother worked in a private research lab. As the only child, she'd felt the full force of the high standards they set for her. It was expected that she be a straight-A student. There was no acceptable excuse for even a B-plus. Their house was quiet, dull, and tedious, a home where spontaneity and lightheartedness were frowned upon. Her mother had checked her homework every night, all the way through the twelfth grade, as if she were still a child. Tests and report cards were scrutinized. Her every movement, her every act, had been inspected by them.

They were not a family that hugged or kissed or said *I love you*. She remembered being so surprised the first time she'd gone to her friend Julia's house, which was filled with kids and laughter. Julia's mother had been warm and welcoming, pulling her into a hug. It was a complete revelation to her that families lived that way, enjoying each other and having fun together. She had only short glimpses of this, however, because her own parents had been firm about time spent away from home. She had to come straight home from school and get right to work on homework, which usually lasted three or four hours. Going out on school nights was strictly forbidden. Saturday was the only day she was allowed to see friends, and that was the day she tried to spend as much time as possible at Julia's.

Of course, she'd left as soon as she graduated from high school, moving away from Annapolis for good. Now, after her years studying psychology at University of California and the work she'd done in the field of recovery, she realized what a cold and barren upbringing she'd had. It was probably part of the reason she'd never really wanted children of her own.

How ironic that, once again, she had married a man with kids.

| 32 |

JOANNA

"Here," I said, handing the two photographs to Celeste. "Pictures of Evie and Stelli from last Christmas." At our last session Celeste had asked me to choose a memory for today and to email it to her beforehand. I chose last Christmas, when we were still happy and together. One picture showed Evie in her bright red Christmas pajamas, a llama bedecked with a tree-light necklace smiling on her PJ top. She was laughing, her hair still messy with sleep, while peeking out from inside her princess tent.

Celeste studied both of the photographs for a minute, and then looked up at me. "Your recounting of this memory was very evocative, Joanna. Haunting almost. I read it several times. How did it feel to put it into words?"

I thought about it for a moment before answering. "It was difficult to write," I admitted. "The day itself was so wonderful. We put the children to bed on Christmas Eve and stayed up late putting Stelli's new bicycle together and arranging all the furniture in Evie's dollhouse. I didn't get to bed until after one. Of course, the children were up early to see what Santa brought them." I smiled as I pictured the two of them rushing to the mantel and grabbing their stockings. "Evie exclaimed over her heart locket and silver bracelet, and Stelli was already setting up his army men. There was wrapping paper everywhere, and it was all a big glorious messy ball of happiness."

Celeste nodded. "And the rest of the day?"

"We let them play with all their toys, of course, and Leo and I just sat watching them, enjoying all the fun they were having. I remember bringing French toast with syrup and fresh strawberries into the den and letting everyone eat breakfast there for once so that they wouldn't have to leave their presents. The four of us sat on the floor in front of the fireplace. Evie kept her new stuffed tiger on her lap while we ate."

"Can we talk about Stelli and what you wrote about reading to him?"

My stomach twisted at the thought. "They were both exhausted by bedtime, and so was I. Stelli asked me to read one of his new books to him—*The One and Only Ivan.* He insisted I read it a second time, which I did, but when he asked for a third time, I snapped at him and said I was too tired. I gave him a peck on the cheek, turned out the light, and left the room." I felt tears fill my eyes. "I'm so sorry I was impatient with him. I would give anything to read it to him again now, as many times as he wanted."

"You said Leo's family came over later in the day, but you didn't mention your own mother. Was she there?"

I shook my head. "No. I invited her, but she backed out. I wasn't surprised, really. I didn't think she would come."

"Why is that?"

"Mom never liked Christmas much. I guess I can understand in a way." I sat there as silence filled the space between us.

Celeste finally spoke. "Tell me about that."

"The Christmases of my childhood were very different. You wouldn't understand. You probably had a dad who was around and who cared about you. I never did."

Celeste tilted her head at me. "We're talking about you. What I had or didn't have has no bearing on my understanding of your hurt or your painful memories. You realize that, don't you?"

I wasn't sure about that, but I continued anyway. "I would characterize my father as a sort of ghost spirit who came and went like the wind. When he was with us, it was so obvious that he wanted to be anywhere else. Even on holidays, he spent just a few hours with us and then left, supposedly for business, but like I told you before, it all turned out to be a lie. Always claiming he was seeing clients, but half the time, his trips were to see his girlfriend. Another woman that he cared about more than us. He was just putting in his time, I guess, waiting for me to finish high school so he could appease his conscience."

"And you told me that your mother never knew."

"Yes. She knew he'd been unfaithful, but not that he was with one particular woman all that time. They didn't have a good marriage. When he was home, she was constantly on his case, complaining that he was gone too much, that she was sick and needed him. But even when he tried to do things for her, she was never happy. But still, what he did . . ."

"If I remember correctly, you told me he was lying to them as well as to you?"

"Yeah. Great guy, huh? Who knows what he was telling his girlfriend until he could leave us for good, since she never knew he was married or had a kid."

"He's never told his new wife the truth?"

"He still pays my mother alimony, so she keeps her mouth shut. She can't work, so she needs his money to live on. Her disability isn't enough."

"Do you and your mother ever talk about what happened and how it made you feel?"

"My mother only talks about how ill-treated she was. It's always only about her. I have to admit that I was glad when she didn't show up last Christmas. Leo's family is so loving and full of fun. My mother would have changed the whole dynamic of the day, turning it into a gloom-fest." I shifted in my chair. "I don't want to talk about my parents anymore. I want to tell you what I found out in San Diego."

"Okay."

"When I met the ex-wife of Piper's dead husband, she had a *lot* to say about Piper. Or Pamela, depending on who you ask." I gave her a long look so that my words could fully register.

"Go on."

I recounted to Celeste everything Ava had told me. "Ava Dunn is convinced that Piper deliberately killed Mia. It would certainly explain why she changed her name and why she seems to be in hiding here."

Celeste frowned. "Joanna, sometimes an accident is just an accident. It's not uncommon for a grieving mother to need to place blame somewhere. If Piper were a murderer, she would be in jail."

"Why are you defending her?" I asked. "She's dangerous. She has a sailboat here, too. What if the same thing happens to Evie and Stelli as happened to Mia?"

"First of all, you are jumping to conclusions. You've told me yourself Leo has a boat and that Evie and Stelli have been taught water safety and wear life jackets. I know it's concerning, but it's out of your control for the time being. And you're working to get joint custody, so hopefully your fears will be alleviated soon."

"As long as Piper is around my children, my fear is going nowhere." I leveled a look of determination at her, and I could tell she was becoming exasperated with me. "I know that might sound irrational to you—I know that—but I just . . . I can't leave the children with that woman when I know in my bones something is going to happen. Maybe I need to start following her when she's out with the kids."

"You can't do that, Joanna. What if someone sees you? You could jeopardize your chances for custody."

"I'd stay far enough back. I wouldn't be breaking any laws. But I could take pictures. Build a case against her."

She seemed to ponder this. "I'm worried that this is turning into an obsession."

"You cannot possibly understand what I'm going through. Maybe I should see a therapist who has children . . ."

A tight look crossed her face. "Of course, that's your prerogative. But I hope you won't. I think we've established a good rapport. It's not necessary for me to have children in order to empathize with you. I'm on your side, remember?"

I took a sip of my water. "Let me ask you something. If you found out that your husband had a disease, would you leave him?"

She squinted at me and pursed her lips. "I don't see the similarities between a genuine disease and your ex-husband marrying another woman."

"His depression. That's what's made him vulnerable. He thought Piper was his medicine. But that medicine is killing him and killing our family. If he were suffering from a physical illness and I knew the cure, I would move heaven and earth to help him."

I could tell by her expression that she didn't agree, but I sensed the veil of detached professionalism descend upon her as she changed the topic. "We have only a few minutes left today. Is there anything else on your mind? How is the exercise plan going?"

Great, I wanted to say. *I'm planning to never do it.*

Instead, I told her what she wanted to hear. "Good. It's helping a little."

33
PIPER

Piper sat on the metal park bench, iPad on her lap and a hot latte in her hand, glancing up now and again as Stelli and Evie ran back and forth from the swings to the sliding board. Stelli was a whirlwind, never stopping, always pushing the limits, and Evie watched over him like a little mother. Their personalities were so very different. Stelli exhausted Piper. There were times her stomach was in knots at the prospect of his return from school in the afternoon, but she had decided recently that on Thursdays she would leave the center at three in the afternoon, pick the kids up from school, and take them to the park, giving Stelli a chance to expend some of his energy and perhaps allowing the two of them to forge a bond.

Now, she watched as he scrambled quickly up the steps to the slide and whooped while whooshing down it. She shook her head and turned her attention back to "Getting Our Best," the blog post she'd been working on. She was almost finished, just needed a powerful closing paragraph, when she heard a scream followed by crying. She looked up to see Stelli sitting at the foot of the slide, blood running down his chin, and Evie trying to comfort him. Piper jumped up, and the iPad slid to the ground as she ran to them.

"Oh my gosh, what happened?" she said, lifting his face so that she could examine the injury. A woman who seemed to be another mother was next to her now, handing her some tissues, which she gratefully accepted. As she used them to blot his face, she exposed a deep gash right under his lower lip.

Piper turned to the woman. “It looks pretty deep.”

She nodded. “Probably needs stitches. By the way, he went down the big slide. That’s for older kids. I guess you didn’t notice.”

Great. Was she supposed to be watching them every second of every day? How were kids ever supposed to self-actualize with all these helicopter moms around? Piper suppressed the panic and irritation that was rising in her and told herself to stay calm and focused. She put her arm around Stelli. “It’s going to be fine, sweetheart. We’re going to go see the doctor, and you’ll be good as new.”

He looked up at her and his chin trembled, and she could tell that he wasn’t completely convinced, but he took her hand, and with Evie on his other side, they made their way to the car. She looked at her watch. It was just past five, and the pediatrician’s office wasn’t open, so she drove straight to the urgent care in town. Fortunately, the wait was short and a friendly physician’s assistant asked some questions as she settled Stelli on the exam table and told them a doctor would be with them shortly. Evie stood next to Stelli, holding his hand, and Piper tried to think of something to do to make the time pass while they waited.

“How about if I read you one of your books? Evie, is there anything in your backpack?”

Stelli shot her a dirty look. “My chin hurts.” Tears filled his eyes, and his lip trembled.

Piper went to put an arm around him, but he pulled away.

“It’s okay, Stelli. The doctor will make you all better. Maybe you’ll even have a cool scar, like a pirate,” Evie said.

His eyes lit up just as the door opened and the doctor walked in.

He smiled at Stelli and held out his hand. “I’m Dr. Stanley.

I hear you hurt the ground with your chin. You must be pretty strong."

Stelli gave him a watery smile.

The doctor examined the wound, then turned to Piper. "It's not too bad. I'm going to clean it up and put some glue on it. That will be less painful than stitches, and he'll be good as new." He turned back to Stelli. "While you're here, how about I take a quick look to make sure you didn't hurt anything else?"

Stelli nodded and Piper watched as the doctor gave him a full examination. He turned to Piper. "He looks a little pale, has he been sick lately?"

Piper shrugged. "Not really. Just a cold a few weeks ago."

The doctor's brow furrowed. "That might explain it. As long as he's been feeling okay." He smiled at Piper. "Everything else looks good. Do you want to bring him back here for a follow-up or take him to his regular pediatrician? Who is that, by the way?"

"One of the doctors at Westport Pediatrics."

He gave her a questioning look.

She quickly continued. "I'm his stepmother, and I haven't taken him there yet, so I'm not sure which doctor. I can call them in the morning."

"Okay, then. I'll have the report from today's visit sent over to their office."

The ride home was quiet, and after explaining to a disapproving Rebecca what had happened, Piper went upstairs to change. Her phone buzzed, and she looked at the unfamiliar number.

"Hello?"

"If you had been watching the children like you should have, Stelli would never have been hurt. Why would you let him go on a slide that was clearly too dangerous for someone his age?" The voice on the other end was at full volume.

Joanna! How had she even gotten this number? "Leave us alone, or I'll call the police," Piper said firmly.

"I want to talk to Stelli," Joanna pleaded.

Piper hit the End button and threw the phone down, shaken by the rage she'd heard in Joanna's voice. When she got downstairs and she still hadn't heard from Leo, despite having left him two voice mails, she and the children sat down to dinner.

"Hot dogs tonight, Stelli, since they're your favorite. And as a special treat for being so very brave today, you can choose a movie to watch, even though it's a school night."

Stelli sat up straight and gently fingered the bandage on his chin. "*Captain America*!"

As soon as they finished eating, Piper settled them in the den, wrapping an afghan around each of them, then brought in two mugs of hot chocolate.

Evie reached out to grab a mug, but Piper stopped her. "That one is for Stelli. I put extra honey in it, just the way he likes it. This one is yours." She picked up the blue mug from the tray and handed it to Evie. "Careful, it's hot." She watched as Stelli took a sip from his. "Sweet enough?"

He nodded.

Satisfied that he'd actually drink it, she went back to the kitchen and was making herself some tea when Leo walked in.

"Hey, beautiful. Sorry I'm late. Got tied up in a deposition." He put his arms around her and nuzzled her neck. "How was your afternoon at the park?"

She sighed. "I tried to call you a bunch of times. I'm afraid Stelli had an accident."

Leo went white. "Where is he? Is he all right?"

"He's fine. Just a cut on his chin. He's in the den with Evie, watching a movie."

He moved away from her, but she grabbed his arm to stop him. "He fell from the slide. He's okay, but I need to talk to you."

Leo shook off her grip and strode to the door. "I need to see him," he said, before she could say another word.

Piper gave him a few minutes before following him into the den. He was sitting next to Stelli, his arm around him, while Evie sat on Leo's lap. The three of them looked so at ease with one another that Piper felt more like an intruder than she usually did. She wondered if she would ever be a real part of this family.

Leo looked up at her and beckoned her toward them with a nod, but she held back, unwilling to break into the tight circle. Finally, Leo stood. "You finish your movie, Stel, and I'll tuck you in afterward. I hope you thanked Piper for taking such good care of you," Leo said.

Stelli looked up at Piper. "Thank you," he said flatly, and turned his eyes back to the screen.

Piper and Leo returned to the kitchen, and Piper fixed a plate for him. He cleared his throat. "Can you tell me again exactly what happened? Evie mentioned something about Stelli going down the big slide." He looked up at her from his plate. "Were you watching him?"

This again, the accusation that an accident was somehow *her* fault. Piper's pulse quickened. "Of course I was watching them. I was sitting right there. Accidents happen, Leo. I didn't realize that only certain pieces of the playground equipment were age appropriate. You have to remember all this is new to me. I'm trying my best." As she looked at him, her eyes filled with tears.

He sighed. "I know, honey. It's just that Stelli doesn't always have the best judgment. Just try to remember he's only six."

"I'm sorry. You're right. I'll be more careful in the future. There's something else, though." She paused. "Joanna called again."

His eyes narrowed. "When?"

"Today. This afternoon. She yelled at me. Said I wasn't watching the children. That Stelli's accident was my fault." She paused. "Leo, she had to have been at the park, watching us. What if the children had seen her?"

A muscle in his jaw tensed. "Maybe I should talk to her, remind her of the judge's order."

"No. You can't do that. That's exactly what she wants—to talk to you. You'd be playing right into her hands."

"I don't know what else to do. We can't have her coming near the kids."

"Let's think about this before you do anything. Talk to one of the judges you play golf with. See what they say. I'm worried that if you call her, she might get the wrong impression."

He reached across the table and caressed her cheek. "Okay, I'll talk to Judge Barrows and see what he thinks we should do."

After he finished eating, they went back to the den together to watch the end of the movie and then put the children to bed. Piper went into Stelli's bedroom after Leo tucked him in. "Stelli, you were a really brave boy today. I was very proud of you. May I give you a kiss good night?"

"My stomach hurts," Stelli said, his eyes filling with tears. "I want my mommy."

Piper clenched her nails into her fist. Stelli was going to have to learn, one way or another, that you don't always get what you want.

| 34 |

JOANNA

I watched her yesterday. Sitting there, pretending to be their mother, while completely ignoring them and typing on her iPad. She didn't see me; she wasn't paying attention to anyone, was just hammering away on her stupid tablet, likely writing more platitudinous tripe. I am incensed that she has the nerve to keep me away from the children when she clearly doesn't even care about them herself.

As she sat ignoring them, I wanted to yell: *Put down your damn iPad and watch the kids.* I'd told Stelli time and time again he had to be older before using that tall slide—it was for sixth graders and up. But when he'd looked over and seen that Piper wasn't watching, he'd tromped right toward it. I wanted to run over and stop him but couldn't risk going against the court order. Before I could decide what to do, he went flying down on his stomach and hit the ground hard. It had taken everything in me not to run to him and sweep him up into my arms. I cried as I watched her finally get up off that bench. Another mom had run over, too, but I'm the one who should have been there comforting him.

Tears streamed silently down my face as she hustled them off to the car. I couldn't tell how badly he was cut, or if he needed stitches. After they left, I sat in the car for another half hour, seething, then drove myself home.

When I got there, Mom was in bed and complained that she was too tired to get up for dinner. I took a bowl of soup up to her, then poured a glass of wine for myself and carried it outside to the tiny back porch, where there was barely enough room for two folding metal chairs. As I sat in one of them, I noticed that the plastic weaving was fraying in several places. A chain-link fence ran around the perimeter of the narrow yard, and untrimmed grass was a half foot high against its edges. My mother said you could always tell which houses in the neighborhood didn't have a man around by how neglected they looked, and I guess our house was Exhibit A. I sat and sipped, watching the sun go lower into the sky, and thinking more about Stelli's accident, and grew increasingly angry. He could have hit his head, gotten a concussion, broken an arm—the possibilities were terrifying. What if there was a next time and the injury was more serious?

The blood was pounding in my temples as I downed the rest of the wine, took the cell phone from my pocket, and called her. I had copied her number from Leo's phone while we were still together. The minute I heard that soft tentative hello, I told her she needed to take better care with him, but she started yelling at me, telling me to leave them alone. I begged her to let me talk to Stelli, to make sure he was okay, but she refused, telling me he was just fine, and then the witch screamed at me not to call her, saying she would call the police if I bothered them again, and disconnected the call.

She's got Leo right where she wants him, and he's blind to her game. I recalled my conversation with Ava, when she'd told me Piper had hated her stepdaughter, and began to wonder if Piper's intention had been to get rid of only Mia. Maybe Matthew had been collateral damage. Was she planning to kill Stelli and Evie, too, so she could have Leo all to herself? I went inside, my head still pounding, and lay down on the sofa as darkness began to fill the room.

I must have fallen asleep, because the next thing I knew, my mother was gently shaking my arm.

"You should go up to bed."

I sat up and looked outside. The sun was just coming up. "Why are you up so early?" I asked her.

She shrugged. "My leg hurt, and I came down to get some aspirin. I called for you, but you didn't hear me." She sat down next to me. "Honey, you need to get yourself together. It isn't like you to mope around this way."

She was right. It was more like her, but I didn't say so. "I had a bad day. Stelli got hurt."

"Oh, honey. Is he . . . Wait, how do you know?"

I told her what I'd seen at the park. "I think I'm going to call Leo and tell him what she did."

"Don't bother, Joanna. She's already told him her version of events, and he's not going to listen to yours. You need to forget about him once and for all."

"What are you talking about? I can't forget about him. Leo and the children belong with me."

She waved her hand dismissively and shook her head. "He *married* her. Men always get what they want, and we're left with nothing." She reached out and clasped my hand. "At least we have each other."

I looked at her in her rumpled robe and matted hair, the forty extra pounds she carried on her doughy body, and thought, *No wonder my father left*, and then was immediately struck by guilt. She couldn't help that she was sick—even if she may have milked her condition over the years—and that my father *had* turned out to be the liar she'd always claimed him to be.

I stood up. "I'm going to go get dressed."

"Good. Maybe you ought to start looking for that job you

talked about, now that I'm feeling better. Get your mind off things."

On some level, I knew she was right, but I couldn't devote my energy to job hunting right now. If only I'd listened to my head instead of my heart. Instead of taking care of Leo and the kids all these years, I should have followed my own dream. I could have been a good lawyer—at least as good as Leo, maybe even better. I took some pre-law courses in college. After I got my associate's degree, I was ready to go on to get my bachelor's, but problems with Mom always seemed to come up. Some emergency or other. It was too much, trying to work full-time, take care of her, and go to school all at once. I just couldn't do it. I have always regretted it.

| 35 |

PIPER

Piper got up from the lounge chair and glanced at her watch. It was close to four, and Rebecca would be home with the kids soon. If she hurried, she could get in some laps before they got back. September was her favorite month in Connecticut—the air still warm but without the stifling humidity of August.

The water felt good, and after ten minutes in the pool, she felt the stress in her muscles begin to dissipate. Leo had promised her he'd be home early and the two of them would go out for a romantic dinner. It had been weeks since they'd been out alone together, and she was pulling out all the stops. She'd bought a new dress and lingerie for the occasion, made reservations at their favorite local restaurant, the Artisan, and booked a room at the Delamar. She was going to surprise him with the hotel. She didn't want any interruptions to their lovemaking tonight. Evie had gotten into the habit the last few weeks of coming into their bedroom at night, claiming she'd had a nightmare. The first couple of times Piper had been sympathetic, but it was almost every night now. When she'd tried to ask Evie what the nightmares were about, the girl got quiet and said she didn't want to talk about it. Tonight she'd have to knock on Rebecca's door instead.

The sound of giggling made her stop in mid-lap and look up. Evie was chasing Stelli, who was holding his sister's ballet case behind his back, laughing at her as she yelled for him to give it back. Piper was about to tell him to stop when Rebecca ran over and started chasing him, too, laughing along with him and turning it into a game.

"Come on, Evie, let's get him!" she yelled, and just like that, Evie went from being upset to laughing along with her brother. How did Rebecca always seem to know how to handle them?

Piper walked up the steps of the shallow end, exiting the pool, and reached for her towel, but before she could pick it up, Stelli dropped the ballet bag and grabbed the towel.

"Keep away from Piper!" he yelled, running toward the house.

Was she seriously supposed to go galloping after him? She felt annoyance fill every pore of her being. Rebecca and Evie were watching her quietly. Was Rebecca trying to make her look bad by just standing there waiting for her reaction? She forced a smile.

"Stelli, dear, I'm too wet to chase you. I could slip." That's probably what he hoped for.

He made a face at her and walked back toward her, then tossed the towel on the ground at her feet. "You're no fun."

Rebecca finally stepped in. "Stelli, you apologize."

Piper put a hand up. She didn't need Rebecca to make her look any worse "No, it's fine. You're right, sweetie. I haven't been much fun. Why don't I run up and change, and then we can go out for ice cream?"

His eyes lit up.

"But . . . they haven't had dinner yet," Rebecca stammered.

Piper turned to Stelli. "Now who's no fun? Who says you can't have dessert first, right?"

"Yay! Ice cream, ice cream," he began to chant. After a minute, Evie joined in.

Piper gave Nanny Tight Ass a triumphant smile.

When they returned from town, Leo was waiting in the kitchen, snacking on a brownie. Piper was really going to have to speak to Rebecca about all the crap she baked for the house. Although, considering the stunt she had just pulled with the ice cream, Piper decided she'd better wait a few days.

"Hi, babe." He kissed her on the lips, then crouched down and opened his arms. *"Pethia mou,"* he called in Greek as the children ran into his arms.

"Piper got us ice cream!" Stelli told him.

Leo laughed. "I can see that. You've got a chocolate mustache."

"I'm going to go get ready. Our reservation's in an hour." Piper smiled, her mood lifted further by this rare good time with Stelli and the prospect of an entire evening alone with her husband.

"Where are you going?" Evie asked.

Piper stopped and turned around. "Out for dinner. Remember, I told you this morning?"

Stelli stomped his foot. "I have my family tree project. You were supposed to help me," he whined to Leo.

Piper felt her heart skip a beat. This could not be happening.

Leo's expression was puzzled. "I thought that was due *next* Friday, right, buddy?"

Stelli, his arms crossed, shook his head. "No, tomorrow. And you said you'd help me find pictures of Mommy!" He doubled over. "And I don't feel good. My stomach hurts again."

Leo looked at Piper. "Can you move the reservation a little later?"

She probably could, but what was the point? They hadn't even started on the family tree, and they'd be at it for hours. Plus, she was sure it was going to end in tears anyway, given the subject matter.

She forced a smile. "No worries. I'll reschedule it for next week. This is more important."

Leo looked at her gratefully and gave her a peck on the lips. "Thanks, babe. You're the best."

Sure she was, she thought, as she walked up to the bedroom and shut the door. Taking a deep breath, she grabbed a pillow from the bed, went into the bathroom, turned the water on, and screamed as loud as she could into its feathers.

| 36 |

JOANNA

I'm not making any headway. I still can't see the children. And I sent a letter to Stelli and Evie, but I've heard nothing back."

Celeste shook her head. "I can only imagine how difficult this must be for you, but your attorney is working on trying to get you visitation rights, correct?"

I nodded.

"Okay, then. What did we talk about last time? The things you can control?"

"That doesn't seem like a very long list these days."

Celeste cocked her head. "Well, for one thing, how about getting back to the gym regularly? The endorphins would help your mood."

I shrugged. "Maybe. I just can't seem to find the motivation."

She nodded, her expression soft. "I understand. I could refer you to a psychiatrist we work with to evaluate you for antidepressants."

I thought about it for a moment. "I don't know. I don't want anything that's going to change my personality."

Celeste shook her head. "No, of course not. I'm just talking about something to 'take the edge off,' as you put it." She lifted her hands to make air quotes. "We don't have to decide now. Just something to think about. Tell me about things with your mother. How are they going?"

I sighed. "Being together in the same house night and day is exhausting. She's really okay on her own, even though she tries to make it seem like she's not. But at least I have the time now to build a case against Piper. I know she has more skeletons in her closet."

"We've talked about this, Joanna. It's not good for you to be so focused on Piper." Celeste tapped her pen on her pad for good measure. "You have to accept the fact that Leo has remarried. You have to get on with your life. Regardless of whether Piper is hiding something or not—your marriage is over. Why don't we try to focus on something positive, like what steps you can take to get at least some visitation with Evie and Stelli?"

"But that's just it. Leo and Piper have built a case against me. It's all lies, but the court believes them. How can I fight that?"

"Well, for one thing, you can talk to your lawyer about making some overtures to Leo's lawyer. Or maybe petitioning the court to allow you visitation, even if those visits have to be monitored. Wouldn't that be better than not seeing them at all?"

"I have talked to her, and she's tried. So far, we're getting nowhere."

Celeste gave me an encouraging smile. "There's always a chance. You can't give up. And if it would help, I'd be glad to speak with your attorney."

"Maybe I could see them at Christmas. Wouldn't that be wonderful?" I said, trying to change the subject. "But too much could happen between now and then. Will they even be alive in three months? Piper has them all fooled. Today, her center's blog post was about gratitude."

"Joanna . . ."

I put a hand up. "I know, I know. But I can't help it."

"Fixating on Piper and these implausible fears is only hurting *you*." She looked at me with resignation. "How did reading it make you feel?"

I bit my lip. "Furious! She's making herself sound like a good person, and she's not! And she's got no right to lecture about gratitude to others when everything in her life is stolen. I felt like putting that in the comments."

"I'm glad to hear that you didn't. What can you do with that anger instead? Is there a way to channel it into something positive?"

"How would you channel your anger and terror if someone was a threat to your husband and children and then wrote upbeat blogs about life?"

She looked at me with pity. "The best thing you can do is to talk to your lawyer and take the steps necessary to make some changes that are within your power. I'm here for you."

When I got home, there was a large brown envelope sticking out of the mailbox. I pulled it out, and my heart raced when I looked at the California postmark. I opened it, pulling out a handwritten note along with a marriage certificate. The note was from Ava:

Dear Joanna,

I was able to rush a copy of Matthew and Pamela's marriage certificate. You were right. She was married before. I feel like such a fool for not knowing this sooner. Good luck with your investigation. Let me know what you find.

Best, Ava

God bless her! I put the note down and picked up the certificate. Reading it, I stopped short:

Matthew Dunn, Divorced, *and Pamela Rayfield Sherwood,* Widowed.

Widowed? Another dead husband? What the hell?

I ran to my bedroom, document in hand, and opened my laptop, typing "Pamela Sherwood" into the search bar. After skimming through the first few entries, I saw a link to an obituary that mentioned a Pamela Sherwood. All of my senses were on high alert as I clicked on it.

Ethan Sherwood of Los Angeles, California, age 21, passed away Wednesday, July 12, 2006, from injuries sustained in a fall during a hiking accident. Sherwood was born on December 19, 1985, in Annapolis, MD. He was a graduate of the Key School and was planning a career in the arts. He is survived by his wife, Pamela Sherwood of Los Angeles, CA; his parents, Donald and Patricia Sherwood of Annapolis, MD; and a brother, Ted Sherwood of Chicago, IL. Funeral services are private.

My mind was racing. It *was* her. She'd buried not one but two husbands? Married twice before and both husbands had *died*? My foot was tapping nervously under the table as I thought about my next move. Annapolis, Maryland. Pamela's hometown, too. It looked like I'd be taking another trip soon.

I next typed "Ethan Sherwood" into the search bar, but there was nothing else on him. Had he been alone on that hike, or had Piper been with him? I went back to the obituary, to the names of Ethan's parents, Donald and Patricia Sherwood. It was easy to find an address and phone number for them in Maryland. I sat and looked at that number for at least a half hour. What would I say to them? Their son had died fourteen years ago. How would I feel if a stranger called me out of the blue with questions about my dead child?

37

PIPER

Piper had left the office early and looked once more through the items she had laid out. Navy slacks, a long-sleeved white T-shirt, wool blazer, and her black Agent Provocateur kimono, which Leo hadn't seen yet. She'd bought it especially for this weekend trip to Rhode Island, their first real getaway. They'd finally have some time alone together without the children.

Her plan was to pick Leo up from the office at six and drive the two hours to Newport. They'd check in and have a romantic dinner around eight thirty. The whole night would be theirs, and then they'd have all day and night Saturday, too. Since the October temperatures were still moderate, she'd booked them a cruise around Newport Harbor. Maybe they'd do the touristy thing and go to the Cliff Walk, see a mansion or two, then take their time getting home Sunday morning. She couldn't wait.

After zipping up her weekend bag, she carried it downstairs and into the kitchen, placing it by the door to the garage. Piper heard a door slam and then the high-pitched voices of the children.

"How was school today?" Piper asked, sitting down at the round table with them.

"We got to go to the media center and pick any books we liked. I brought home *The Hidden Staircase* and *Black Beauty*." Evie's eyes were filled with excitement, her smile wide.

"That's wonderful."

"Can we read together tonight?" Evie asked.

Piper hesitated. "Well . . . your father and I are going away for a few days. Remember?" She saw Evie's face fall and hurried on. "But we'll be back on Sunday. We can read them together as soon as we get back."

Stelli glared at her. "I have a sore throat. I want Daddy to look at it." He scowled. "And my stomach hurts, too."

Great, thought Piper, rising from her seat and going over to Stelli. "Open your mouth," she said, leaning toward him.

He opened it obediently and stuck out his tongue. His throat didn't look red or inflamed, and he seemed to have no trouble swallowing the cookie. "When did it start to hurt?" she asked.

"Just now," he said, then cocked his head. "I think it was hurting this morning, too."

"Did you tell the nurse at school?" Piper asked.

"It stopped hurting at school."

"When did your stomach start bothering you?"

"I don't know," he said.

This was ridiculous. Piper stood up straight. "I guess you'd better go to bed then. You should rest if you're getting sick. We'll take your temperature. Go on upstairs, and I'll be there in a minute."

"Okay," he mumbled as he shuffled toward the stairs.

After he left, Piper walked down the hallway to Rebecca's suite and knocked on her door. She had just gone off duty for the rest of the day, but Piper wanted to get something off her chest.

Rebecca opened it right away. "Do you need me?"

"I just wanted a quick word."

"Yes?"

"The kids are having too much sugar. It's not good for them. Stelli's complaining of a stomachache. Starting next week, I'm going to take over making their lunches and preparing their afternoon snack."

"Oh, okay. I'm sorry. I didn't realize—"

Piper put a hand up. "I know. It's just, sugar lowers the immune system, and that's the last thing they need. I'll give you some recipes and options for healthier breakfasts as well."

She walked away before Rebecca could respond.

Piper and Leo strolled hand in hand back to their suite after their candlelit dinner. The night was cool and clear, with thousands of stars glittering in the dark sky. She leaned her head against Leo's shoulder as they stopped so he could unlock the door. Soft light from a bedside lamp bathed the room in a golden glow; the bed had been turned down for the night. She put her arms around his neck and reached up to kiss him. "This is perfect." She dropped her arms. "I'm going to take a bath. Why don't you join me?"

He grinned at her. "I will. I'm just going to call home and make sure everything's okay. I'll be right in."

Piper sighed, went into the bathroom, and sat on the edge of the tub as it filled, feeling guilty for being annoyed. Of course he would want to call home—any parent would—but Stelli was a smart kid and knew exactly how to manipulate his father. She'd done the right thing to show him he couldn't get away with that kind of thing with her. Maybe this would set a precedent and he'd stop trying to control Leo with invented ailments.

She undressed and got into the water, lying back and closing her eyes. She hadn't been this relaxed in she didn't know how long. She felt like she might fall asleep when suddenly there was movement and a splash and Leo slid into the tub behind her. He began to kiss the back of her neck.

"Everything all right at the house?" she asked.

"The kids were asleep. All is well." He continued his caresses, nibbling at her ear. Every nerve ending was tingling, and she leaned back against him, savoring the feel of his body against hers. Much later, after they'd made love, she fell into a contented sleep, nestled in the crook of his arm.

They were awakened early Saturday morning by the ringing of Leo's cell phone. "Rebecca, hi. Is everything okay?"

Piper leaned up on one elbow, now wide awake. She watched his eyebrows knit together in a frown, a knot forming in her stomach.

"No, no. You did the right thing. So they filled the prescription for you, right?"

She watched him as he listened carefully, her alarm growing by the minute. When he hung up, Piper looked at him expectantly.

"Stelli threw up in the middle of the night and woke up with a sore throat. Rebecca called the pediatrician this morning and took him in. They did a rapid strep test, and it was positive. He's had this before."

She sat up in bed. "What's the treatment for it?"

"He'll be on an antibiotic for the next ten days. It's highly contagious, so we need to be careful, especially with Evie."

"But he'll be fine, right?" she asked.

Leo put his hand over hers. "You're concerned about him. That makes me glad. And yes, he should be fine." He rose from the bed. "We should pack up. Stelli's asking for us."

Leo was being kind. Piper knew Stelli wasn't asking for "us." He wanted his father, which was completely natural . . . even though she was hugely disappointed that their romantic getaway was disintegrating before her eyes. She hesitated a moment, wondering if she should say anything, then decided to plunge ahead before he heard it from Stelli. "Stelli complained of a sore throat when he got home from school yesterday. I thought he was making it up."

"What?" Leo's voice was sharp.

"He was fine and totally perky when he came in, but as soon as I reminded the children that we were going away, he said that his throat was sore and his stomach hurt. I asked him if it had hurt him when he woke up that morning, and he said he thought so, but he never complained at school. He said it didn't hurt at school. I looked at his throat, and it wasn't red or inflamed. When I took his temperature, it was practically normal. I thought he was just saying that to keep us from going away."

"What do you mean 'practically normal'?"

"It was ninety-nine point two."

"Ninety-eight point six is normal. *Practically normal* doesn't cut it. I can't believe you. You put my child's health at risk because you decided he was lying?" Leo's face was red, and a vein in his neck was throbbing.

She understood he was upset, but she *had* thought Stelli was making it up. And Leo was overreacting by saying she'd put his son "at risk." Strep throat was totally treatable. He'd be fine in a few days. Nevertheless, she needed to calm Leo down. "I'm sorry. I would never do something to hurt Stelli. You must know that."

"I don't know *what* to think. You ignored my son's symptoms and what he was telling you. It astounds me that you could have even thought about leaving the house knowing he might be sick, let alone that you wouldn't tell me before we left." He shook his head and looked disgusted.

Piper didn't know what to say, so she just sat there.

Finally, he spoke again. "Let's get packed. I'll check out and meet you at the car." Leo's voice was cold as he hurriedly dressed, threw things into his bag, and left the suite.

As soon as they arrived home, Leo ran upstairs to check on Stelli. Piper didn't know what she should do—give them space or go in as well. She decided she'd wait a bit and headed to the kitchen to grab a cup of coffee to find Rebecca was preparing lunch—grilled cheese sandwiches. She looked up as Piper walked in.

"Welcome back."

"Hi, Rebecca. So sorry for not mentioning Stelli's sore throat to you. I had no idea this was a recurring issue for him."

"Yes, well, in the future, if there's something going on with one of the children, I'd appreciate your letting me know, especially if you're going away."

Even though she may have deserved the chastisement, Piper felt her back go up. But now was not the time to make things worse. "Yes, of course, it won't happen again. How's he feeling?"

"A little better since starting the antibiotics. He's a real trouper. To be fair, he probably seemed okay to you yesterday, but it takes a lot before he complains. His mother used to call him her little soldier."

Piper already felt inadequate; she didn't need to hear about his sainted mother. But she wanted Rebecca on her side, so she pretended it didn't bother her. "I know he misses her a lot."

"They both do. But it's especially hard on Stelli. He's struggled with some anxiety . . . I don't want to speak out of turn, but it's one of the reasons his mom stopped working—so she could be with him. He got very used to having her around."

Whose fault was it that she was gone? Piper wanted to ask. *If she loved her children so much, she wouldn't have left them.* But of course, she just gave Rebecca a sad smile. "I'm sure he did. I think I'll go check on him now."

"Piper . . ."

She stopped and turned back to face Rebecca. "Yes?"

"I know it's not easy if you're not used to raising children, especially stepchildren. But you're doing a good job."

Piper smiled at Rebecca, though the term *stepchildren* rubbed at her, bringing an image of Mia to her mind. "Thank you for saying so. I appreciate it." When she got upstairs and peeked into Stelli's room, he was sleeping, and Leo was sitting by the bed watching him.

"How is he?" she whispered.

Leo stood and tiptoed out of the room into the hallway. "He's better. Fever's gone."

She put a hand on his arm. "Leo, I feel just awful. Please forgive me. This parenting stuff is new to me." She nestled closer to Leo, pressing herself against him.

"It's all right, my love. I know you didn't do it on purpose."

She tilted her head up and kissed him slowly. "How about we go take a little nap together before dinner?" She put her hand on his fly, pleased to feel him respond.

"That sounds like the perfect idea," he whispered, his voice thick with desire.

After dinner, she and Leo went upstairs to check on Stelli again, Piper carrying a cup of tea with honey. Leo was about to read him a story, but she asked if she could instead. He'd looked at Leo, who nodded, and Stelli unenthusiastically agreed. Leo leaned down to kiss Stelli on the head.

"Good night, my boy. Love you to the moon and back."

Stelli grinned up at his father. "Love you more than all the stars."

Leo withdrew from the room, and Piper took a seat on the edge of the bed and held the tea out for Stelli. "This will help ease your sore throat."

He took a few sips then made a face.

"Thanks for letting me read you a story. Which one would you like, Stelli?"

He held her gaze a moment, and she had to admit that he was a beautiful child. His normal rambunctiousness had been dampened by the illness, and she realized that this was the first time she'd really had the chance to sit quietly with him.

"I don't know," he said.

"How about this one?" she said, sliding *The Giving Tree* from the bookcase next to the bed.

He shook his head. "It's too sad. That one makes me cry."

She smiled at him. "Aww. You're right. It *is* sad."

He pointed. "That one."

"*The Lion, the Witch, and the Wardrobe*?"

He nodded. "Mommy was reading it to me."

She felt her face flush with annoyance, but she kept her expression impassive. "Sure, honey." She picked up the leather book and flipped to where the bookmark was. "Looks like you left off when Edmund went missing."

Stelli nodded again. "He didn't listen. The Witch got him."

For a minute, Piper wondered if Stelli was trying to tell her something, comparing her to the White Witch, but no, she was being ridiculous. It was just a coincidence.

38

JOANNA

One dead husband could be an accident, but two? After reading Ethan Sherwood's obituary, I had called his parents. Their house sitter informed me that they were visiting their son in Chicago but were scheduled to return the day before Halloween, and I promised to try them again then.

I'd tried reaching Leo, too, but his new legal secretary wouldn't put me through. I wondered if Missy had been let go because she was too sympathetic to me. I tried to find a home number for Missy, but she was unlisted. I still hadn't been able to get Leo's new cell phone number. I even showed up at his office once, but he had instructed security to escort me from the building. So I thought about the only other person I might be able to get on my side—Rebecca. I knew that Piper had probably done her best to turn Rebecca against me, but if there was a chance she'd seen through Piper, too, I had to try. Maybe together, somehow, we could stop her.

Rebecca's routine rarely varied, and I knew that she did the grocery shopping on Wednesdays and Fridays, hitting Fleishers butcher in Saugatuck last. When I pulled into the parking lot of the shop, I saw her red Honda CRV parked there, but all the other spaces were filled. I anxiously circled the block three times before a black Mercedes finally pulled out of Fleishers' parking lot and I was able to grab its spot. By that point Rebecca was coming out of the store, two brown paper bags in her hands. I jumped out of my car and walked over to her.

She looked up, her eyes wide in surprise. "Joanna. What are you doing here?"

"I need to talk to you."

She looked around nervously, then nodded.

I followed her to her car and waited while she put the bags in the back. She turned to face me. "How are you?" she asked, her eyes kind.

I felt mine fill. "I'm really worried about Stelli and Evie. I've found out some things about Piper."

Her eyebrows shot up. "What?"

"She was married before. Twice. Both of her husbands died. One fell off a cliff. The other died in a sailing accident along with his daughter while she was with them. The police couldn't make anything stick, but they definitely suspected foul play."

Her mouth dropped open. "Oh my . . . that's horrible. Does Leo know?"

I shook my head. "I can't get through to him. I printed out the articles and mailed them to his office, but I don't know whether or not his new assistant gave them to him. You're my only hope. Has she done anything worrisome that you've seen?"

She bit her lip. "Well, not worrisome so much as insensitive. She and I had a run-in when she tried to get rid of some furniture without telling the children first."

My blood boiled. She was already redecorating the house. "The kids must have been awfully upset."

Rebecca nodded. "Although in her defense, once she saw how upset they were, she sent it all back." She hesitated then went on. "One other thing. She insisted on taking over making the kids' lunches and afternoon snacks. Stelli has been getting a lot of stomachaches lately."

"What do you mean? Do you think she's putting something in the food to make him sick?"

"Well . . . I wouldn't go that far." Rebecca put a hand up, suddenly appearing worried again. "I've really said too much."

"Can you get Leo to call me? *Please?* I need to tell him about her past."

"I don't know, Joanna. Maybe he already knows about her past. I mean, if nothing was proven against her, maybe she was just really unlucky. I'm already on thin ice with her, and if I go accusing her of things, I could lose my job."

I thought for a moment. She was probably right, and if she was fired, then the kids would have no one else at the house looking out for them. "Okay, listen. Can you please be extra vigilant? Watch out for them and call me the minute you see anything suspicious. I'll have to try to figure out something else in the meantime."

She nodded. "I'll do my best." She leaned over and hugged me. "Take care of yourself, Joanna. It was good to see you."

At least I'd put Rebecca on alert. I could only hope she'd be able to protect them. That and I would continue watching from afar. Maybe I could even get Ava to call Leo, try to make him see the light. I'd call her later and see if she would. Something had to work. Leo was a good father, a better father than I'd ever had. Despite all his faults, he would always take care of his children—unlike my own father, who'd left me to deal with my mother and never looked back. I tried to forget about him, not to care since he so obviously didn't care for me, but I found that I couldn't put my father out of my mind.

Over the years, I'd started obsessing over the woman who had lured him away from us. When I was in my twenties, I decided

I needed to see her for myself. I found out that he was living in Woodstock, New York. He'd been careless when he put the return address on a tax document he'd sent to my mother. I drove there on a Saturday, expecting a little cottage in the woods somewhere, so it was quite a surprise to see a beautiful wood house built high on a hill. It had to have been at least four thousand square feet, with multiple decks overlooking a lake. There were no cars in the driveway, and I debated getting out and taking a look around, but in the end I just got back in my car and drove into town. I wandered in and out of the shops, wondering if I'd run into him.

I asked around, figuring everyone knew everyone, and finally a waitress at a cute little restaurant called Bread Alone told me that he and his wife owned a little bakery called A Bun in the Oven, a few doors down. I went to take a peek inside and saw a friendly-looking woman behind the counter. The shop was crowded, and I went in, looking at the items in the glass display case. I watched her as she interacted with a customer. She hadn't turned out to be the siren I expected the other woman to be. Just an average-looking lady in her forties, not all that much younger than my mom. Her brown hair was short and pushed behind her ears, and she wore no makeup except for a light pink lipstick. What made her stand out were her beautiful blue eyes. When she smiled and spoke to customers, they sparkled with kindness and good humor—so very different from my mother's usual expression. As much as I didn't want to admit it, I could understand just from her demeanor why my father would have been drawn to her, but it still didn't excuse his lying and duplicity, and it certainly didn't excuse his abandoning his only child and adopting another woman's. I couldn't bring myself to buy anything, not wanting to waste a cent on either of them. I turned and left without a word.

39

PIPER

The mouthwatering aroma of chocolate chip cookies filled the kitchen, and Piper checked the timer—ten minutes to go. Rebecca was picking the children up from school today, and the treats would come out of the oven, warm and delicious, just as they got home. She set out two small plates, two glasses, and two napkins on the kitchen table.

She heard their voices even before the door leading to the garage opened, and a moment later, they burst into the room, backpacks flung off their shoulders and coats shrugged off.

"What smells so good?" Stelli asked, his eyes on the baking sheet cooling on a rack. "Chocolate chips! Can I have some?"

"Of course. I baked them for you and Evie. But first, you need to drink your smoothies. We need to make sure you get your vitamins, too." She handed them each a glass.

Stelli made a face. "Do I have to? I got a stomachache the last time."

Piper nodded. "That's only because you're not used to so many fruits and vegetables, which is not good. Drink up, and then you can have a cookie. It's a small glass." He put his mouth around the straw and drank. Piper watched to make sure they both finished, then put the plate down in front of them. "Now you can have cookies." She looked over at the nanny. "How about you, Rebecca—would you like one?"

"No, thank you. If you're okay with the children, I wouldn't mind checking my emails."

"Certainly. We're fine. You go ahead," Piper said.

"These taste different," Stelli said, still chewing.

"I used carob chips instead of chocolate. They're healthier." She didn't mention that she'd also substituted honey for the sugar and coconut flour for the wheat. Their palates were definitely accustomed to junk.

Stelli took another bite. "They're okay, I guess."

"Can I help you next time?" Evie asked.

"Absolutely. I would love that."

Just then, the head of the maid service that came twice a week entered the kitchen to let her know she was leaving. Piper grabbed her wallet and followed the woman to the door to pay her. When Piper walked back to the kitchen, she heard the children talking and hung back.

"These cookies aren't as good as Mommy's," Stelli told his sister.

"They're pretty good," Evie said.

There was a long silence, and then Stelli spoke again. "I hate it here without her." He sounded angry.

"I know," Evie said. "But we have to get used to it. She's never coming back."

"Why not? My Sunday school teacher said that Jesus died and came back. Maybe Mommy could come back, too."

"I don't know, Stelli. I don't think so."

"She will. I know she will." Piper could hear the quavering in his voice, as if he were about to cry.

"Don't you remember? Dad said she's never coming back. And anyway, Piper is here now. What would she do if Mommy came back?"

"Who cares about stupid Piper? She could go away."

Piper closed her eyes and leaned against the wall. Every time she thought she took a step forward with Stelli, she immediately took three steps back. He was almost worse than Mia—at least with Mia, though, Piper had always known where she stood. She guessed it was true about the connection between boys and their mothers.

It bothered her that he was building a fairy tale in his head. Even though he was only six, it wasn't healthy. She and Leo would have to figure out how to put these childish fantasies to rest once and for all.

She stood a moment longer, until they'd stopped talking, and entered the room. "Well," she said, trying to keep her voice bright, "looks like you're all finished. Why don't you go upstairs and change, and then you can go outside and play?"

Stelli was up and out of the room in a flash, but his sister lingered. "Thanks, Piper. The cookies were really good."

Piper smiled at her. She was such a lovely child, who was obviously missing her mom, too, but wanted to be kind to Piper. Stelli's backpack still lay on the floor where he'd dropped it, and Piper picked it up and pulled out his lunch box. He'd left carrots and a half-eaten box of raisins in it, which she removed, then wiped out the inside.

She put the lunch box aside and checked Stelli's backpack to see if there were any notices from school. A folded piece of paper lay on top—a note about a field trip to the Bronx Zoo, asking for money and chaperones. Maybe she would try to arrange her schedule to sign up for that, she thought, putting the paper on the counter next to her phone. She smiled as she pulled out three small army men and a few Legos. There were also two library books and a crumpled crayon drawing, which she smoothed out—a large orange pumpkin with smaller pumpkins around it—a drawing for, obviously, Halloween. And then her fingers skimmed a small slick square of card stock, and she pulled it out. She looked with dismay at the photograph of their mother.

For the rest of the afternoon, while Rebecca played outside with the children, Piper was online in her study, reading articles and studies on talking to children about the death of a parent. She was still in front of her laptop at seven, when Rebecca fed the children dinner and took them upstairs for their baths. She didn't turn off the computer until they came downstairs in their pajamas, freshly scrubbed and ready for bed. By the time she had finished, she felt she had some concrete information to give Leo when he got home from a late meeting at the office tonight. After tucking the kids into bed, she decided she could use a long relaxing bath. As the tub filled, she lit a few candles and put on the classical station she liked. The house was quiet except for the strains of classical music coming from the speakers, and she lowered herself into the warm water. All the tension left her body as she soaked, her head resting on a bath pillow, her eyes closed, and her nostrils filled with the soothing smell of sage from the burning candles. She concentrated on her breathing—in through her nose and out through her mouth—emptying her head of all troubling thoughts.

When she finally rose from the water, it was close to nine. Leo would be home soon. She gently massaged hempseed oil all over her body and slipped into a nightgown and robe. While the cookies had been baking earlier, she'd made a big pot of red lentil soup, knowing that he would probably want a light dinner at such a late hour. She was in the kitchen heating it up when he came in, and she turned the flame off and went to him.

"Mmm. You smell delicious," he said, drawing her into a hug.

She kissed him and took a step back. "Sit. I've just warmed some soup for you."

"That sounds great." He sat.

"How was your meeting?" she asked, as she placed the soup and a bowl of kale chips in front of him.

"Good. We finally have that Sanders case figured out. It's horrifying what that poor woman went through. Her husband abused her for years, and she was too terrified to leave because of all his connections in law enforcement. She doesn't deserve to be in jail for what she did. I had three different psychologists talk to her, and they all agree that she was in the grips of PTSD when she killed him."

"She's lucky that you're generous enough to take her case pro bono."

"She deserves a good defense, and the state is not easy on cases like this. They don't want to appear as though they condone vigilante justice. But she really feared for her children's lives and her own."

Piper nodded and listened as he went on. If work was going to keep him away from home so much, she was glad that at least it was for a worthwhile cause. When he finished his meal, they cleared the dishes together, and he pulled her into another embrace before they turned out the kitchen light. "Thank you for dinner. I'm going to go shower. Meet you in bed?" he mumbled, as he kissed her neck.

They went hand in hand up the stairs, and Piper waited with some trepidation as he showered. She was sitting in one of the armchairs in front of the bedroom fireplace when he emerged from the bathroom. "Come and sit with me for a few minutes. I want to talk to you."

He frowned. "Something wrong?"

"Well, not wrong exactly. But there is something we need to address."

She recounted the conversation between Stelli and Evie this afternoon. "I'm concerned about how we handle this going forward."

He sighed. "Piper, we've gone over this. You have to stop taking it personally. It's natural for him to miss his mother. Time will ease his sense of loss."

She felt her face grow hot. She couldn't let herself lose her temper. That would only alienate him, make him less likely to listen to what she was going to suggest. "Yes. Time will certainly help. But in the meantime, there is something we can and should do."

He looked dubious.

"Hear me out. I still think Stelli should see a therapist. I know you've been balking at it, but you remember what the principal said. He's still got a lot of anger that he needs to find a way to release. And he needs to let go of Joanna as well. Even though I'm not his real mother, he needs to see me as a mother figure. It's important if we're going to be a happy family."

"But a therapist will be invasive. Given that we haven't exactly told the kids the truth about their mother, how would we handle that? I don't want this person to judge us."

She'd thought about that already, but she paused briefly before answering. "Look, all we have to say is that she died and Stelli is having a hard time accepting it. And a therapist could help him to be less hostile toward me. Evie's accepted me, and it's time for Stelli to do the same."

"I just don't know about Stelli talking to a stranger about—"

"Trust me. It will be good for them, you'll see. We have to make Stelli truly understand that she's not coming back, that it's impossible. Right now, it's like he's waiting for her to walk in the door. It's not good for him."

"I guess you're right."

"One other thing," she started.

He raised his eyebrows. "What?"

"I don't want you to get the wrong idea, but I think maybe we should start replacing some of the photos around the house with ones of the four of us."

He started to speak, and she put a hand up.

"I'm not saying we need to get rid of all the pictures of her, but it's not healthy for them to see her face wherever they turn."

His face softened. "You're right. I hadn't thought about it that way."

Piper was relieved. "Good. I'm glad we're on the same page." She rose from the chair and let her robe drop. "Now"—she leaned down and gave him a long kiss—"let's go to bed."

| 40 |

JOANNA

I planned to leave early tomorrow for the five-hour drive to Annapolis. When I'd called Ethan's mother, Trish, pretending to be the sister of Pamela's, a.k.a. Piper's, fiancé, I told her that I was concerned Pamela was still heartbroken over what had happened with Ethan, thinking that would make Trish more likely to talk to me. Sure enough, she told me she'd be happy to meet with me. I didn't want to ask too much on the phone, so I made arrangements to go to their house. I didn't mention that Pamela had changed her name, of course, and I thought again about *Reynard*. I reread the definition I'd found when she first came into our lives, which I'd recently printed out and taped to the wall.

> *Though Reynard is sly, amoral, cowardly, and self-seeking, he is still a sympathetic hero, whose cunning is a necessity for survival.*

Sly, amoral, and self-seeking certainly fit the bill. The coward part I still had to figure out. But sympathetic hero? Hell no.

Before I went any farther down this rabbit hole, I had to go. I had an appointment with Celeste, and though she'd asked last week if we could devote this session to talking about my father, the new information on Piper was all I could think about.

When Celeste called me in, I took a seat, eager to get started.

"Thank you for the email," she said. She'd asked me to write up a timeline on my father's departure and our scant contact since. "I'd like to talk about some of the similarities between Leo and your father. How about we explore those today?"

"Before we get to that, I'd like to get your take on some new information I found." Celeste nodded, though I was already plowing ahead. "I've discovered that Piper was married at least two times before Leo."

She nodded again. "Go on."

"Her first husband died in an accident, too. Pretty coincidental, isn't it?"

If she was shocked, it didn't show on her face. "What kind of accident?"

I handed her the obituary, which she read and handed back to me. "It says he fell during a hike. Do you know if Piper was with him when it happened?"

"Not yet, but I'll find out more tomorrow. I'm going to go see his mother."

"I suppose that's fair enough. Let's see what she says. In the meantime, back to your father and Leo. Can you tell me the ways in which they are alike?"

I resisted the urge to roll my eyes; it felt a little condescending for her to prompt me like this. "Both of them are hardworking."

"Good. What else?"

"I suppose both are more vulnerable than they let on."

She leaned forward. "How so?"

"Both of them succumbed to the charms of a woman outside of their marriages. That suggests to me, if not a weakness in character, at least a weakness in resolve." I wondered if Celeste's husband had such a weakness and if she trusted him or not.

"I find it interesting that you refer to a weakness in character as 'vulnerability.' Why do you think that is?"

It was because I still believed in Leo and didn't want to admit his character might be flawed. And, in my father's case, it was because he'd lived in a miserable marriage for over twenty years. But I shrugged, not ready for her to try to disabuse me of my ideas. "I'm not sure."

"Most women would vilify their husbands and call them names. Yet you continue to defend Leo, to say you want him back. By continuing to believe that Leo was coerced into infidelity, don't you think you're letting him off the hook too easily?"

"Maybe. I guess I haven't wanted to allow myself to feel that anger, because I'm afraid if I do, it will swallow me up. But he *is* responsible. And he did wrong me."

She was nodding. "Yes. He did. And it's okay to feel that anger. This is a safe place."

"How could he do that to me? After the way I took care of him and the children? My father might have had a reason to leave, but Leo didn't."

She rotated her hands, palms up. "These things happen sometimes. Why do you think it's still so hard for you to forgive your father when you've said yourself that you understand what he did?"

"I forgave him a long time ago for leaving my mother—even for leaving me. After all, I was eighteen. But what I can't forgive him for was replacing me."

She looked puzzled. "Replacing you?"

I nodded at her. "With a new daughter. Four years younger than me. She wasn't even his biological child, but I found out a few years after he left that he'd adopted her."

"How did you find out?"

"My mother told me. She started following him, and she saw them together a year after he left. He told her everything then. How he was starting a new life with a new family."

"That must have been very hurtful."

Why did therapists always do this? It must be to prompt their patients to say more, but it always felt like a ridiculously obvious statement. I took a deep breath before responding. "Yes, it was. He even paid her college tuition, something he told my mother he couldn't afford for me. He was more concerned about the future of a child who wasn't biologically his. That's what I can't forgive. When all my friends left that August for colleges all over the country, I had to enroll at the community college, because without my dad I couldn't afford the tuition for BU. Sometimes I wonder if he did it on purpose, to make me stay home and take care of my mother. He knew what she was like, that she'd be pestering me constantly with her complaints about how sick she was and how she needed help. What kind of man does that to his own child?"

"You're right. That's not fair at all."

"The only reason I found out was because my mother told me—more evidence of what a bad person he was."

"That was a terrible thing to do."

"Terrible that he didn't pay my tuition or terrible that she told me about it?"

"Both. They both let you down."

I looked past her to the framed degrees hanging on the wall behind her. A bachelor's from Springfield College and a master's in social work from Syracuse University. "Did your father pay for your undergrad?" I asked, cocking my head.

She looked a bit surprised. "I'm not sure how that's relevant."

"I was just curious."

Celeste rubbed her hand across her chin. "Would it be accurate to say that both your father and Leo abandoned you and gave their affection and resources to someone else in your place? And that perhaps, in Leo, you chose someone with the same character traits as your father?"

Please don't pull any punches for my sake, I thought. "No, I don't think that's accurate," I said, crossing my arms.

My father was a liar, a cowardly liar, I thought to myself. Leo was an honorable man who'd already been dealing with depression and feelings of inadequacy when he got caught in a web of someone else's deceit—someone who was out to hurt my family. Was he responsible for his actions? Of course. But you could only blame the person for inviting the vampire into your home—you couldn't blame them for falling victim to the bloodsucker's thrall.

41

PIPER

We're going to have a family game night," Piper called out to the children, who were coming downstairs with Rebecca, fresh from their baths.

"Fun!" Evie said.

Piper had already set up the board for Sorry in the family room. As they took their seats, Rebecca brought in a plate of store-bought brownies.

The kids each grabbed one, as did Leo, who stuck his right in his mouth. "These are good!"

This woman really was getting on her nerves. Piper would have to talk to her again about all the sugar.

Stelli looked inside the Sorry box. "I want red. What color do you want, Dad?"

Leo shrugged. "You pick."

"You can be yellow. Evie's blue. You're green, Rebecca."

There was an uncomfortable silence for a long moment, then Rebecca spoke. "No, sweetie, the four of *you* are playing."

"This whole idea was Piper's, remember, pal?" Leo said, ruffling Stelli's hair.

"Yeah," Stelli mumbled.

Piper knew her face had flushed. "I guess I'm green." She forced a cheerful tone into her voice. "Stelli, why don't you go first?"

He picked a card. "Three!" He moved his pawn onto the board.

As they started to play, Rebecca withdrew from the room, and Piper felt the tension in the room dissolving.

"Are you looking forward to the long weekend?" Leo asked. "You get to skip a day of school."

"I am," Evie said. "I got a new Nancy Drew book, and I'm going to read all weekend."

Piper smiled. "I have a surprise for you."

"What?"

"I found all my old Nancy Drew books in a box I'd put in the attic. I took them with me when I left home. The whole series. They're yours if you want them."

Evie jumped up and down. "Really? Yes, thank you, Piper."

Leo gave her a warm smile and reached out to squeeze her hand.

"Are we playing or talking?" Stelli interjected.

Leo laughed. "My little man. Soon you'll be ready for poker."

Stelli bit his lip as he picked up his card, then a grin transformed his face. He lifted his pawn and brought it down hard on one of Piper's, knocking it from the board. "Sorrrrryyyy!" he yelled with glee.

"Geez, Stelli, you knocked her piece off the board," Evie said.

"It's okay," Piper said, leaning to retrieve it from under the table, where she could grit her teeth without being seen. She sat back up again. "Good move, Stel."

"It's Stelli," he corrected her.

Even Leo was starting to look annoyed. "Stelli, be nice."

The boy looked at his father, then burst into tears. "I don't want her here! I want my mommy!" He ran from the room, and Leo jumped up and ran after him.

Piper looked over at Evie, whose eyes were filling. So much for game night.

"Are you okay?" Piper asked.

Evie looked down at the table and shrugged. "I miss her, too, but I know she's not coming back. Stelli doesn't understand. He thinks she'd come back if you weren't here."

"I wish there were some way I could help him," Piper said.

Evie pushed her chair back from the table. "I'm gonna go see how he's doing. Mommy told me that I have to look out for him."

Piper shook her head as Evie walked away. This was getting out of hand. She took her wine, grabbed a fleece, and went outside to sit. Things were not going as planned. She hadn't realized when she married Leo that Stelli was going to be such a thorn in her side. When she'd gotten together with Matthew, she'd anticipated that Mia might be difficult—after all, she was the spoiled preteen daughter of a mother who hated Piper. But Stelli and Evie were so young and adorable, she really thought they'd accept her and the four of them could be a family—especially without the influence of a mother poisoning them against her.

But Stelli just couldn't let his mother go. She stayed outside for another half hour, stewing, until she saw a shadow moving through the house and, looking, saw that Leo had returned to the first floor. The screen door opened, and he came out and took a seat in the rocker across from her.

"Is he okay?" she asked.

Leo nodded. "Yeah. You just need to give him time."

Once again, Piper had been relegated to second best by the man in her life. When was she going to learn that the children always came first? She'd seen it with Matthew. No matter what kind of trouble Mia caused between them, it was always, *Poor Mia, she's having a hard time with the divorce.* Or, *Poor Mia, it's so disruptive going back and forth between two houses.* Mia had made up her mind from the minute Piper began dating Matthew that she was going to do everything in her power to come between them. Whenever they'd go somewhere in the car, Mia would jump in the front seat and scream *Shotgun*, and Matthew would give Piper a tilt of the head while wearing that sappy expression that begged her not to say anything. Mia would try on Piper's clothes and leave them in a heap on her closet floor, take naps in their bedroom, and she even borrowed, then lost, her wedding band. Matthew never did a thing about any of it.

And still, Piper tried. She offered to take Mia for mani-pedis, or to drive her and her friends around, but Mia told her that's what she had a mother for. Fortunately, they had her only on weekends, so weekdays were blissful—just Piper and Matthew in their sprawling house on the Pacific Ocean. They'd fall asleep with the balcony door open, listening to the crash of the waves, the smell of salt air filling the room. And then the day that brought it all to a screeching halt—all because of Mia.

Things would be different this time. Piper was going to make sure of that.

"Why don't we go inside?" Leo said.

Piper was about to stand when she felt her phone vibrate in her pocket and, pulling it out, put it to her ear. "Hello?" She froze when she heard the voice on the other end.

"Hello, Pamela."

"Mom?"

"Yes, I'm afraid I have somber news."

She gripped the phone tighter, stood, and walked to the far end of the deck. "What is it?"

"Your father passed away. He had a cerebral hemorrhage in his sleep. I'm told he didn't suffer, that it was instantaneous."

Leave it to her mother to convey even this news in her robotic, unfeeling manner.

"When?" was all she could manage to get out.

"He expired last Tuesday."

Expired? As if he were a carton of yogurt. "Why didn't you call me then? I would have come right away."

"Why? Your being here wouldn't have changed anything."

"I could have been with you. I could have said goodbye to him," Piper choked out.

"I told you. Your being here was unnecessary. Everything's been taken care of."

Piper went cold. "Did you have the funeral without me?" She was incredulous. "Why are you bothering to call me at all, then?"

She heard an intake of breath. "You haven't been home once in all the years since you left, so I didn't rush to call you. I just thought you ought to know, that's all."

Piper was silent.

"There's an online obituary. If you want to leave a comment there, you may, but since you weren't interested in being in touch while he was alive, I don't see why you want to pretend to care now." Her mother hung up, and Piper began to cry.

Leo looked at her with concern. "What's happened?"

"My father died."

A wave of dizziness overcame her; she walked back over to the rocker and lowered herself into it. Her heart was beating furiously, and tears were running down her face. Leo was suddenly next to her, pulling her into his arms. She didn't know what she was feeling, except that deep, racking sobs were shaking her now.

So that was it. Her father was dead and gone, and her mother hadn't even thought to call her until a week later. Even though she'd left her childhood home with no intention of ever going back, she realized now that she'd always hoped for some kind of reconciliation, for a time when her parents might realize their own part in abandoning her, first emotionally, and then literally, by never looking for her when she took off. Now, that hope was dead and gone, along with her father. How could her mother be so cold? Was she so unlovable that, even now, when her mother was grieving and utterly alone, she didn't want Piper's company?

Leo led her back into the house, and she sank down into the living room sofa. He sat next to her, holding her while she focused on her breathing, willing herself to calm down. She would put it behind her, like so many other painful episodes in her past. Her mother may now be alone, but *she* wasn't. She had Leo. And Evie and Stelli. They were her family now, her perfect family, and she would pour all her efforts into them.

42

JOANNA

I can't remember the last time I'd taken a long road trip, and I found the drive to Annapolis calming. Cruising along and watching the scenery roll by gave me time to think and reflect. As I discover more and more about Piper and her past, Leo's behavior seems less of a betrayal than I first thought. He could never be accused of being naive or easily fooled, but it's obvious to me that there is something about Piper that allows her to insinuate herself into even the smartest man's affections. Leo is the type of man women find intriguing. He's strong and masculine, and at the same time solicitous and generous—of men and women equally. His only fault, as far as I'm concerned, is that he's a workaholic.

Hard work and long hours came naturally to him by way of his father, who kept the restaurant open seven days a week. I thought about the last time I saw the family. They were all at the house, Leo's parents and his two brothers with their wives and children. It seemed there were kids running around everywhere, and Evie and Stelli were having a great time with all their cousins. I spent most of my time in the kitchen with Leo's mother. She and the other women in the family had brought trays and trays of delicious and aromatic Greek food, and we were busy heating things and transferring them to platters. It was a veritable feast, as it always was when the family got together.

It always astounded me that a family could be so large and so close, since my upbringing was singularly lonely. It was fascinating to watch them all together, and it was apparent that they adored Leo. He was the one who had made it big, the first to go to college. And then, when he continued on to law school and became a lawyer, he really became the golden boy.

My thoughts were interrupted by heavy traffic on the New Jersey Turnpike, and I had to concentrate more carefully on my driving. Eventually, I crossed into Delaware and then decided to stop at a rest area for lunch once I hit the Maryland border. When I pulled into the parking lot, I punched the address into my phone's GPS and saw that I was about an hour away from Ethan Sherwood's parents' home.

I'd never been to Annapolis, and when I finally pulled off the highway at exit 28, I began to see why it had been called one of the most charming cities in the country. I passed by large rivers and meandering creeks as I drove to their house, which was at the end of the road on a small peninsula. I pulled up to a beautifully landscaped lot, with seagrasses and graceful trees, and parked on the street. The house was a three-story yellow shingle with a turret room and large front porch.

I breathed in, feeling nervous, and paused for a moment before ringing the bell. Almost immediately, the door opened, and a woman who looked to be in her late sixties stood in front of me.

"Hello, I'm Joanna."

"Yes, hello, I'm Trish," she said, running a hand through her silver hair. She had a nice smile and warm brown eyes that put me at ease. "Please, come in. Why don't we go sit in the living room?"

I followed her down a wide hallway to the back of the house. "Can I get you something to drink? Perhaps some coffee? Or something cold?" she asked.

"Are you having anything?" I asked, not wanting to put her to trouble.

"I usually have an herbal tea in the afternoon."

"That sounds perfect," I said.

Trish returned with a tray holding two cups of tea along with milk and sugar and set it down on the coffee table. She handed me a cup, took her own, and then sat in a chair opposite me. "Now, dear, what is it I can help you with?"

I had thought about this carefully beforehand. Since I wasn't sure of the Sherwoods' feelings for Piper/Pamela, or if they were even still in contact, I didn't want to reveal my suspicions, so I'd come up with a slightly different scenario to present. "I'm not sure if you know that Pamela's living in Connecticut now."

"Actually, we lost touch a few years after Ethan died. The last time we spoke she was living in California. San Diego."

"I am sorry about your son. That must have been a terrible time."

Trish took a sip of tea, and her hand shook as she placed the cup and saucer back on the coffee table. "Yes. It's something you never really recover from, the death of a child." She sat back in her chair and gazed at the floor, as if peering into the past. "Ethan was my firstborn. He was bright as a button, full of imagination." She looked up at me then, her eyes shining. "He loved to tell stories. He'd keep us on the edges of our seats with his tales. He wanted to be a screenwriter, you know. That's why they went to California."

"They were awfully young, weren't they?"

"Well, yes, they were." She smiled sadly. "Don and I were not the most attentive parents in those days. We should have given Ethan a lot more guidance than we did. We made up for it with Ted, Ethan's younger brother."

"And Pamela?" I asked.

"Ah, Pamela. She was such a lovely young girl. Polite and kind.

So pretty. And smart. A straight-A student. We didn't know her parents then. We traveled in quite different circles, but I knew her father taught at the Naval Academy, and they were very strict. I always felt sorry for her. She always seemed so in need of love and affection. How is she doing?"

It was a good thing I hadn't begun by denigrating Piper. Trish obviously still thought highly of her. "She's well. But I am a little concerned about her. As the wedding day approaches, she seems to be more down. I think she may feel guilty about remarrying," I lied.

"Poor dear." She took another sip of tea.

I continued. "She still seems to be carrying heavy grief over Ethan's death—I thought perhaps speaking with you might shed some light so I can help her move forward."

"I see. I'm sorry to hear that she's suffering. How long has she been seeing your brother?"

"About a year and a half."

"I'm sure it hasn't helped her state of mind that her father died recently," Trish said.

I disguised my surprise and pretended that this was old news. "Yes, that may be what set her back into a depression," I agreed. "If it's not too difficult to talk about, would you mind telling me about Ethan's accident?"

"They were hiking. Ethan was doing something foolish, goofing around at the edge, and he fell. Pamela was destroyed. As we all were." Her eyes were filled with grief. "As soon as we got the call, we flew to California. We called the Rayfields, Pamela's parents, but they never responded. Didn't go to California and didn't reach out to their daughter, as far as I know. Ethan was cremated, and Pamela kept some of the ashes to spread there, while we brought some home so that a part of him could be in the waters here that he loved so much."

So Piper was there when Ethan fell to his death. I took a deep breath to make my voice even. "The funeral was here in Annapolis?"

"Yes, a private service. Pamela didn't come since she had a service for him in California."

"And how long did you stay in touch?"

"Not long. The last time we spoke, she was still single and still in California."

"I guess it must have been hard for her. Being so young and alone in a new place with no money to speak of," I said.

"Oh, she had some money. Ethan's trust matured the week he died. Don and I were both thankful for that, at least. But you know, she was our son's wife. We would never have let her go without."

So Piper had known from the get-go that there was money to be had, if not from a trust, then from his parents. The poor little girl who needed "love and affection" so badly.

"Thank you so much for your time and hospitality, Trish. I appreciate it," I said, rising. "I think this will be really helpful as I do my best to support her."

"Not at all. Any friend of Pamela's is always welcome here. Please give her my love and tell her I'd be so happy to hear from her."

"I'll do that," I said, as we walked to the front door, but of course, even if I were her friend and I did tell her to get in touch with Trish, Piper would never do so. It was pretty clear that she threw people away when they were of no more use to her. Why would she write off this wonderful woman who had obviously thought the world of her, unless she had had something to do with Ethan's death?

As soon as I got in the car, I looked up another number on my smartphone. I had a feeling there was someone close by who could give me a much truer picture of Pamela Rayfield.

43

PIPER

Leo told Piper he'd take the children to the aquarium, instead of going to the office, so she could have some time to herself to absorb the news about her father. They'd already given Rebecca the day off, and, as luck would have it, the kids were off as well due to a teacher conference day, even though the Thanksgiving break was in just three weeks. Piper had tossed and turned all night, finally falling into a fitful sleep sometime after two. She was still groggy when she got out of bed and checked the time on her phone. Ten o'clock. She couldn't remember the last time she'd slept so late.

She got dressed, then went to the kitchen and made a cup of espresso. The first floor was dark and silent, and she realized she kind of liked it. It seemed like ages since she'd felt free to do whatever she wanted, whenever she wanted, without worrying about someone seeing her and judging her.

She was becoming more convinced part of the reason she wasn't connecting better with Stelli was because of Rebecca. She was probably stoking the fire of his missing his mother. Did they really need a live-in nanny? The lack of privacy was bothering her, too. Just the other night, Piper had gone into the kitchen after dinner to make a cup of tea and seen Rebecca shrink back from the door. Was she eavesdropping on them?

Her mind returned again to her father. Opening her laptop, she looked up the obituary she hadn't been able to bring herself to read the night before. It was a nice piece, chronicling his accomplishments in his career and in the community. A deep sadness hollowed out her stomach when she looked at his picture. His hair had thinned, and his face was lined—he'd aged a lot since she'd last seen him. Of course, it had been over fifteen years ago.

His long-standing career as a professor at the Naval Academy and his popularity with his students were evident from the seemingly endless condolences they left in the comments section. Piper read them with growing bewilderment.

Professor Rayfield was my favorite professor. Always made the class fun and interesting.

Professor Rayfield always took the time to explain things, very patient, great teacher.

Prof Rayfield encouraged me to follow my passion. Amazing teacher.

Were they really talking about her father? When she was growing up, he hadn't had much patience with her, and as for encouraging a passion? That was a joke. How was it possible that he'd been able to connect so well with his students when he had never attempted to understand his own daughter? She felt cheated and closed her laptop, not wanting to read any more.

She walked into the living room, where she could look out at the expanse of woods. Her father was dead at sixty-eight. A ticking time bomb in his head had gone off. Had he had any warning? she wondered. Any premonition that it was his last day on Earth? She thought of the way he had lived such a careful, sequestered life. He and her mother never relaxed. Both of them brought their work home with them; they never spent time around the table just talking, or playing a game after dinner. He took his "morning constitutional" every day, but it had never seemed to her that he enjoyed the time outdoors, rather that he was just checking off another item on his list so he could feel good about being responsible with his health. He loved his work, she supposed, although how anyone could get excited about mechanical engineering was a mystery to her. His only concession to what he called a "frivolity" was his weakness for Laurel and Hardy. It was the only time she heard him laugh with abandon. Her mother used to roll her eyes and tell him to turn the volume down, muttering under her breath about how stupid the movies were. But it had made Piper glad to see that he had a lighter side. She sighed. She hoped he was at peace.

Restless, she decided to write a new blog post for the center, maybe something about living every day as though it were your last. It was an expression everyone had heard but few took to heart. She hadn't updated the blog in a few weeks, and she noticed that there were comments on older posts still to be approved. She read through each one, approving the appropriate comments and deleting the spam. She froze as she came upon a comment posted a week ago.

> Found you! Did you think just because you left California, I'd forget all about you? I wonder what your clients at the "recovery center" would think if they knew you were a murderer. Good thing you're not still teaching sailing, at least. Now that I know where you are, I'll be making sure that everyone knows exactly who you are, including that new husband of yours.

Piper took a screenshot and filed it away, then deleted the comment. How had Ava found her? She'd been so careful, even making sure that the business transfer had gone through several holding companies so it couldn't be publicly traced to her real name. If Ava showed up here, she would make Piper's life impossible.

She had to think . . . It must have been Brent. She knew he'd recognized her when she'd seen him in town. Damn it! He must have gone home and called Ava. But still, how had Ava so easily found out her new name and her role at the recovery center? One thing was for sure—Ava wasn't going to drive her out of Westport the way she'd driven her from San Diego. This time, Piper would find a way to stop her.

She looked up Brent's office number online and, taking a deep breath, dialed.

"Pacific Investments," a male voice with a British accent answered.

"Brent McDonald, please. Pamela Dunn calling."

"One moment."

She drummed her fingers while she waited.

"Pamela?" He sounded tentative.

"Hi, Brent. I owe you an apology." She dove right in, her tone calm and apologetic. "I'm sorry for pretending it wasn't me when I ran into you in Westport. I was worried about what Ava might do if she found out where I was."

There was a weighty pause before he responded. "I'm not sure I understand."

She sighed. "Surely you remember how she acted after Matthew and Mia . . . She blamed me and made my life a living hell."

He cleared his throat. "Um, I know she made a scene a few times at the club, but she was grieving. I mean, you have to cut her a break. She lost her daughter."

"I know, I know. But she started stalking me, following me

everywhere I went, making a scene. She spray-painted 'Murderer' on my car."

He made an odd throat-clearing noise, but she pushed on.

"You know as well as I that what happened was an accident—the authorities were clear on that. But she was never going to let it go, so I needed to disappear, start over again. And now she's found me. I have to ask: Did you call her and tell her you saw me in Westport?"

She heard a long exhale and papers shuffling. "Listen, Pamela, or Piper, or whatever your name is now, I'm really not comfortable giving you any information. In fact, I'm beginning to wonder if Ava was right."

Fear shot through her. "You can't be seri—"

He cut her off. "I'm dead serious. After I saw you on the street, I had a long talk with Ava. She told me some things about you that I never knew. If I'd have known the way you treated poor Mia . . . Look, I have to go. Don't call me again." The line went dead.

This was no good. If Ava knew where she was, she'd start calling Leo and tell him awful things about her—things that would make him suspicious, that would make him doubt her just as Brent was doing. She wasn't going to let that happen.

Leo knew, of course, that Piper was a widow. She'd told him when they first started dating that she'd moved here from California for a fresh start after she'd lost her husband and stepdaughter in a tragic sailing accident. When she'd opened up to him about the accident, he'd been sympathetic and respectful of her wish to leave the past behind and hadn't pressed her for details. She'd also told him that she'd changed her name because of a stalker, but she hadn't volunteered that the stalker was Ava. She needed to clarify this with Leo right away, so that if Ava did reach him, he wouldn't entertain her ravings.

As soon as he and the kids walked in the door, Piper greeted them in the foyer and wasted no time telling Leo she needed to talk to him alone.

"Everything all right?"

She held a finger up. "Hey, guys. How about I put a movie on for you and then bring in some lunch for you in a little while?"

"Okay," Evie answered, and Stelli didn't make a fuss for once. She got them settled, then led Leo into the kitchen.

"Do you remember when I told you that I had a stalker in California?"

Alarm filled his face. "Of course. Has he found you?"

"I think so. But it's not a *he*." He looked startled, but she kept going before he could ask questions. "I didn't tell you the whole story because I didn't want you to get the wrong idea."

He leaned back, giving her an appraising look. "O-kay . . ."

He was wearing his attorney persona now, and she knew she had to be careful. "Ava, Matthew's ex-wife, was stalking me. They were separated when I met him. In fact, *she'd* cheated on him long before I came into the picture. But when he and I started dating, she went crazy."

Leo wasn't saying anything, only watching her carefully.

"I didn't think that it was any more than petty jealousy, and I assumed that she'd eventually get over it, but she never did. She made up lies about me, embarrassed me at the country club—essentially, she made my life a living hell."

"Couldn't your husband do anything about it?"

"He thought it was better to ignore it, that his involvement would only escalate things. I mean, you can understand because of what we've been through with Joanna." She put up a hand. "When he was alive, it wasn't too bad. We just made sure we didn't go to club events that we knew she'd attend, but Matthew and Ava had joint custody of Mia, so we had to deal with some of it for Mia's sake." She reminded herself to take a deep breath. "After Matthew and Mia died, Ava really lost it. She thought I was responsible, and that's when she started following me and telling other people that I had stolen him from her for his money. She'd lived in the community all her life, so most people believed her—or at least humored her. It got so bad that I had to leave and change my name." She began to cry, and Leo came and sat next to her, putting his arm around her.

"No one is going to hurt you. Tell me, what's happened now? How do you know she's found you?"

She told him about running into Brent months back and discovering Ava's comment on her blog this morning.

"I'm sorry, my love. You don't deserve this."

She leaned her head on him. "Just promise me you won't talk to Ava if she calls you. I don't want her filling your head with her vile lies. I couldn't bear for you to think ill of me."

"Don't worry. That could never happen. But I won't speak to her, I promise."

"Thank you," she said. Her relief was so extreme she nearly collapsed.

| 44 |

JOANNA

Marion Rayfield had agreed to meet me at the medical laboratory's coffee shop the next day. I got there early after spending the night in a local hotel, and as I sipped my coffee, I thought about what I wanted to ask her. I had gleaned from Trish that Marion hadn't approved of her daughter running off to California with her boyfriend, and that, apparently, Piper had been estranged from her parents ever since.

I decided to be upfront with Marion about the reason for my visit. At promptly eleven a.m., a woman strode in purposefully, craning her neck. She had short brown hair cut in no real style, and she wore wire-rimmed glasses and a lab coat. It had to be her. I waved, and she walked over.

"Mrs. Rayfield?"

She looked at me without smiling. "It's *Dr.* Rayfield."

"Apologies. Thank you for taking the time to meet with me. I hope I'm not taking you away from your patients," I said, trying to ease the tension.

"I'm in research. Microbiology. It's fine."

"I see. May I get you some coffee?"

She shook her head. "I would prefer to make this quick. You said it was urgent that you speak to me about my daughter?"

She was certainly no-nonsense. "Your daughter goes by the name of Piper now."

"Yes, I'm aware of that. I recently had to get in touch with her when her father died. I found her number through a friend she still keeps in touch with. Piper! What a ridiculous name."

"I'm sorry about your husband." And I was—it was terrible that it had happened so recently and suddenly—but the woman seemed to take it in stride.

"Thank you," she said in a clipped monotone.

"So then you've seen her? I assume she came down for the funeral."

She stared at me. "Why is any of this your business?"

I pulled my spine as tall as I could and dove in. "She married my ex-husband, and my children are living with her. I have some concerns about that, and I would like your help."

"I see." She cleared her throat. "I haven't seen her since she took off the night after her high school graduation. She wanted to come back and see me after she learned about her father, but I told her not to. She broke her father's heart. He had such high hopes for her, but all she cared about was herself."

"I'm sorry," I repeated, not sure what else to say. "Were you aware that she remarried after Ethan died?"

Marion shrugged. "No, but it's not surprising. She was so young when she ran off with him. I'm really not that interested, to tell you the truth. We did everything for her, and she thanked us by running away without so much as a goodbye. She was supposed to start at Virginia Tech in the fall. We'd been counting on her going there, on her making us proud."

It was obvious that she was still very angry, but I couldn't tell if she genuinely thought Piper didn't—couldn't?—truly care for others, or if these were the words of a mother whose only child had rejected her.

Before I could formulate a response, she continued. "We always had to work so hard to ground her. She was too vain for her own good, always primping in the mirror and trying to charm people. She was elected homecoming queen, of all the anti-feminist, frivolous things . . . We wanted her to focus on her academics, her intelligence. She's a brilliant girl, but she threw it all away. Thought she'd run off to Hollywood and get discovered."

"I didn't realize she'd wanted to be an actress."

"Oh yes," she sneered. "Thought she was quite the little star. Even when she was little, she always wanted to put on plays for us with her friends, insisted on being the center of attention. We'd tell her we weren't interested. I mean, really. It does no good to coddle children, to lull them into a false sense of security about unattainable goals. Do you realize how minuscule the chances are that she would be able to support herself by acting?" She didn't wait for me to answer, clearly warming to the subject. "Close to zero. We wanted her to go into a meaningful field, be a doctor or an engineer. We thought we'd talked sense into her when she chose Virginia Tech, but then she ran off with Ethan. A spoiled rich boy."

I jumped in. "Her second husband was rich, too. He and his daughter also died in an accident."

I watched her face as that sank in.

"What kind of accident?"

"Sailing. Apparently the daughter fell off the boat, and her father jumped in after her. They weren't wearing life vests, and they both drowned."

She raised her eyebrows. "Very odd, indeed. Pamela was with them?"

I nodded.

"I can't imagine why they weren't wearing life vests. That's sailing 101."

I decided to plunge ahead. "I have to wonder if maybe it wasn't an accident."

She narrowed her eyes. “Are you accusing my daughter of murder?”

“No. But you have to admit, two husbands with untimely deaths is awfully coincidental. Ethan died while the two of them were hiking, and she inherited the money from his trust fund. And her second husband, Matthew Dunn, left her an estate worth twenty million. Don’t you think that’s suspicious?”

“It may be, but what do you expect *me* to do? I don’t have any influence over her any longer. If you’re so worried, you should go to the police. I can’t help you.”

I leaned forward. “Dr. Rayfield, please. Just tell me: Do you think she’s capable of murder?”

She leaned back in her chair, clasped her hands together, and closed her eyes. “Honestly, I don’t know. I never really understood her. There was one incident . . .”

My heartbeat quickened. “What?”

“There was graffiti spray-painted on a teacher’s blackboard, threatening to kill him. It was the same teacher who’d given her a bad grade.”

“You thought she might have spray-painted the threat because someone failed her?”

“No, no. He’d given her a B, and we’d grounded her for two weeks, so she had to miss the homecoming dance. In the end, they crowned the runner-up since she couldn’t go.”

They’d grounded her for a B and made her miss homecoming when she was selected queen? It was a wonder she hadn’t threatened to kill *them*, Joanna thought.

Marion shook her head. “She swore she had nothing to do with it. But there was black spray paint in our garage.”

“Had she bought it?”

“No, it was my husband’s. But as you say, very coincidental.”

This woman was a real head case. "Anything else?" I asked.

"Not that I can think of. I'd have to say that anything is possible. I washed my hands of her a long time ago. If there's nothing else?"

I shook my head and stood to leave. "Thank you so much for your time."

If anyone had the recipe for raising a sociopath, it was Marion Rayfield.

45

PIPER

Leo's family was coming over for Thanksgiving dinner in a few hours, and Piper was nervous. She'd wanted to have help here today so she could focus on her guests, but Leo had cautioned her against it, saying his mother wouldn't think well of her if she did.

She'd met Leo's family only once before, on their disastrous would-be wedding day. Leo had confided to her that his mother thought he was getting remarried too fast. Piper would have preferred if he'd have kept that information to himself. Why couldn't men tell when discretion was the better part of valor?

The house was blessedly quiet. Rebecca had left to spend the day with her father, and Leo had taken Evie to the Compo Beach playground, but Stelli had complained of another stomachache and was resting upstairs. Soon enough the house would be filled, though, with Leo's parents, his brothers, their wives, and their kids. There would be sixteen for dinner, including Piper, Leo, and the children. She hoped today would be a time when she might ingratiate herself with the family.

She tied an apron around her waist and went to work. She'd put the turkey in early that morning and was putting the finishing touches on the homemade pie crusts. She had made the mashed potato and sweet potato casseroles last night, and they were in the refrigerator, ready to be popped into the oven. Now she was organizing appetizers and veggies for before the feast. She'd decided to tackle a Greek appetizer, hoping it might endear her to

Leo's parents, and settled on spinach pie, painstakingly filling the filo she'd gotten at the grocery store with what she hoped was the perfect balance of spinach and feta cheese.

She put the three pies in the oven, set the timer for forty minutes, and went into the dining room, where she put together a simple centerpiece—a row of seven low glass vases with a single white mum in each—simple and elegant. Straightening one of the place mats, she moved a wineglass a tad, and left the room feeling satisfied. Now she could go upstairs and get herself ready before Leo and Evie returned.

It was nearly three by the time they got home, just enough time for Evie to change before everyone arrived. Piper had laid out Stelli's clothes but saw when he came downstairs that he'd chosen a different pair of pants and shirt. A silent act of defiance? she wondered. Evie, who was old enough to choose her own clothes, had picked a cranberry-colored sweater dress.

"Evie, you look so pretty. Would you like to come help me in the kitchen?"

"Sure," Evie said, following Piper.

"Here you are," Piper said, putting two boxes of crackers on the kitchen table. "Will you put these crackers on this cheese board?"

The dessert pies were cooling, and the spinach pie would soon be ready to come out of the oven. Piper opened the oven door to check on it. It needed a few more minutes to brown on the top, so while Evie was busy with the crackers, Piper pulled the shrimp platter out of the refrigerator. As she turned around, she almost bumped into Leo.

"Boy, you've been busy. The house smells amazing."

She smiled. "I've loved every minute of it. I hope everyone has a big appetite."

"You don't need to worry about that," he said, and grabbed a shrimp from the platter. "My family loves to eat." He popped it into his mouth just as the doorbell rang. "Speaking of which . . . I'll get it."

Piper wiped her hands on the apron before taking it off, turning to Evie, and motioning her toward the foyer. "Let's go see who's here."

They must have come as a convoy, Piper thought as the entire family came trooping through the door.

"Leo, *agape mou*," Evangelia said, hugging her son to her.

His father moved in for a bear hug as soon as Leo's mother let go. They stood together looking at Piper. Evangelia gave her a forced smile. "Peeper," she said. "Very nice to see you."

"It's Piper, Ma," Leo said, and Piper heard Stelli snicker behind her. "What have you got?" Leo pointed to the three shopping bags they'd brought with them.

"Happy Thanksgiving, Piper," Stelios said as he enfolded her in his strong arms. At least one of Leo's parents was nice to her.

"You know, Ma never goes anywhere empty-handed," Gus said.

Piper looked at the bags in alarm. Had the woman brought food?

"Take, take. Into the kitchen," Evangelia ordered them.

With a sinking heart, Piper picked up one of the bags, which was quite heavy, while Leo picked up the other two. His mother and father followed them into the kitchen, where Piper and Leo set the bags on the counter. Piper's heart sank as the others unpacked the contents from two large insulated bags—a huge platter of sliced lamb, a pan of roasted potatoes, a deep tray of rice. It was the entire dinner. She was too upset even to look as they started on the second bag. What was Piper supposed to do with everything she'd cooked? What kind of crazy people brought an entire meal to a home where they'd been invited to dinner? As they unloaded the last bag, Piper saw a tray of baklava and another of something they called *koulouraki*, some kind of braided cookie. She wanted to cry—or scream.

She looked pleadingly at Leo, but he seemed completely oblivious, as if this were the most natural thing in the world. As her kitchen was taken over, she grew impatient and asserted herself. "This is so generous of you, Evangelia. Thank you so much, but I've already cooked our dinner." She gestured toward the large turkey on top of the stove, where it was waiting to be carved. "We're having turkey. It's traditional on Thanksgiving. And I've made potatoes, both white and sweet, and lots of vegetables. I don't think we really need all the food you've brought, but I could wrap it up and put it in the refrigerator for you to take with you later."

Evangelia turned to Leo and began to speak rapidly in Greek.

"What?" Piper said. "What is she saying?"

"You've hurt her feelings. She was only trying to help you, so you wouldn't have so much to do with the whole family coming."

Great, Piper thought. Now the woman would hate her even more. "I'm sorry, I didn't mean to hurt your feelings," Piper said to her. "I just wish I'd known before I did all the cooking." She noticed Leo's jaw tick just a touch, and she plastered on a smile. "But, of course, we'll have lamb *and* turkey. Thanksgiving dinner is supposed to be a feast, right?" She tried to make it sound like she meant it.

"*Kala.* Good. Turkey is for the Americans. Lamb is tradition."

Toula and Angela, her new sisters-in-law, helped Evangelia take the food into the dining room, and Piper grabbed Leo by the arm, holding him back. "Why didn't you tell me she'd be bringing all the food? Why the hell did I spend two days cooking?"

"I'm sorry. She always brings something, but not the whole meal. I don't know why she did that this time." He seemed sheepish but nowhere close to bothered, which made her anger flare. It was just like when Matthew would shrug at Mia's antics or tell her to relax about Ava's behavior—it seemed unbelievable that men had so little idea of how manipulative and cruel women could be.

"She did it because she hates me."

"Piper. That's not true."

"She doesn't even say my name right. She doesn't like me, Leo."

He put his arm around her. "Stop this. She just doesn't know you yet. Come on, let's go have a drink in the living room."

Everyone else went into the other room, where the shrimp, cheese, and crackers had been put out. Piper took the spinach pie from the oven and gave it fifteen minutes to cool, then transferred the pre-cut pieces to a platter. She could hear laughter and talking and took a deep breath to steady herself. Leo's family was so Greek. He'd assimilated so well that she almost forgot his roots. But when his family came around, he fell back into the role of adored son to a mother who clearly thought that Piper wasn't a suitable wife to him.

When she walked into the living room, Leo stood up from his seat on the sofa next to his mother and walked over to her.

"Ma, look what Piper made," he said, pointing at the spinach pie she was holding. "*Spanakopita.*"

Evangelia looked up in obvious surprise. "But I brought mine."

Leo took a piece from the platter Piper was holding and put it on a napkin. "Here, try it."

She took it from him reluctantly, examined it, then brought it to her mouth. She made a face. "What kind of filo you use? From a store?"

Piper felt her stomach tighten. "Yes. I got it at Trader Joe's."

"What does Joe know about filo?" Everyone laughed while Evangelia shook her head. "You have to make it yourself. And if you too lazy to do that, at least you get at Greek grocery store." She stood up. "Come. I show you what real *spanakopita* tastes like."

Piper could feel the heat in her face, and Leo mouthed *Sorry* but said nothing. Piper put the platter on the coffee table and smiled. "That's okay, I'm not really hungry."

"Ma, come sit down," George said, trying to take her arm.

She shooed him away. "I'm going to heat up the *spanakopita* and the *tiropites* I brought. Leo, show me how to start your oven, please."

Angela, Gus's wife, gave Piper a sympathetic look as Evangelia left the room. She picked up one of the pieces of spinach pie and took a bite. "It's delicious. Thank you so much for having us here today. She means well . . . I hope you won't let it ruin your day."

Piper smiled warmly at her. "Thank you."

"Who wants to see my new remote-control helicopter?" Stelli asked, and for once, Piper was grateful for his interruption. His cousins Michael and George, along with their fathers, followed him from the room, leaving Piper alone with Toula and Angela.

Toula, George's wife, lifted her wineglass. "To Piper, may she survive Hurricane Evangelia."

Piper laughed despite herself and clinked her glass with Toula's.

"She'll come around. She's tough but fair. It took her a while to warm up to us. You know Greek mothers and their sons," Angela said.

Piper arched an eyebrow. "But at least you're both Greek. That's one strike against me. And the other is that I'm not the children's real mother. She really dislikes me."

Angela tilted her head. "It's true, the two of them were very close. But you have to give her a chance to get used to you, that's all."

But Piper knew she was right. The woman couldn't abide her, and she proved it when they all sat down to dinner.

Evangelia looked over at Stelli. "Stelios, my boy. Come to Yiayia."

Stelli obliged, and Evangelia put her hand under his chin, turning his face from side to side. "You don't look so good. You're pale. You feeling okay?"

Stelli shrugged and looked at his feet.

"You're embarrassing him, Ma," Leo said. "He's fine."

Evangelia raised her eyebrows and put her hand on his forehead. "He's not hot. But still keep an eye on him," she replied. Then she turned to her granddaughter. "Evie, my *koukla.* That is a beautiful dress you are wearing."

"Thank you, Yiayia. Mommy bought it for me last year. It was too big then."

"Your mama, she had wonderful taste. She buy for me this shawl I am wearing today. One of my favorites."

There was an uncomfortable silence, and Evangelia went on, looking at Evie. "You remember, you and me and your mama, when we would make baklava together? She was good cook."

"Ma," Gus said, "maybe we should change the subject."

"What? The children can't talk about their mother?"

Piper felt her face get hot. "Of course they can. But maybe we should talk about the things we're grateful for *today.* That's what Thanksgiving is all about. It's tradition. And since we're in America, we'll follow American traditions."

All eyes were on her, and she feared she'd spoken too rashly, but what the hell. How much was she supposed to take from this woman? How dare Evangelia come into Piper's home and insult her? Piper raised her glass and looked around defiantly. "Here's to family," she said, "old and new. *Both* old and new."

Leo raised his glass with a smile and looked across the room at her, but his eyes were cold.

46

JOANNA

I've begun to follow her. She left the house at eleven and drove to the mall in Stamford, a half hour away. She parked near the entrance, and I found a space two rows over, watching as she and Evie got out of the car. My breath caught in my throat when I saw her take Evie's hand and watched as they swung their clasped hands back and forth while they walked toward the mall entrance. I rested my head on the steering wheel and closed my eyes.

Did this mean Evie was getting close to her and forgetting me? With a feeling of alarm, I opened the car door, grabbed my handbag, and marched to the mall, trying to talk myself out of the fear I felt. It took a bit of walking around before I caught sight of them sitting in the food court. They seemed to be deep in conversation, which meant they didn't see me, but I was heartbroken that they seemed to be bonding. Evie looked so grown up sitting there, with her shiny brown hair past her shoulders and parted in the middle. She wore a white sweater that I hadn't seen before, black leggings, and a pair of pink Uggs that I'd picked out for her last year.

She looked like she was enjoying herself, laughing and gesturing with her hands as they talked. Piper, too, looked like she was having a good time, but an image popped into my mind of a smiling Mia in that photograph, and then a deadly spider spinning its web, a web that looks so inviting and enticing until its victim is trapped and fighting for its life. Beside myself, I stood there, trying to decide if I should ignore the court order, run over, and grab Evie away from her. But before I could take a step, I saw Leo and Stelli, hand in hand, heading toward the food court. With a shaking hand, I pulled my sunglasses out of my bag and put them on, kicking myself for not having brought a baseball cap.

I needn't have worried, though. They only had eyes for each other as Leo walked briskly to the table and leaned over to kiss Evie and Piper before sitting down. Anyone else looking at them would think them the perfect family. Even Stelli was smiling. Had she won him over as well? A crushing jealousy choked me, taking my breath away. I thought my heart would break. But then I realized—Piper wasn't being sweet to the children because she wanted a mother-daughter or mother-son relationship. She was lulling everyone into complacency. How much easier to put whatever her plan was into action if the children felt safe with her? I fought the feeling of helplessness that was making me lightheaded and unsteady and ran to the parking lot.

By the time I reached my car, I was sobbing hysterically, and I leaned my head against the steering wheel and cried and cried. When I was finally able to stop, I took a deep breath and started the car. The clock on the dash said one thirty. My appointment with Celeste was at two, which gave me plenty of time to get there. I arrived with five minutes to spare and took a seat in the small waiting room. I felt so alone. I needed desperately for someone to hear me, someone to tell me I could protect my family.

Celeste opened the door to her office. "Hello, Joanna. Come in."

She sat down in the familiar red chair and waited for me to seat myself before she began. "You look like you've been crying. Has something happened?" she asked gently.

I tried to control my breathing. "Yes . . . I mean no, not really, but something is going to happen. Something bad. I went to see Piper's mother. And even her own mother didn't really defend her when I voiced my suspicions about the two dead husbands."

"Did her mother indicate she'd ever been violent?"

"Not in so many words, but . . . And now Evie seems to be trusting her."

She crossed her legs and looked at me intently. "What do you mean?"

"Piper took Evie out to lunch. At the mall. Leo left work early and met them there. He had Stelli with him."

"And you know this how?"

I bit the inside of my lip. "A friend of mine saw them. She called to tell me." There was no way I was going to admit I was following Piper. Even though our conversations were confidential, I didn't want to lose credibility in Celeste's eyes.

"Okay, let's think about this. It's not helping you to hear from other people what Piper or Leo or the children are doing. It upsets you needlessly because there's nothing you can do about it. I think it would be wise of you to tell your friends that you don't want to hear any more stories or gossip."

"My friends are as disturbed as I am at what's going on—they're only trying to help me."

"But here's the problem. It doesn't serve you in any way. It only makes things worse for you. I think you have to accept that Leo is not going to leave Piper, for your own sanity."

"I can't simply stop thinking about my family, especially not when my friends and I see Piper all over town acting like the adoring wife and mother we know she isn't. No way in hell."

"Maybe that's the issue—seeing her around. What would you

think about getting away somewhere? Somewhere you wouldn't run into her. You could take some time on your own, maybe think things through without all the noise. You might even come back with a fresh perspective."

The heat started in my chest and rose to my face. "This woman is dangerous. She's planning something bad. She's got two dead husbands *and a dead child* in her past"—I could hear my voice turning toward the hysterical, so I took a breath—"and who knows what she has planned now? The children are in danger, and you're telling me to take a *vacation*?"

Celeste said nothing for a minute, pursing her lips. "You say you believe Piper has divulged nothing of her past to Leo, is that right?"

"Why would he be with her, let her be around the children, if he knew?"

Celeste locked her fingers together and brought her hands to her chin, seeming to ponder this. "Your concerns could be legitimate. Her past doesn't look good, I agree. On the other hand, it *is* possible to make assumptions that are false."

"So I should just give her the benefit of the doubt and wait until something horrible happens? I don't think so."

I could see sympathy in her eyes as she looked at me. "You've told me yourself that the accidents were investigated, and that Piper was cleared. She's done nothing to give you cause to worry as far as the children are concerned. Yes, Stelli had that accident at the playground, but children fall every day. I really think you need to begin to focus on yourself and your own well-being. It might do you some good to take a step back just for a few days."

I was incredulous. "You must be joking." I stood up from the chair, the blood rushing through my veins like a raging river. I felt like I was being gaslighted. I had seen the looks on the faces of all the people in Piper's past, had seen the havoc she had wreaked. How was *I* the one being told to stay away?

I left without saying anything else. This would be my last session with Celeste.

47

PIPER

Piper knew before she even looked at the date that it was Ethan's birthday. She always got a weird feeling in her stomach and woke up knowing something was bothering her, and then she'd remember. She supposed it didn't matter how many years had passed—the feelings of guilt and regret would always bubble up when she thought of him.

Their lives together had started with such romance and excitement. She and Ethan had run away at eighteen, driving cross-country in the Jeep he'd gotten as a high school graduation present. They'd left with twenty-five hundred dollars between the two of them—his trust fund wouldn't mature for three more years.

Piper had been suffocating under the viselike control of her high-achieving parents. She'd had to be in all honors and advanced placement classes. They didn't care that that meant she was up past midnight every night studying, and then up at six to be at school by seven every morning. She played a sport in every season, was in debate club and model UN. She had no free time, and that's exactly how they liked it. When they sat around the dinner table, they'd grill her about her coursework. She felt like they were automatons, devoid of emotion, only there to account for her movements. By the time she graduated, she knew she had to go far away. She'd been accepted to all seven universities she'd applied to, but her parents had insisted she choose Virginia Tech.

Ethan's home life was vastly different from hers, but no happier.

His father had struck gold when he'd invested heavily in Microsoft and was able to retire early, buy a huge sailboat, and stay home and manage his investments. By the time Ethan was old enough to be somewhat self-sufficient, his parents decided to recapture their lost youth and cram in all the fun they'd missed. Instead of family dinners, he'd come home to a fifty on the table with a note telling him to order in and look after his younger brother. Don and Trish Sherwood spent most of their evenings at the Annapolis Yacht Club and were often too hungover in the mornings to get the boys up for school. Ethan said it was like living in a frat house. The two of them used to joke that if they could somehow merge their sets of parents, they might end up with one decent pair.

They made a plan to leave together on the Fourth of July, their own Independence Day. Piper's parents would be ensconced on the Naval Academy grounds watching the fireworks, and Ethan's parents would be anchored in the Severn River, partying as they took in the show in the sky overhead. She had left a note for her parents telling them that they should not look for her, that she was going to start her own life. As they sped away from Maryland, she'd kept a tight hold on her cell phone, expecting them to call and insist she come home. But they never did. It was as though she'd ceased to exist for them. After a week with no attempt on their part to contact her, no call to Ethan's parents or to any of her friends, she decided they were dead to her forever. At least Ethan's parents had wished him luck on his "adventure" and showed a modicum of interest in his life by giving him a check for two thousand dollars to get him started.

It had taken them ten days to reach Los Angeles, and they'd been awestruck when they arrived. It was a bustling mix of high-end stores, gorgeous and fashionable men and women, scruffy vagabonds, and snarling traffic. Crazy exciting, but not quite the shining, palm-tree-lined paradise Piper had expected. She kept her eyes peeled all the time at first, looking for a celebrity at every corner, but that instinct wore off after they'd lived there awhile.

Ethan's friend Wally let them stay on his pull-out couch in West Hollywood. Piper got a job waitressing, while Ethan began work on his screenplay, and after a couple of months, they'd saved up enough to get a small studio apartment of their own. They reveled in their freedom, staying up late, drinking wine, smoking pot, and spending hours in front of the television—all the things she'd never been allowed to do at home. For the first time in her life, she felt free and happy. They decided to get married, and she was eager to shed her last name and the last vestiges of the family she'd been born into. Wally and his girlfriend, Carina, were their witnesses on the beach that night, as another friend officiated, and then they drove to Santa Monica for the weekend to honeymoon. They stayed in bed the whole time, making love and making plans for their bright futures.

Three years passed. Ethan finished his screenplay and tried to sell it, becoming more and more depressed with each rejection. Piper was getting disillusioned as well, losing out at every audition and wondering if she was going to spend the rest of her life waiting on other people. They began to argue, mostly over money. Piper told him it was time for him to get a real job. He called her a dream killer. But she was just being practical: it wasn't going to happen for either of them, and she'd already decided that she was going to go back to school in the fall. He needed to grow up.

By the time of his twenty-first birthday, they'd negotiated a tentative peace, and they planned to head to Cahuenga Peak in the Hollywood Hills to see the Wisdom Tree. The three-mile hike would give them time to talk without all the distractions of the city. And the view from the top was supposed to be spectacular.

Piper liked the idea of the Wisdom Tree, hoping it would somehow impart some sage guidance to them.

The day started out on a good note. It was beautiful and sunny—not too hot, not too cool. They were both in happy moods, playful and teasing each other. When they reached the top and looked down, she felt like anything was possible and was hopeful for the first time in months. They'd embraced and kissed—a real kiss, not the quick pecks they'd become accustomed to in recent months—and she lingered in his arms for a few moments, enjoying the feel of the sun on her face and the breeze in her hair.

She forced herself to remember the good part of the day, the part where they had reconnected and everything felt good—the part right before he went flying off the mountain to his death. She didn't like to think about what came after, either. The police. Their suspicious looks as she told them how he had been standing at the edge of the precipice, and that when she called out to him to be careful, he'd given her a mischievous smile and balanced on one leg, then lost his footing. She would never forget the sound of his scream as he fell eighteen hundred feet.

After he was gone, she'd wanted to leave L.A. immediately, but she had to wait until the investigation into his death was closed. Then she quit her job at the restaurant and moved to San Diego. The hundred and seventy-five thousand dollars she'd inherited from his trust fund was enough to help her forge a new life.

Snapping back to reality, Piper sighed, dragged herself out of bed, and threw on her workout clothes. Yoga wouldn't cut it today. She needed a long run. Something to clear her head and get those endorphins flowing. As she laced up her Nikes, she caught a glimpse of her face in the mirror. Smiling at her reflection, she recited the words she'd spoken to herself every year for the past fourteen years: "You're not responsible. Don't let the past drag you down. Life is for the living."

Standing, she walked briskly from the room, shutting the door behind her and pushing the memory of that day from her mind. She hadn't hiked since then, but when she'd discovered that Leo had a house in Bar Harbor right near Acadia Park, she'd thought it would be the perfect opportunity to get back on the horse, so to speak. She'd always loved to hike but had stopped after Ethan; it was time to embrace it as a hobby again.

She'd seen pictures, and the house was stunning. Nestled in acres of green, it perched on a cliff overlooking the ocean. The gray-shingle facade was all windows and white trim with decks boasting views of the water from all sides.

She wanted to go the day after Christmas and have a nice holiday break, where they could really start to bond as a family, and had brought it up to Leo back in November.

"It'll be perfect. A wonderful getaway for our new family to spend some time together bonding. We can play board games with the kids. Go hiking. Just relax. What do you say?"

"It will be too cold to hike in December. Besides, I've already booked our trip to St. Barts. The children like to get away somewhere where they can swim and be warm. It's really much nicer at the Maine house in the spring and summer; we can go there then."

She'd let the subject drop and resigned herself to heading to St. Barts the day after Christmas. A couple of days before the twenty-fifth, though, she'd checked the forecast for Maine and seen that it was supposed to be unseasonably warm all week—in the fifties. Later that evening, right after she and Leo had made love, she ran a finger lightly up his arm. "I want to talk to you about something."

"What is it, my love?"

She leaned up on one elbow and looked into his eyes. "It's something I want for Christmas."

He smiled. "I've already gotten your presents."

"I'm not talking about presents. You know how much I want for Stelli and Evie to accept me, to think of me as a mother."

His expression grew serious. "Of course."

"Well, I think it's important that we have some quiet time together to reflect and plan our goals for the new year. Going to the islands is your old tradition. The children are still going to see me as an intruder replacing their mother there. I want to start a new tradition. Instead of airports and hotels, let's finish the holidays in a more old-fashioned way. Board games, popcorn, and movies. And hiking together as a family experience. It's going to be in the fifties in Bar Harbor all week."

He sighed. "I can see your point. I can cancel the trip to St. Barts if you really want, but I don't know about hiking. I worry about Stelli. He's not great with boundaries, and the trails are so high up. If he fell . . ."

"We'll watch him. We'll make sure he's safe."

"I'm not so sure about that. He didn't know better with the slide . . ."

Was he really bringing that up again? "Well, *I* know better now. We won't take our eyes off him. I want us to make new memories there. Family memories."

He got a faraway look and was quiet. "Maybe it would be good. But I know the kids were really looking forward to the island."

"I'll talk to them tomorrow," she said, nestling back against his chest. "If they really object, then we'll go with the original plan, okay?"

The next day, she gathered the children around the kitchen table. She'd given Rebecca the afternoon off and had made their snacks—green smoothies with some liquid vitamins—and they sat contentedly, Evie swinging her legs back and forth under the table.

"This looks weird. Why is it so green?" Stelli asked when she put the glasses down on the table.

She'd forgotten to buy blueberries, which made it purple normally. "Because I put in Hulk powder," she said, smiling.

His eyes widened. "Like the Incredible Hulk?"

She nodded. "Yup. It will make you strong like him. And it's got yummy fruit, so it's sweet. Try it."

He reached for the one farthest from him, but she stopped him. "Not that one. That's Evie's." She pushed the other one toward him. "Different vitamins for different kids. This one's yours."

He took a sip with the straw. "Not awful," he said.

"Told you," Piper said, taking a seat. "Listen, Daddy and I were talking yesterday, and we thought it would be fun for us to do something different for Christmas break this year. How would you like that?"

Evie stopped drinking and sat up straighter. "What do you mean?"

"Well, we were thinking it might be fun to go to the cottage in Maine."

"That sounds boring. I want to go to St. Barts," Stelli said.

"If we do go to Maine, I was thinking we could get the new Oculus Rift virtual reality system and play games together. We could get the new Xbox, too," Piper told him.

Stelli's eyes lit up. "Really?"

Piper turned to Evie. "And we could read by the fire, and watch lots of movies."

"That does sound kind of fun," Evie said.

"And we'll do some hiking, too. There are some beautiful trails with wonderful views," Piper added. "Stelli, what do you think?"

"Okay, I guess, if you let me pick out the games to buy. But I don't want to go hiking! What if I fall?"

"Well," Piper said, "I will keep you safe. It'll be fun, and we'll all be together."

"I fell at the playground. Rebecca said you should have been watching me better."

Piper felt her cheeks burn. What else had Rebecca been filling his head with? She would deal with her later. "You did know that you weren't supposed to go on that slide, right? You won't do something silly like that on the trails, will you?" She was sick and tired of being blamed for something that wasn't her fault.

"I guess," Stelli replied slowly.

Piper smiled at him. "Good. It's going to be so much fun. We can even build a fire in the pit outside and make s'mores."

"We used to make s'mores with Mommy," Stelli said.

Why did he have to keep bringing her up? Piper thought. But before she could steer the conversation in another direction, Evie piped in. "Mommy used to like Maine until the last few times. She was sad there."

Piper frowned. This was news to her. "Do you know why she was sad?"

"I think because they had a lot of fights that time."

"You mean the last time you were all there?"

"Yes."

Piper tried not to sound too curious. "What did they fight about?"

"I don't know. I couldn't hear what they were saying. I could only hear how loud their voices were. It made me cry. Daddy was yelling at her, and she was crying."

They both became quiet, and Piper stood. "Finish up your snacks, and then you can bundle up and go outside to play."

Stelli slurped down the rest of his smoothie, then picked up the tangerine Piper had peeled for him and put a slice in his mouth. "If we go to Maine, maybe Mommy will come and make s'mores with us again."

"Oh, sweetie," Piper said. "Mommy won't be there, but she will be watching you from heaven. She sees you all the time and knows what you're doing. She's happy for you."

"I don't want her in heaven. I want her here." His shoulders began heaving as he sobbed. Piper wrapped her arms around him and held him until he was cried out.

48

JOANNA

I woke up early on Christmas morning, thinking of the kids and wondering if they were missing me as much as I was missing them. My phone rang, and I wondered who could be calling me on Christmas Day. I was surprised to see Rebecca's number on the screen. My pulse quickened. "Rebecca, hi, are the kids okay?"

"Yes, but I'm worried about them."

"What's going on?"

She cleared her throat. "After what you told me, I've been watching Piper a little more carefully. Stelli's still having a lot of stomachaches. They may just be due to all this green-smoothie and sprouted-bread stuff—it's a lot of food he's not used to . . ."

"How often is he getting these stomachaches?"

"Every day."

I felt my blood run cold.

Rebecca continued. "But the reason I'm calling . . . well, after what you told me about her first husband, I thought you should know . . . They're going to Bar Harbor tomorrow morning."

"In the winter? Leo never goes there this time of year."

"I know. They were supposed to go to St. Barts. In fact, we all were, but at the last minute Piper talked him into going to Maine instead. And she told me I didn't need to come, that I could take the week off."

Why would Piper cancel a trip to the beautiful tropics to drive up to freezing Maine? It didn't make sense. "When did all this happen?"

"Just last night. And that's not all. They're going hiking. I overheard her talking to Leo about it. I keep thinking of how high that house is, and about those trails, how easy it would be for someone to fall," Rebecca went on.

Stelli was afraid of heights, and Leo knew that. Was Piper planning something like what had happened to Ethan Sherwood? "Thanks so much for calling me, Rebecca."

"Please, you have to keep this between us," she pleaded.

"Of course," I said. "Don't worry—they won't find out you called me. Just please, stay close to the kids until they go. I'll drive up there tonight so I can keep an eye on things."

"Of course I'll watch them today. But be careful, Joanna."

I assured her I would be. If I hadn't already been convinced that it was time to act, the phone call from Rebecca cinched it. Who goes to Maine in the winter? And Piper was planning a hike? Acadia would be practically deserted, so there'd be no witnesses if she did something. I had to cut her off at the pass.

After showering, I pulled out a few things and threw them in a suitcase. I'd have to figure out my plan on the drive; I always think better in the car anyway. There was no way Piper was going to kill another child, especially not the ones I loved so much.

Mom was asleep, so I left her a note on the kitchen table. She wouldn't be happy to be alone on Christmas, but I had no choice. I made myself a quick coffee, shaking. I had to get to Leo before they went on that hike. Maybe even before that. She could be planning to push him down the mountain behind the house.

I looked at my watch, almost eight. I had one more thing to do before leaving, one thing that was going to serve as insurance and justification for at least one part of my life if all of this went south.

Opening my laptop, I clicked on a desktop folder and opened a file. Going to Facebook, I logged in and posted the document. Methodically, I went through the other thirty-one files in the folder and did the same. When I got back from Maine, there would be—as my mother would say—a shit show waiting.

49

PIPER

Christmas morning had been quiet, Leo wanting little pomp and circumstance as the children were still missing their mother. They had showered the kids with gifts, hoping to distract them from the one thing they wanted most. On Christmas Eve, Leo had given Piper her present in private—a beautiful diamond-and-emerald infinity band.

Later that night Piper helped Evie pack. "Let's not forget these boots, they're perfect for hiking," Piper said, taking them from the closet and putting them in the suitcase. "Now, what else?"

"Can I take my Nancy Drews?"

"Of course. What kind of trip would it be without books?" She smiled as Evie added two of the yellow hardcovers to her suitcase. "Okay, I think we're finished. Why don't you get your pajamas on, and I'll go check on Stelli?"

She walked down the hallway to his bedroom and found him sitting on the floor, the empty suitcase open next to him. "Let's get you packed for the morning, Stelli."

He leaned his head on his knees and wrapped his arms around them. "I don't feel good. I don't want to go," he mumbled.

"Does something hurt?"

"My stomach. I want to stay home." He kept his head down as he spoke.

"I'll fix you something to help your tummy and make it all better."

He looked up at her, tears running down his cheeks. "Why do we have to go to Maine? It's cold there."

She leaned down to wipe a tear from his cheek. "It's going to be nice this week, and it will be fun, Stelli. I promise. And after we go hiking, we'll roast marshmallows and have hot chocolate. We'll build a big fire in the fireplace and play games. You'll have a good time."

He put his head down again and didn't answer.

"I'm going to pack some things for you, and then I want you and Evie to come downstairs. I'm going to show you pictures on the computer of the really neat trails we can go on. That way you can see everything ahead of time. We'll all decide together which trails we're going to take. How does that sound?"

He looked up at her again. "Okay, I guess."

"Good," she said, ruffling his hair. "Your pajamas are on the bed. Why don't you put them on while I pack your suitcase? You can run downstairs and tell Daddy to meet us in the kitchen."

Piper finished packing Stelli's suitcase, closed the lid, and called to her stepdaughter as she passed her room. "Evie, come to the kitchen. We're going to take a look at the trails we want to hike. Your dad and Stelli are waiting for us."

When they got downstairs, Piper made some ginger tea for Stelli. "Here you go, this will help your tummy."

He took a sip and made a face. "Yuck."

She took the mug, went over to the counter, and put a spoonful of honey in it. "Try it now," she told him.

He took a tentative sip.

"Better?"

He nodded.

"Drink it all down. It's good for you."

Evie took a seat, and Piper opened the laptop. "Take a look . . . I was thinking of Ocean Trail and Flying Mountain Trail."

"Flying Mountain!" Stelli said. "That sounds scary."

She looked at Leo. "It's a very moderate hike." Turning to Stelli, she continued. "It was named by the Wabanaki Indians because it looked like it flew off a nearby mountain."

"I've done that trail. It's pretty tame, but before the summit, you do have to walk over some exposed ledges. It might be a bit much for Stelli," Leo said.

"It's okay to have fear, but we all need to face our fears and get past them. Let's sleep on it and see how we all feel once we're there." Before anyone could disagree again, she plowed on. "Time for bed, guys. Make sure you brush your teeth, and Daddy will be up to tuck you in." She was in no mood to read bedtime stories. Leo could do that tonight.

"Do we have to? Can't we stay up a little longer?" Stelli whined.

"Well . . ." Leo looked at Piper, and she shook her head. "Piper's right. We have a big day tomorrow. You need to get your sleep." He rose from his seat. "Let's go."

She could have done without his making her look like the bad guy, but she wasn't going to quibble in front of everyone. After they'd gone upstairs, she studied the website and thought about the kids' reaction. The way Stelli had been overindulged by his mother had made him anxious and fearful. Evie had seemed to escape the worst of their mother's neuroses, but Stelli had obviously picked up some of them. It was tragic, really, what some mothers did to their children.

She closed her eyes, rubbing her forehead. She thought she'd finally be part of the perfect family when she met Leo and he'd introduced her to the kids. They needed a mother, he said, and he wanted a wife. Evie and Stelli were young. It wouldn't take long for them to accept her, she'd thought. But lately, Stelli had reminded her more and more of Mia. She hadn't realized that a child so young could be this manipulative, but Stelli was proving it to her, and just as Matthew had been unable to see through Mia's subversions, so Leo thought Stelli was completely innocent of any undermining.

This trip had to be a turning point in her marriage—she would make sure that things were going her way sooner rather than later. She focused again on the computer, picked up a pen, and began to list the trails in order of difficulty. Stelli was going to learn his place this week, and Evie? Well, she hoped Evie would stay as sweet as ever.

| 50 |

JOANNA

The ache in my back and neck grew more intense the closer I got to the Maine state line. I'd stopped only once, for a large cup of coffee, but the caffeine had only made my already-jangling nerves even worse, and that wasn't good since I knew I needed to stay calm and focused. Ava had called me last night to tell me that she'd been unable to reach Leo on the phone, despite leaving several messages. Piper had to be responsible for that, I felt sure.

After another hour, I pulled into a rest area to use the bathroom, returning to the car with a granola bar and getting back on the road. I was set to reach the house just before dark. I thought of the last time I'd been to the house. By the time we'd arrived, everyone was happy to be there, and I'd cooked us a warm meal, after which we'd roasted marshmallows outside over the fire pit, the sound of crashing waves in the background. Had I known it would be the last time we'd all be there together, I'd have soaked it in even more.

It was dusk when I got there, and as I pulled up the long driveway and the house came into view, it felt as though I could finally expel all my pent-up breath. I killed the engine and got out of the car, breathing in the salty sea air. The wind blew my hair in front of my eyes, and I tucked it behind my ears, hurrying to the front door. I entered the key code and was relieved when the door opened. Walking through the rest of the house, I examined every room, every knickknack. The living room still had the family portrait over the fireplace. A red frame caught my eye, and I walked over to the coffee table to look at the picture it held. It was a picture from last winter of me with Stelli and Evie in front of a snowman we'd made in Connecticut. I thought about how much they'd grown since then, and my heart squeezed almost unbearably. I kissed the picture and put it back down. The sun had gone down now, and the house was dark.

I went to the kitchen and found the key to the guest cottage. I'd sleep there tonight. Even though they weren't expected until tomorrow, I didn't want anyone to drive by and see lights on. Getting back in my car, I drove to Mountain Peak Café, one of the few spots that I knew was open year-round. I'd have dinner there, then drive back in the dark and park my car a little farther down the road, where it wouldn't stand out.

The cottage was pitch-black, and I used my phone's flashlight to illuminate the way as I pulled down the blackout shades. I'd also bought a small lantern that wouldn't be seen from the outside with the shades drawn. I knew the woods provided enough camouflage so no one would find me here, but that I, using my binoculars, would be able to see up to the house and watch until the opportunity came to act. I pulled out my iPad and tried to read a novel, but I just couldn't concentrate. I kept thinking that I should be in the main house, sleeping in the master bedroom, not hiding like a criminal in the guesthouse. I was suddenly filled with a hatred so intense that I could barely contain it. Images of Piper and Leo together taunted me, and I clenched my fists so hard that my nails dug into my skin. Why did it seem that I was always the one left behind?

Maybe Celeste had been right about the parallels between Leo and my father. After all, my father had replaced me with a younger woman, too. But at least his wife hadn't been a psychopath. I was going to stop Piper—or die trying.

| 51 |

PIPER

Piper hadn't realized how difficult it could be to travel with young children. Evie and Stelli were querulous the entire way to Maine. They must have stopped at least five times on the seven-hour trip, either for a bathroom break, a snack, or just to stretch their legs. Stelli was complaining yet again that his stomach hurt. By the time they reached Bar Harbor, she needed a break. The charm of the town soon restored her good humor, though, and she couldn't wait to go meandering downtown and visit the little shops. When they pulled up to the house, she actually gasped—the pictures hadn't done it justice. It was magnificent. A sprawling gray house high on a cliff overlooking the crashing waves. The kids ran from the car and to the front door ahead of her and Leo.

"I have to poop again!" Stelli called as he jumped up and down.

Leo ran to the front door, punched in the code, and opened it. Piper took it all in as she entered. This house was everything their Westport one wasn't—open and sleek, with beautiful wood floors and moldings, enormous windows with views to the water below, and inviting French country decor. She dropped her bag on the staircase and walked into the living room, where almost an entire wall was taken up by a charcoal-colored stone fireplace. She froze when her eyes traveled up to the portrait above it, which must have been taken at least four years ago. Stelli was a toddler, and Evie looked to be about four. She moved in to examine it more closely—handsome husband, adorable kids, beautiful wife. Piper took in her long, dark hair, the luminous brown eyes framed by long, thick eyelashes. The same eyes that Stelli had. They looked like the perfect family. Leo's arm was wrapped protectively around his wife, her hand on Stelli's shoulder, his on Evie's. Piper really didn't want to have to look at it all weekend, but she didn't think she could ask him to take it down without seeming insensitive.

Sighing, she walked into the kitchen and was pleased to see there were no reminders here. It was smaller than she'd anticipated, almost rustic, but with top-of-the-line appliances. There was a granite island with four stools neatly lined up, and Piper found herself wondering about all the meals the four of them had shared here, as a family, before she'd come along.

She had to stop this. Leo had had a life before her, just as she had had a life before him. The difference was that he didn't have to live in the shadow of her last husband. She was starting to understand his reluctance to bring her here. She took a deep breath and decided that it was time she began leaving her own imprint on this house. Tomorrow, she'd begin by picking up some housewares and replacing a few things—just a few. Over time, she could make sure that very little remained of another woman's touch.

Continuing her tour, she opened a set of French doors to the sunroom, a cozy space that looked out to the immense deck spanning the entire length of the house. Moving through, she walked outside, where the bracing sea air made her hug herself even though it was unseasonably warm. Tomorrow it was supposed to be in the fifties again, which would be perfect for their hike.

Breathing deeply, she took in the panoramic view. She could see herself spending hours out here, looking at the water, meditating, doing yoga. Walking to the steps, she went down and walked closer to the edge, looking down at the ocean. She could see why Leo was nervous about the kids wandering too close to the edge.

They were at least three hundred feet above the jagged rocks. She shuddered and turned back to the house.

Everyone was already installed in the kitchen when she walked back inside—Leo stirring something on the stove, Stelli building a Star Wars Lego set, and Evie coloring.

"What smells so good?" she asked.

"My famous chili."

"How did you get the groceries? We haven't even gone to the store yet." She walked over to the sideboard, poured herself a glass of wine from the open bottle of Rutherford, and took a sip.

"I called ahead, my dear. Lloyd, our caretaker, filled the refrigerator for us. I even made sure he got the carrot juice and some of that other rabbit food you're so fond of."

"Well, thank you. I guess after we eat, we can just relax and get a good night's sleep so we'll all be ready for our hike tomorrow."

Stelli looked up from his Legos. "What hike?"

"We're going on the Gorham Trail tomorrow. It's very easy; it even has steps in places. It's going to be a lot of fun."

"How high is it?" Stelli asked, his voice shaking.

Piper groaned inwardly. "Around five hundred feet. But it's perfectly safe. We'll all be together."

He looked skeptical. "I don't know. I don't really like hiking." Looking past her to his father, he said, "Daddy, I don't wanna go."

"It looks fun," Evie said.

Before Leo could respond, Piper spoke again. "You know, Stelli, I used to be afraid of swimming."

He looked at her, eyes wide. "But you're a really good swimmer. You always do laps in the pool."

She nodded. "Yup. But I wasn't always. I didn't learn how to swim until I was ten."

"How come?" he asked.

She shrugged. "My parents never taught me, and my mother was afraid of water. She passed that fear along to me. But I decided one day that I wasn't going to let fear ruin my life. You see, I wanted to learn how to sail, and you can't do that if you can't swim."

Both children gave her their full attention.

"How'd you learn?" Evie asked.

"I talked my father into taking me for swimming lessons. At first, I was afraid even to put my face in the water, but I took it one step at a time, and within two months, I could swim. And now, it's one of my favorite things to do."

"Well . . ." Stelli bit his lip.

"How about if we try tomorrow? It's an easy trail, and if you don't like it after an hour, we can turn back. But I think you will. I'd hate for you to miss out on something really terrific because you're scared. Deal?" She stuck her hand out.

"Okay," he said, and shook her hand.

She looked over at Leo, and he winked at her, a pleased expression on his face.

"Dinner will be ready in an hour."

"I'm going to take a little walk; I'm feeling stiff after the car ride. Anyone want to join me?"

The kids begged off, and Leo shook his head. "Thanks, but I'm good."

She went out through the back deck, pausing a moment to admire the view again. The temperature was dropping, and she zipped her down jacket, pulled a knit hat over her head, and put her gloves on. She walked fast, eager to get in a couple of miles before dark. She loved being outside. Hopefully there wouldn't be many other hikers around tomorrow, so they could take in the scenery in peace.

As she walked, she reminded herself to stop and live in the moment. Mindfulness was what they taught at the center, but lately she had been having a hard time practicing it. *Breathe deeply, listen to nature, absorb the sights and sounds around you*, she told herself. Her mind began to clear, and she heard a snapping branch underfoot, the screech of a snowy owl, the feel of the wind on her face.

It was working. The stress lifted from her like a blanket tossed from her shoulders, and she felt lighter with every step. As twilight began to settle, she decided to turn around. The guesthouse was in view, and seeing it made her glad once again that she'd had Rebecca stay home. She didn't need the woman's prying eyes. As Piper began the walk back, a movement at the guesthouse caught her eye.

Had the shade in the window moved? She stood very still for a moment and then decided her mind must be playing tricks on her, but as she headed back to the house, she was strangely unsettled.

After dinner, Stelli bounced up to Leo. "Can we watch a movie tonight?" Stelli asked. "Maybe *Star Wars*?"

Was he kidding? A two-hour movie? "Well, maybe just a show tonight, Stelli. You and Evie both had a lot of screen time today in the car," Piper answered.

Ignoring her, he turned to his father. "Please, Dad?"

"Piper's right, buddy. That's a long movie, and it's already close to six. I think a show, a hot bath, and bedtime for you two *maimou*."

"We're not monkeys!" Evie said.

"Yes, we are!" Stelli said, jumping up from his chair and making screeching sounds. Leo got up and chased him, the two of them laughing until Evie joined in as well. They ran into the next room, then back, until they collapsed in a heap on the sofa, their giggles lingering. Piper sat there watching, the familiar feeling of not belonging filling her once again.

So far, this was not going at all her way.

Finally, Leo stood up and came back to the table, oblivious to her discomfort. "Come finish eating," he called to the children, and they returned, still smiling.

Much to Piper's relief, they went to bed without a fuss at nine o'clock. Leo emerged from their room and joined Piper by the fire, where she sat reading *Jane Eyre*. He poured himself a glass of the pinot noir she'd opened and sat next to her on the sofa.

"How about we light the fireplace in the bedroom and take the wine in there?" he asked, nuzzling her ear.

She spun around and kissed him. "That sounds perfect." She could fix this; she just needed this time with Leo to get started.

They shut off the gas fireplace and walked through the house, turning off the lights. Once they were upstairs, Leo put the wine on the dresser.

"I'm going to go slip into something more comfortable." She winked and went into the bathroom. She'd bought new lingerie especially for this trip, and she slipped the nude-colored camisole over her head. Her stockings and garter belt came next, and then a slash of red lipstick to complete the picture. Her hand was on the doorknob when she heard the bedroom door opening and the sound of little feet running in.

"Daddy, I had a nightmare! Mommy was falling from the cliff, and I couldn't save her." Evie's voice was choked and halting. "Can I sleep with you?"

"Of course," Leo said. "Go get Stelli, too. If he wakes up all alone, he'll be upset."

Piper's blood was boiling. Why was Leo such a pushover? Okay, Evie had had a nightmare. You calm her down and put her back to bed. Now *both* kids were going to sleep with them? She grabbed a tissue and rubbed the lipstick off, then pulled off the garter and stockings. She grabbed the robe hanging off the back of the door and put it on.

"Everything okay?" she asked, coming out of the bathroom. Evie and Stelli were already under the covers.

Leo gave her an apologetic look. "Nightmare. Rain check?"

She pressed her lips together in an attempt to smile. "Sure."

"There's not enough room for her, too," Stelli said.

She swallowed her anger and took a deep breath, afraid of what she might say if she didn't calm down. Was it going to be like this forever? The three of them together, with her on the outside looking in? Even though the queen-sized bed *was* small for four, it galled her that Leo remained silent. After it was clear that he wasn't going to object, she spoke. "I'll go sleep in one of the guest rooms. It *is* a little crowded in here."

Leo gave her a grateful smile. "Thanks for understanding."

Piper forced herself to say something nice to Evie. "I'm sorry about your bad dream, honey. I'll see you in the morning. Good night, all." Before she left, she grabbed the bottle of wine and her glass.

She walked down the hall to the last room on the end and went in. Turning on a lamp, she sat by the window in one of the cushioned armchairs and filled her glass. This was definitely not the vacation she'd envisioned. She may not be the children's mother, but she was their father's wife. It was about time he got his priorities in order. She was tired of being second fiddle to the children in her husbands' lives. She thought about Matthew and Mia.

If Matthew hadn't let Mia get her way all the time, maybe they'd both still be alive.

| 52 |

JOANNA

Their car pulled in late this afternoon. As I watched through the slender space between the curtain and the window frame, I could feel every nerve ending pulse, and I held my breath as if doing so might make me invisible. Leo was the first one out of the car, followed quickly by Piper and the children. I almost cried out when I saw them. Leo grabbed a knapsack and suitcase from the back of the Range Rover and followed Piper and the kids into the house. I moved away from the window and sank into a chair, suddenly filled with fear and self-doubt. What if she outsmarted me? I breathed in deeply. I had to think positively, get my thoughts in order, and go back over my plans.

Years ago, Leo had installed cameras outside the house so he could check on it remotely. I'd never deleted the app from my phone, and while it didn't allow me to see into the house, if I turned on the audio, I could hear what was going on in most of the rooms. I kept the sound turned up all night, so that even when I fell asleep, I would be awakened by anything unusual. I doubted I'd get much sleep anyway. The night sounded a fitful one in the main house, but after the kids were settled in bed with Leo, all had been quiet. I could tell from her voice that Piper had been angry at being kicked out of the bedroom, and though I felt some satisfaction about that, I mostly worried that it might add more fuel to her crazy fire.

The next morning, I heard them as they woke up and had

breakfast. After some fancy footwork, Piper persuaded Leo to take them to Gorham Trail in an hour. My heart broke hearing the fear in my poor Stelli's voice and Leo's lame attempt to comfort him. I couldn't believe the way he was allowing Piper to run roughshod over the children. I knew this was my one chance to act. Grabbing my backpack, I slung it over my shoulder and walked into the woods. I pulled out my binoculars as I approached the back of the house and scanned the windows. The kitchen was empty, so I figured they must be getting dressed upstairs. I was debating whether to go in through the garage or the front door when my heart leaped at the sight of Stelli and Evie coming down the stairs to the first floor. They were so much bigger than they had been just a month ago. They already had their outdoor gear on, and when they came out onto the back deck, I realized it was the sign I'd been waiting for.

I ran to them. I could see the shock on both of their faces when they saw me. Stelli stood still, but Evie took a step back.

"Shhh. We're playing a game," I whispered. "Come with me."

Stelli scrambled down the steps and threw his arms around my legs, but Evie, rooted to the spot, looked hesitant. "Stelli, wait."

But he was already holding my hand.

"What are you doing here?" Evie asked.

"I came to save you from Piper. Come on, Evie."

She was looking at me with suspicion. Piper had fooled her, that much was clear. "Stelli, you have to come back in the house," she said, putting her hand out as she moved back toward the French doors.

He'd turned around to look at his sister, so now I stood behind him, my hands on his shoulders. I bent down, holding him, and put my mouth against his ear. "Stelli, Piper wants to push you off the mountain. You need to stay with me."

He looked at Evie and then tilted his head back to look at me, and I could feel the hesitation in his body. I tightened my grip on him.

"You let him go!" Evie yelled again. "I'm going to tell." She turned away and ran into the house.

"I don't think I should go with you, Joanna. Daddy will be angry. Please . . . let me go!" He started to pull away, and I had no choice.

I pulled the stun gun from my coat pocket and gave him a quick zap on his hip. His eyes widened, and then he went limp. I couldn't understand why Evie had betrayed me, but I didn't have time to dwell on it. Instead, I hoisted Stelli into my arms and ran into the woods. He was growing heavier with each step. My arms began to shake, and my lungs were burning. I had to slow to a brisk walk when I heard the sound of footsteps and shouts behind me. Taking my eyes from the path, I looked behind me, then tripped over a branch on the ground.

Stelli fell from my arms as I registered Leo running toward me. I was panting, my heart going wild. Stelli lay on the ground next to me, and I knelt, putting a protective hand on his chest.

"What have you done?" Leo crouched down by Stelli's unmoving body. "What did you do to him?" His face was white, and there was terror in his eyes.

"He'll be fine in a little while, Leo," I said, and I pulled out the stun gun. "But stay back, or I'll use it again."

"You're insane! Get away from him!"

"Not until you listen to me." I pointed the stun gun at Stelli with one hand and pulled a folder from my backpack with the other. "Move away from me," I ordered him.

He hesitated a few seconds, looking from me to Stelli, and then took a few slow steps backward, never taking his eyes off me.

"Here," I said, and tossed the folder to him. "Take a look, Leo. You're angry at the wrong person. Piper is the dangerous one, not me. Did she tell you how she got rid of her last family? And another husband before that? She moved to Connecticut to hide. Changed her name, whitewashed her past. She's lied to you. Don't you get it? She's going to kill Evie and Stelli . . . maybe you, too. She belongs in jail. You need to come back to me."

He shook his head. "Back to you? I was never *with* you. I knew all about Piper's past before I married her. She told me everything."

He took a step toward me.

"Stop!" I screamed at him. "Don't come any closer."

He ignored me and reached for my arm, trying to grab me. "Give it up, Joanna. Piper's called the police. They'll be here any minute. Give me that." He took another step toward me, and I pressed the stun gun into his chest and watched him go down.

My hands were shaking, my breath coming in short gasps. I picked Stelli up and ran once again, this time toward the house. Leo was never going to believe me. He was going to stay with that bitch until she killed them all. But she wasn't going to get Stelli. He was mine. I knew then what I had to do. Stelli writhed in my arms, beginning to rouse. "Shhh," I said, and kissed him on the head. "Don't worry, sweetheart. We're going to see Mommy. That's what you wanted, right? Everything's going to be okay."

I stumbled along, holding Stelli against my chest, until we reached the edge of the mountain. I turned to the house for a final glimpse and then looked back over the cliff to the sea. It was beautiful down below.

Stelli's eyes were open now, and I could see the fear in them, but I didn't want him to be afraid. "Stelli, it's all right. Don't be afraid. Your mommy's gone, but she knew I would take care of you, that *I* would be your new mother." I took a deep breath and closed my eyes, saying a little prayer.

Olivia was waiting for us, I knew. *I tried, Olivia. Leo wouldn't listen. But I'm protecting Stelli, bringing him to you, and we can share him.* I opened my eyes and took one last look at the splendor below, at the black, howling ocean that would soon be our home.

I lifted my foot to step forward, holding Stelli against my body.

"Stop!"

I turned around. Piper was standing there with Evie next to her, crying.

"Joanna, please. Talk to me. Step away from the ledge."

I laughed. "You'd like that, wouldn't you? You must derive some sick pleasure in killing. You can't have Stelli. He's mine."

"You're right."

"What?"

"He's not mine. I should have never come between you. Just come back to the house, and we can talk about it." She took a step toward me.

"Don't come any closer, or we'll jump right now. I'm not an idiot. You're lying."

"No, I'm not," she said, tears rolling down her cheeks. "Please, let him go. Take me with you instead."

"Why would I want to take you?"

"He's young. Too young to die. You don't want me to have them, and that's fine. I'll go away. Let Stelli stay with his sister. Please."

She looked sincere, but she'd fooled a lot of people.

"No deal," I said, and turned back toward the ocean.

"Wait!" she screamed.

I whipped around. "You think I'm stupid, don't you? I don't believe you. Leo's just like my father. He's taking your side against mine. But Stelli belongs with me. You and Leo can't have him."

Stelli was now squirming, though sluggishly, in my arms. I was having trouble holding on to him. I looked over my shoulder. The edge was only two feet away. I could make it over with Stelli before Piper had a chance to reach me.

I hitched Stelli up, wrapping my arms more tightly around him. "Stay still!" He was crying now and calling Piper's name. "Stop, you can't trust her. Stay with me."

Here we go, I thought, as I took a step and leaned back.

"She's going to push Stelli just like she pushed Mommy!" Evie yelled.

I froze. *What did she say?* What had she seen that night? Suddenly, nails clawed at me, ripping into my flesh. I fell to the ground and Stelli rolled from my arms. I was too stunned to understand what was happening at first, but then I saw Piper pick him up and push him toward the house.

"Run," she said, following behind him.

I had no choice. I'd never wanted to use the real gun, but I couldn't let Stelli run away. He belonged to me and to Olivia. She was waiting for us. I'd promised her that I would never let him go. I withdrew the gun from my pocket and aimed at Stelli. Taking a deep breath, I tightened my finger on the trigger and fired. The next bullet would be for me, and then we'd be together forever.

| 53 |

PIPER

"Come on, Stelli, hurry," Piper cried, catching up to him and grabbing his hand. She turned to look behind them and saw the glint of the gun in Joanna's hand. The veins in Piper's neck pulsated, and her heart was hammering in her chest. She squeezed the tiny hand in hers and steered Stelli's body in front of hers as they continued to run. Stelli was crying, and his legs were faltering. Piper turned once more, panicking, heart thumping, as Joanna raised her hand, the gun pointed at Stelli. Without a second's hesitation, Piper pushed Stelli to the ground and threw her body on top of his, just as a gunshot tore through the morning air. With Stelli's small, shaking form beneath her, she could hear his sobs and feel his terror. The musky scent of grass filled her nostrils, and as she wrapped her arms and legs around his little body, a searing pain registered, shooting through her upper arm.

Suddenly, someone was lifting her up and she heard sirens and voices as she was loaded into a big vehicle with flashing lights.

"Stelli," she croaked, as the ambulance doors closed.

"Your little boy is fine," the EMT said to her. "You saved his life."

Piper closed her eyes in relief. "Thank God," she said. "Thank God."

The next time she opened her eyes, Leo was in a chair next to her bed—a hospital bed, she realized, as she looked around the room. The pain in her shoulder brought everything into sharper focus.

"You're awake," he said, leaning forward to take her hand. "How do you feel?"

"Some pain. What happened? Where are the children? Is Stelli all right?"

"Stelli's fine. He and Evie are with the Mortons, friends who live about a mile down the road from the house. The kids will be more comfortable there."

She swallowed, her mouth dry. "Water?"

Leo picked up a lidded cup and brought the straw to her lips.

She drank greedily and then rested her head back on the pillow, exhausted by the effort. "Joanna?"

"She tried to kill Stelli. Almost killed you. The police have her now." His voice sounded raw.

"She never stopped following us, did she? She knew we'd be at the house in Maine," Piper said.

"Rebecca told her we were going there. She—"

"What? Rebecca was talking to her about us?" Piper asked before Leo could finish.

"I called her a little while ago, to let her know what happened. Apparently, Joanna had gotten in touch with her, feeding her lies about you. Rebecca thought the children might be in danger, so she told Joanna about the trip. Joanna had told her about Ethan's death and then the accident with Mia and Matthew."

Piper shook her head, disbelieving. "All this time Joanna thought I was a murderer?"

Leo took her hand again. "She convinced Rebecca of it, too. Ava got to Joanna and clearly convinced her." He took her hand again. "I'm furious that Rebecca called Joanna. I told her to pack her things and leave."

"That's probably for the best."

"She should have come to me. We could have avoided all of this." He shook his head.

She sighed, thinking about Joanna again. "I knew Joanna had problems, but I never imagined she could go as far as she did."

"It's my fault. I never realized how unbalanced she was. All the years she was at the firm, she was invaluable to me. She was the perfect assistant." His eyes clouded over. "I should have seen what was happening. She was just such a help after Olivia died, offering to get the kids from school, packing their lunches, cooking their meals. All I could think about was my wife and how much I missed her. I let it go too far by allowing Joanna to stay in the guest wing and spend weekends with the kids and me. Nothing ever went on between us, trust me. That was the last thing on my mind," he was quick to add.

"Joanna thought that because you let her stay at the house and help with the children that she was meant to be your wife?"

"I guess so. But I knew something was off when she started acting like it was *her* house—rearranging the kitchen, questioning me about my plans, looking at my emails. I guess because she was living at the house until Rebecca could come back she started to feel like it was her house. I wrote it off as her being pushy. She ran everything at the office, so I thought she was just trying to help . . . or at least I told myself that. I was grieving, and I needed the support. But then she got so weird and angry that I was seeing you. Stupid me, I assumed it was because she was worried about the kids and felt it was too soon after Olivia's death. When she told me that she loved me, I felt guilty. I told her I didn't feel the same way, but I had to handle her with kid gloves. I mean, how would it look? My assistant staying over at my house."

"I never understood how she got so intertwined in your life in the first place."

He leaned back in his chair and ran a hand through his hair. "It started when Olivia's depression escalated, and Joanna became her confessor. Olivia confided to Joanna that she believed she was a bad mother, that her depression made it impossible for her to care for the children the way she should. I see now that Joanna saw it as her mission after Olivia died to become the mother she thought they needed. I knew the night she came downstairs in Olivia's red dress that she was taking things too far." He shook his head. "When Joanna left to take care of her mother, it seemed like the problem had been solved—she would go home and I would ease her out of our lives slowly. It was so stupid of me."

"You were trying to be kind, and the children loved her. You couldn't have known that she'd escalate things the way she did."

He stared past Piper, unblinking. "No. I'm a criminal lawyer. I should have seen it. All I saw was a lonely woman professing her love. I thought she'd get over it with time."

"Stop beating yourself up, Leo. There's no telling what caused her to snap the way she did. We're safe now. And together. That's all that matters." She paused. "Why didn't Olivia get some professional help?"

"She should have, but she insisted she could fight it by herself. The despair would take over one minute, and the next she'd be on a manic high. I never knew who she would be when I got home. She wanted to prove that she was strong enough to do it on her own, with no medication, no help with the children . . . but obviously, it was too much for her." His face sagged. "I should have insisted."

"Leo, you can't force someone to get help. You couldn't have known that she would take her life." Piper looked at him, her expression grave. "One day, when they're much older, we're going to have to tell the children the truth about her suicide."

He stood up suddenly and started pacing, his face tormented. "Piper, we were wrong. Evie said so. She remembered."

"Remembered what?"

"The weekend she died, Olivia had taken Evie to the Maine house for some mother-daughter time. The day after they got there, the police found her body at the bottom of the cliff, and discovered a note in the bedroom. I didn't even have time to be sad, I was just so furious that she would do something like that, especially to let Evie wake up and see that she was gone."

Piper was confused. He'd confided this to her when they had begun dating—why was he going over it again? "I'm sorry that this has brought all of that back to the surface. I was only trying to help you through it by having us come here."

He shook his head. "No, you don't understand. Evie remembers seeing Joanna that night. She woke up to angry voices in the house, saw figures out on the cliff. She saw Joanna . . . push her mother. She buried the memory and thought it had been a dream. That's why she kept having that nightmare."

Piper was horrified. "Joanna killed Olivia? And Evie saw?"

"And then Joanna let me think Olivia had killed herself. Joanna must have forged the note . . ." He had started pacing the length of the hospital room. "After working for me for so many years, she could write my and Olivia's signatures in her sleep."

Piper leaned back, drained. "I'm so sorry."

"The only good thing is that I know now that Olivia didn't intentionally leave us."

"That *is* good. The children will still need help, though, making sense of . . . all this."

He nodded. "I know."

She took his hand. "We'll help them through this. We'll all help each other through this."

"We have time," he said.

Yes, fortunately, they had a lifetime to figure it out. Her eyes fluttered shut. For now, she needed to sleep.

54

JOANNA

I haven't touched the greasy meat loaf congealing on the tray that the guard brought an hour ago. All I could manage to get down was the lime-green Jell-O. If this is the way the food is going to be in jail, I suppose I will finally lose that extra twenty pounds. They want to charge me with Olivia's murder, and my lawyer has advised me to plead insanity, explaining that it was the best way for me to avoid a prison sentence. But I was only helping Olivia. She came into the office one day to have lunch with Leo, but he'd been called into court and forgotten to tell her. She looked so downtrodden, I was reminded of my mother—the woman who'd kept me from my dreams, from having a life of my own. I knew what having a mother like that did to a child.

I asked if she'd like to go to lunch with me instead, and she said yes, her face hopeful, as though she'd been thrown a life preserver. She poured her heart out to me that day, admitted that she'd been struggling with depression since Stelli had been born. At first, they thought it was postpartum, but it wasn't lifting. She was still depressed two years after Stelli's birth. She'd have her good spells, but then the black days would come—days when she could barely drag herself out of bed. She worried about what it was doing to the children. I tried to help her, to get her to see a therapist, but she refused. She thought she could handle it on her own.

Over the next few months, we became closer, and I checked in on her frequently. Sometimes, when Leo worked late, I'd go over and make dinner for the kids and spend a little time with them while I encouraged her to get up, to take a walk, to do anything. She confided that she'd thought about suicide, that she'd wondered if her family would be better off without her. She begged me not to say a word to Leo, but I worried that it was only a matter of time before she took her own life.

And then that Friday last year, when Leo told me that she and Evie had gone to Maine for the weekend, I panicked. What if she was going to kill Evie and herself? I had to protect that sweet little girl. If Olivia wasn't going to help herself, it was time that I did.

I got to the house late, after eleven, and Evie was asleep. Olivia looked surprised to see me, but she welcomed me in and we went into the kitchen to talk. She said she thought the getaway would help, but she still felt dead inside. I begged her to get help, but she said she'd get through it. We started to argue and moved outside to the deck. We thought Evie was still asleep, but she must have heard us when we were still in the house and then sneaked outside to listen. I told Olivia that she wasn't being a good mother, that if she loved the kids and Leo, she'd go see someone, get medication. She started yelling at me then. Saying I had no right to talk to her that way. She said I was the help, not her friend. I screamed back at her, telling her about how my mother's illness and depression had ruined my childhood, and that she was going to do the same to her own kids. Her eyes blazed with an intensity bordering on insanity, and she ran away from me then, toward the cliffs.

She turned back to me and yelled: "Maybe I'll just jump. End it all now. Then I won't be around to ruin my children's lives." In her eyes was a dare, and I knew then that she needed my help. She wanted to do it. She just didn't have the nerve. So I took a few strides forward and pushed her, watching as she fell like a rag doll, not making a sound, until she hit the jagged rocks below. That was the moment I became their mother, and when Leo got over his grieving, I would be his wife. I wouldn't stay in bed all day or shirk my responsibilities. I would take care of them like they deserved.

I went back to the house, peeked in on a sleeping Evie, and then composed the note that Leo found. Writing as Olivia, I tried to make him understand that I had left to make his life better, and that I didn't want the children to lose the Maine house—they loved it there. I implored Leo not to sell it.

Everything would have all been fine if Piper had just stayed away.

You may think I'm crazy. I'm not. I know that Evie and Stelli weren't born to me, that they're not my biological children. But they are mine, spiritually—no one else could understand so well what they went through. I was always meant to be their mother, and they were always meant to be my children. Their birth mother hadn't been able to live up to her responsibilities. But I could. I had to. When Olivia died, it was crystal clear that Leo and the children had always been my destiny.

I helped him pick up the pieces after Olivia was gone. I was happy to do it. Looking back, I can see I should have given him more time to realize what I already knew—that we were destined to be together. He was still grieving Olivia, and I moved too fast.

Not physically, of course. I knew that we had to wait before making love until he was completely over Olivia and could come to me wholeheartedly. But I didn't think he'd mind if I rearranged the kitchen and some of the furniture. Olivia was not organized, and things needed to be more efficient. I organized the house for him, helped with the kids' rooms. And the children loved me, and I loved them. Then he started talking about boundaries. Said I was getting too involved. I did my best to respect his boundaries, knowing that eventually they'd disappear. But then he met Piper.

He got upset whenever I mentioned her, and eventually he told me it was best if I resigned, offering me two years' severance and a $250,000 lump sum. I took his money because I needed it. Of course, I realized only later that he must have been afraid I'd sue him for sexual harassment, since he'd allowed me to stay at his house. After the police accused me of child abuse when I'd only been trying to keep Stelli safe, Leo got a restraining order against me.

I always knew that Piper's intention was to hurt them, and I still think she will. Maybe she took a bullet for Stelli, but it was all for show. She'll never be their mother. I'll wait for as long as it takes.

My mother called to tell me she'd come see me in jail, but I told her not to bother. The only good thing about being here is that I don't have to feel guilty about not taking care of her anymore. No more cooking and cleaning up after her, trying to cheer her up. I had lived in her dreary, cramped house all my life, but now I wouldn't end up like that pitiful woman in the obituary I read, the one who took care of her mother until she died. Despite the fact that I was in a locked cell, I felt free for the first time in years.

The last person I had to settle the score with was Celeste. She'd be happy to know that I was no longer obsessing about Piper. But she wouldn't be happy to hear the rest of what I had to say. I'd heard from my attorney that Celeste's license had been suspended and her office temporarily closed. I asked him to arrange for her to visit me. At first, she refused; then I told him to tell her that I knew who had leaked her files on her Facebook page, and suddenly she was ready to meet.

She would be here any minute. Finally, the guard opened the door and she walked in. Her appearance was shocking. She was disheveled, her face pale and devoid of makeup, and she had dark circles under her eyes.

"Hello, Celeste." My voice was cold.

She sat across from me and shook her head. "What have you done?"

"I'm sure you're up to speed on why I'm here. Maybe if you'd been a better therapist . . ."

"I don't mean that. What do you know about my computer being hacked?"

"You're really not that quick, are you?"

"Look, Joanna, I don't want to play games here. I only came because your lawyer said you know what happened."

I had to be careful what I said, but I'd prepared for this. I leaned back in my chair. "Well, first of all, you should be careful about opening attachments. You're so fond of emailing your patients, but I guess you didn't know that theoretically someone could add a little Trojan horse to one of the documents they send you and clone your whole computer. Not that I'm saying that anyone did that. But someone could."

Her mouth dropped open. "All that confidential information was posted to my Facebook page. I'm going to lose my license, and I'm being sued."

"What a shame. Although I must say, you're a pretty shitty therapist, so it's no loss to the mental health community."

"You're crazy. I don't know why I didn't see it—*how* I didn't. You lied to me. You told me that Leo was your ex-husband, that Evie and Stelli were your children. You were never even married. I should have recognized that you're delusional."

I rolled my eyes. "I'm not delusional. I always knew he wasn't my husband, you idiot. Of course I lied to you. But they *are* my children. Olivia gave them to me." Now I was getting angry. I had to focus and get back to why I had wanted to see her. I leaned in closer. "Remember when I told you that my father had replaced me with another daughter?"

She looked confused.

"Putting the pieces together yet? Did you ever wonder why your stepfather was gone so much? Why he didn't live with you full-time until you were a teenager?"

A spark of recognition appeared in her eyes. "No . . . I don't . . ."

"Because he left my family for you and your whore of a mother."

Celeste looked at me in shock. "*My* father is *your* father? I . . . I didn't know. He traveled for work."

"He was my father first. But he wanted to spare you and your mother the embarrassing truth of our existence. He didn't give a shit about us. You wanted to know why I never told him how I felt—because he didn't want me to be a part of his family, *your* family." I laughed. "Couldn't let your mom know he'd been cheating on his wife for years with her. Even though she had you out of wedlock, for some reason he thinks she's a saint."

"I'm so sorry. I didn't know, Joanna." She sounded like therapist Celeste for a minute.

"Yeah, well, too late for 'sorry.' He paid for your college *and* your graduate degree. That money was supposed to be for my education. I'd be a lawyer now if it weren't for you. I guess now *neither* of us has the profession she wants."

"You came to me purely for revenge?"

"Ah, for once you're showing some insight."

"You were never interested in therapy," Celeste said, shaking her head. "You didn't actually want help."

"If I had, I'd have chosen someone who knew what she was doing. Tell Daddy I said hello." Before she could respond, I called the guard and then turned to her. "You can go now."

Finally, the playing field was leveled. If I had to lose everything, so did she.

55

PIPER

Piper nestled against Leo as they sat on the sofa and watched the children work on a jigsaw puzzle together. Snow had been falling since late morning, and when she'd peered outside after sunset, there was already a five-inch accumulation, with no letup in sight. A wood fire crackled and gave the room a cozy glow on this wintry evening. She smiled and closed her eyes in pure contentment.

"Piper, look, we're almost finished," Stelli's voice broke through the silence.

She opened her eyes and tried to sit up, but excruciating pain shot through her shoulder, taking her breath away. Sweat broke out across her forehead, and she sat still for a moment. The doctors had told her that a shattered humerus would hamper the movement and use of her shoulder for a long time. She'd been lucky, though, that the bullet hadn't severed an artery or hit the nerves in her upper shoulder. She might have bled to death or lost the use of her arm permanently.

She looked at Stelli. "Wow! What a great job. It's fabulous."

He grinned at her, and Piper was gratified by the happiness she saw in his eyes. So much of what had lain at the root of Stelli's fears had come out after that awful day in Maine. Had it really been only three weeks ago? It seemed like years now, but she remembered the details with stunning clarity.

The night following Piper's release from the hospital, the

children had come downstairs in their pajamas, ready for bed, and Stelli had crawled onto Piper's lap, careful not to touch her shoulder. Evie wiggled in between Piper and Leo.

"You saved me," Stelli said, his big brown eyes staring at her.

She gave him a warm smile. "I'm so happy you're okay."

"Are you going to stay with us forever, Piper?" Evie had asked.

"Yes, Evie, I am."

"Mommy left," Stelli said.

"Mommy didn't want to leave, Stelli," Leo said. "It was an accident."

Stelli sat up, his eyes wide. "Joanna said Mommy told her she was going to go away 'cause she wanted Joanna to be our mommy. But I don't want Joanna."

Leo and Piper had exchanged glances.

"Joanna was just confused. Mommy never told her that," Leo said.

"Mommy was sad, though. She cried a lot, and that made me sad, too," Evie said, tears filling her eyes.

"I still don't like those trails," he'd told Piper. "Mommy told me there are monsters at the bottom. They make you jump and then they eat you."

Piper was shocked that his mother would have told him something so frightening. "That's not true, Stelli. There are no monsters."

He'd looked at her imploringly. "Mommy told me she could hear them. They said her name."

So that was it, she'd thought. No wonder this poor child had trembled in terror at the thought of hiking those trails. She should have talked to him and explored the reasons for his fear. So much could have been avoided if she had.

"Stelli, you know how sometimes you hear the waves splashing against the rocks or you hear the ducks quacking or a bird singing, and it sounds like they're saying a real word?"

He nodded.

"Well, it's just our minds telling us that. Because we know that water can't really say things, and birds and ducks don't know how to speak our language, and monsters are only make-believe. Right?"

He fixed his eyes on Piper's, seeming to think this over, and then slowly nodded his head. "Right."

"You see, your mommy only thought she heard her name." Piper paused. "Stelli, I need to apologize to you."

His eyes grew wide.

"I didn't understand what you were going through, and I pushed you too hard. I promise to do better, to be more patient. And I know I can never take the place of your mommy, but I want to do a good job and be like a mommy to you, if you'll let me." She noticed the look of gratitude on Leo's face.

Stelli thought about that a moment. "Will you stop making me drink those smoothies and eat yucky stuff?"

She laughed. "Yes. No more yucky health food for you, I promise."

That night had been the real beginning for all of them, but especially for Piper. She'd steeped herself in self-help advice and often flippant bromides. She'd even chosen Reynard, an old Germanic name, because of its meaning: *counsel* and *strong*. She'd been overcompensating for a childhood that had been sterile and bereft of any tenderness or affection. She had never been taught that the true essence of the relationship between a parent and a child was understanding and acceptance. She had to stop trying to make others into what she wanted them to be. It sounded so simplistic, even trite. But she knew now that she had to stop, let go of her past, and move fearlessly into the future.

Piper smiled. She would do her best to help Stelli overcome the anxiety that had tied him up in knots these past few years. She was thinking of selling the Phoenix Recovery Center and starting a new counseling practice here. But first, *she* had to recover.

"Dinner will be ready soon," Leo said. "Why don't you two go see how Yiayia's doing in the kitchen?" Leo said.

They ran off together, leaving Piper and Leo alone. He took her hand in his. "Do you know how much I love you?" He leaned toward her and kissed her lightly on the lips. "You saved Stelli's life. And risked your own."

"Stelli has taught me a lot. I saw myself as so evolved and wise. Don't get me wrong—I worked hard to bring myself out of deep grief and self-hatred after Ethan's and then Matthew's and Mia's deaths. But I got a little too cocky, threw around a lot of high-sounding advice without putting anything into action. I want the children to be able to come to us with all their hopes and dreams and fears. I was never able to do that with my own parents, and I won't let the same thing happen to Evie and Stelli."

"You're incredible. The kids are so lucky. And so am I."

She smiled at him and rose from the sofa. "I'm going to see how your mom's doing with dinner."

The children burst out of the kitchen just as Piper entered it. "Whoa, where are you off to?"

"Yiayia said dinner's ready and to get you and Daddy," Evie said.

Piper laughed. "Okay. Go get your father."

She walked over to the stove, where Evangelia was stirring a pot of heavenly-smelling soup. "That smells wonderful. Lemons?"

"*Avgolemono.* Egg and lemon soup," she said. "I hope you're hungry."

"Starving," Piper said.

Leo's mother had come to stay with the children while Piper was in the hospital. She had come up to Piper's bedside the first night after she'd been released. Pulling a chair next to the bed, she had reached for her daughter-in-law's hand. "I'm so sorry, *pethi mou*, I misjudged you terribly."

Piper had been pleased by the sincerity in Evangelia's tone and her use of the affectionate term, *my child.*

"We all made wrong judgments. There were so many things I didn't know. I wish . . ." Piper stopped, too choked with emotion to go on.

Evangelia shook her head. "Shh, it's okay. Don't upset yourself. The important thing is to move forward. You are strong. Just what the children need. And what Leo needs. I will never forget that you risked your life to save my grandson." She'd squeezed Piper's hand. "You are my daughter now."

All Piper had ever wanted was a mother who loved her, who would take care of her. "I would like that very much," she said.

"*Kala*, good. No more misunderstandings between us. If you have a problem with me, you tell me. I do the same. Now, is okay for me to come for a few days to take care of you until you're on your feet again?"

"I would love that," Piper had answered. Now Piper put a hand on her mother-in-law's back.

Evangelia turned from the stove. "Go sit. You mustn't tire yourself. I'm here to help, remember?" Her voice was stern, but she gave Piper a warm smile.

"Okay."

Leo and the kids were waiting in the dining room, and he pulled out a chair for her. Evangelia came in with the soup and set it down on the table.

"Who wants to help Yiayia get everything else?"

Stelli jumped up. "I will."

How different he was after everything they'd gone through. They had turned a corner and the old bratty Stelli was gone. Piper leaned back in the chair, her shoulder beginning to throb. She'd declined prescription meds, having seen too many people quickly become addicted to them. The ibuprofen took the edge off, but it didn't eliminate the pain.

"You okay?" Leo asked.

She shook her head. "Yes. Just hurts a little, but I'll be okay."

Evangelia and Stelli returned with bread and the soup.

"Thank you again, for everything, Evangelia," Piper said.

"It is my pleasure, sweetheart." She stopped a minute, then continued. "I know it is not the custom in America anymore"—she held up a hand—"and is okay if you don't want, but I would love if you would call me Mom."

The children both looked at Piper expectantly, and she hesitated only a moment. "Thank you, Mom."

Evangelia smiled. "Who says the grace?"

"Can I?" Stelli asked.

"Yes, of course," Leo answered.

"Thank you for this food and for keeping us safe. Please take care of Mommy in heaven and thank you for giving us Piper to take care of us. Amen." He got up from his chair and went to Piper, pulling something from his pocket. "I took this. I'm sorry." His eyes were wide, his small hand trembling as he held the glass rhinoceros out to her.

This was a good sign that he was learning, admitting he'd done wrong.

"Thank you, Stelli," she said gently. "You hold on to him right now, and when we finish dinner, we'll put him back with his other animal friends. If you'd like, you can keep the collection in your room. I think they would like it there." She looked around the table at each of them. These two young children whose lives had been so deeply affected by their mother's mental illness; Leo, the man she wanted to spend the rest of her life with; and his mother, who wanted to be a mother to her, too. She knew without question that this *was* her family now. Her perfect family. The one she'd been searching for all along. Perfect. Not like the others, whose flaws and imperfections had brought them tragedy. This time was different. This time they would all be good. And nothing bad would ever happen.

Otherwise, she'd have to start all over again.

ACKNOWLEDGMENTS

As Piper would tell you—*the attitude of gratitude is the highest yoga* (Yogi Bhajan). But in all seriousness, we are truly grateful for the many people without whom this book would not be a reality.

First, to our brilliant editor, Emily Griffin: we are so lucky to have a partner who understands and refines our vision and voice. You make our words so much better than they would be if left unattended. It is a rare gift to work with someone in whose wisdom and instincts we wholeheartedly trust. Boundless thanks to the amazing team at HarperCollins. To our fabulous publicist, Heather Drucker: your passion and talent always yield amazing results and you take such good care of us—thank you from the bottom of our hearts. Appreciation to Katie O'Callaghan for your creativity and dedication to marketing excellence. We are deeply grateful to the HarperCollins global publishing partners for making our work available to readers all over the world. Huge thanks to Jimmy Iacobelli for designing a cover we instantly fell madly in love with. To Amber Oliver for all you do behind the scenes. To Virginia Stanley and your team: thank you for your kindness and continual enthusiasm—you are our champions. And as always, deepest gratitude to Jonathan Burnham and Doug Jones for your continued faith in us and our work.

To our exceptional agent and friend, Bernadette Baker-Baughman: what can we say but we love you to pieces and couldn't imagine anyone better to walk beside us on this exciting journey. To Victoria Sanders: thank you for treating us like family and for always making us laugh with your killer sense of humor. To Diane Dickensheid, Jessica Spivey, and Allison Leshowitz: thanks for all you do to support us.

To our film agent, Dana Spector at CAA: tremendous thanks for your passion, dedication, and brilliant negotiating. We couldn't be in better hands.

To Gretchen Stelter, always our first reader and editor: deepest thanks for your friendship, guidance, and keen insights. You navigate us to our true north.

Much appreciation to good friend Carmen Marcano Davis, PhD, for taking the time to vet our psychological profiles and for assuring us we are not unbalanced when you hear our plots. To partner-in-crime and fellow author Wendy Walker: thank you for help with family law questions and for always being a phone call away for encouragement and advice. Gratitude to our dear cousin, Leo Manta, for instruction and help with sailing terms and all things nautical and for being one of our biggest cheerleaders.

To the community of author friends we gather with each year at ThrillerFest: we are so grateful for all of you and the mutual support and encouragement we have found in our thriller family over the years.

To our readers: your support means the world to us. We hope that we continue to entertain and surprise you. Heartfelt thanks!

None of this would be possible without the love and support of our families. Thank you for tirelessly listening to story ideas, for understanding when we're locked away for hours at a time, and for everything that you do. We love you!

ABOUT THE AUTHOR

LIV CONSTANTINE is the pen name of sisters Lynne Constantine and Valerie Constantine. Separated by three states, they spend hours plotting via FaceTime and burning up each other's email inboxes. They attribute their ability to concoct dark story lines to the hours they spent listening to tales handed down by their Greek grandmother. You can find more about them at livconstantine.com.

EXCERPT FROM *STRANGER IN THE MIRROR*

Addison

I'd like to think I'm a good person, but I have no way of knowing for sure. I don't remember my real name, where I'm from, or if I have any family. I must have friends somewhere, but the only ones I recognize are the ones I've made in the two years since the new me was born—every memory before that has been wiped away. I don't remember how I got the crescent-shaped scar on my knee or why the smell of roses turns my stomach. The only thing I have is here and now, and even that feels tenuous. There are some things I do know. I like chocolate ice cream better than vanilla, and I love to watch the sunset paint the sky in vibrant orange and pink at dusk. And I love taking pictures. I think it's because I feel more comfortable behind the camera and looking out. Looking inward is too painful when there's nothing much to see.

We're celebrating my engagement on this beautiful September day, and I'm surrounded by people who say they love me, but who is it really that they love? How can you truly know someone when their entire past is a mystery? Gabriel, my fiancé, is sitting next to me, looking at me in an adoring way that makes me feel warm all over. He's one of those people whose eyes smile, and you can't help but feel good when he's around. He is the one who is helping me discover the parts of myself that feel authentic. I take pictures. Gabriel tells me that I'm an amazing talent. I don't know if I'd go that far, but I love doing it. When I'm behind the camera, I'm me again. I know instinctively that this is something I've done and loved doing for a long time. It's the thing that has saved me, given me a living, and led me to Gabriel. He's actually giving me my first break—a show at his family's gallery—in October. Soon, they'll be my family too.

The clinking of a glass gets my attention. It's Patrick, Gabriel's best man.

"As you all know, this clown and I have been friends since we were six. I could stand here all day and tell you stories. But since both our sets of parents are present, I'll spare you the gory details and just say that we've had our share of good times and laughs, and our share of trouble. I never thought he'd settle down, but the minute I saw him with Addison, I knew he was a goner." Patrick lifts his glass toward us both. "To Addy and Gabriel. Long life!"

My eyes scan the restaurant and land on Darcy. Her glass is lifted, but her smile seems forced, and her eyes are sad.

We all raise our glasses and sip. Gabriel's sister, Hailey, is my maid of honor, but she cannot regale the crowd with stories of our shared past because, like Gabriel, she's only known me for six months. Despite the festive mood around me, darkness descends again, and I feel hollow. Gabriel seems to sense my mood shift and squeezes my hand under the table, then leans over and whispers, "You all right?"

I squeeze back and force a smile, nodding, willing the tears not to fall.

Then Gigi gets up and takes the microphone from Patrick.

"I may have only known Addison for a couple of years, but I couldn't love her any more. When she came into our lives, it was the biggest blessing we could have asked for." She looks at me. "You're like a daughter to us, and Ed and I are so happy for you. To new beginnings."

I know she's trying to make it right for me, but it's hard to toast to new beginnings when they're all I have. I do it anyway, because I love her too, and because she and Ed try to be the parents that I don't have. Ed will give me away at the wedding, and while I'm grateful to have him, I can't help but worry that I have a father somewhere wondering what happened to me. That's what makes it so impossible for me to fully embrace anyone with my whole heart. What if my parents are out there somewhere mourning for me, agonizing over what's happened to me or thinking I'm dead? Or even worse, what if there is no one looking?

The doctors have told me that I have to be patient. That memory is a tricky thing. The more I try to force it, the more elusive it becomes. I have no real clues to my identity, no identification, no cell phone containing pictures or contacts. My body, on the other hand, shares some clues—the jagged scars that tell their own story—just not to me.